Praise for the first novel in this charming new series by
Nicole Michaels

START ME UP

"Delightfully playful, Michaels's contemporary marks
her as one to watch."   —*Publishers Weekly*

"Sexy and exciting . . . this is a book that makes falling
in love even more fun."   —*RT Book Reviews*

"Cute and crafty! A delightful beginning to a new series
that is sure to charm readers."
                    —*New York Times* bestselling author Jill Shalvis

"Sometimes a book checks off all of your boxes and just
hits the spot. *Start Me Up* did that for me . . . a sweet
contemporary romance that revolves around a single
mom, her blog, and a sexy, younger man. Oh, *Start Me
Up*, you had me at hello!"   —*Romance at Random*

"Sexy, steamy with just the right amount of snark. Nicole Michaels makes falling in love fun."
                    —*New York Times* bestselling author Christie Craig

Also by Nicole Michaels

Start Me Up
Win Me Over

Novella
Blame It on the Mistletoe (e-original)

Draw Me Close

Nicole Michaels

St. Martin's Paperbacks

This is a work of fiction. All of the characters, organizations, and events portrayed in this novel are either products of the author's imagination or are used fictitiously.

DRAW ME CLOSE

Copyright © 2016 by Nicole Michaels.

All rights reserved.

For information address St. Martin's Press, 175 Fifth Avenue, New York, NY 10010.

ISBN: 978-1-250-05817-1

Printed in the United States of America

St. Martin's Paperbacks edition / March 2016

St. Martin's Paperbacks are published by St. Martin's Press, 175 Fifth Avenue, New York, NY 10010.

10 9 8 7 6 5 4 3 2 1

To my sister Lauren, who has become a beautiful
and inspiring heroine in her own story.

Acknowledgments

Hard to believe this is the final book in the Hearts and Crafts Series. What a year! As always, many people deserve my gratitude. Thank you to Sarah Younger, for always being there; Lizzie Poteet, for your incredible insight; Annie Hulkower, you've been amazing at getting my books in front of others; Crystal Ben and Kerri Resnick, the covers have been beautiful; Laurie Anne Bowes and Emily Zoladz (and their lovely subjects), thank you for allowing us use of your art to bring my stories to life. Also everyone at St. Martin's Press and Heroes and Heartbreakers for their help in creating and promoting this series.

To my high school girlfriends. These days we rarely get to chat. In fact years go by, but writing a series about women friends has meant I've called on our past for inspiration many times. Our weekend outings, relationship drama, banter, trouble, and inside jokes. I wouldn't be the same person today without each of you. Heather, Lindsey (thanks for the name also!), Michelle, Jenny, Billie, Beth, Melissa, Erica, Katie, and Breanna.

Thank you to every single person who has read, reviewed, and purchased my books. I can't tell you what it means to me. I hope you join me for whatever comes next!

My amazing friend Sabrina for the initial inspiration, my besties Jennifer and Tracy, my wonderful mom, and all the rest of my family and friends. And most importantly, my boys and husband. Every day the four of you make it possible for me to continue fulfilling this dream through your patience, sacrifice, and unending support. I love you so much.

One

It was bad enough being single on Valentine's Day, but Lindsey Morales was single, alone, and *working*. By her own choice, of course. Work was always her escape from the pressures of the world. Besides being incredibly broke, she had the additional pressures today of lacking heart-shaped candy, cards full of meaningless drivel, and overpriced flowers. Things she'd never received from a man on Valentine's Day before. But it was fine. Candy went straight to your thighs, meaningless drivel was, well . . . meaningless, and flowers wilted and died. No reason to feel sorry for oneself. None at all.

Lindsey let out a sigh and stared through her windshield at the turn-of-the-century, light yellow farmhouse that she'd been hired to help renovate. The headlights of her SUV cut through the night, illuminating the wraparound porch. It was in the process of being rebuilt and everything was coming along nicely. She'd been very specific that it needed to look just like the original and thankfully her instructions had been followed. But it still . . . needed something. Maybe a swing. Or a pair of

rocking chairs. She would suggest that to her friend
Anne, since this was going to be her house when the
work was finished.

And what a gorgeous house it would be. The property was incredibly serene and beautiful. Although it
was now dark, Lindsey had been here enough times to
perfectly imagine the picturesque landscape. The big
barn in the back that nestled up to a wide-open field and
the mature line of trees that ran the perimeter of the
extensive yard. It certainly would be lovely to wake up
to that kind of beauty and peacefulness every morning.

Lindsey turned off her engine, collected her bag of
home magazines and cutouts, laptop, the little cooler
she'd packed for herself, and got out of the car.

The February wind was brutal, biting at her cheeks
as she walked up the front porch steps. This morning's
weather forecast had mentioned a cold front was moving in and that could mean snow—not her favorite. It
wasn't even six in the evening, yet it was already pitch-
black outside. Thankfully whoever had worked here last
had left the porch light on. Lindsey laid down her cooler
in order to pull the key from her jeans pocket and unlock the front door.

She stepped in and took a deep breath of paint fumes
and pine, then went back for her things before shoving
the door shut against the bitter cold. It had been nearly
a week since her last visit and she was excited to see
what had been done.

Flipping on the entryway light, she turned and took
in the space with pleasure. It was spectacular. The
stairs had been rebuilt with the bannister and spin-
dles she and Anne had chosen, and the large entryway

chandelier—full of vintage Swarovski crystals she'd repurposed—sparkled. Despite Lindsey's disdain for the contractor on the project, she had to admit that he knew what he was doing. Or at the very least he knew how to hire good tradesmen. It was difficult to give the man too much credit, even if it was due.

It wasn't that Lindsey had a problem with contractors on principle, just *this* one. She and Derek Walsh had a history, one she'd have preferred never to think of again. That was easier said than done, but not seeing his face helped. Hence the main reason for her nighttime Valentine session.

As she stood here, ready to do manual labor in jeans and an old T-shirt, he was probably wooing some unsuspecting woman with a fancy dinner and flowers. No doubt he was dressed to entice—easy to do for a wealthy man who was too handsome for his own good. She could imagine him in dress pants that perfectly molded his butt and a well-tailored suit jacket that hinted at barely restrained muscles. He probably had no use for sappy cards, chocolate, or overpriced bouquets. It wouldn't take much convincing to lure a woman back to his place.

Lindsey knew his routine all too well, and now that he was divorced it was probably serving him well once again. Men like Derek were exactly the reason Lindsey was better off working and not dating.

And she'd keep telling herself that until she believed it.

With one last glance around the entryway Lindsey headed down the little hallway toward the kitchen. She stopped and peeked into the living room. It was dark, but the hall light cast enough of a glow that she could see the progress. The old shag carpet was gone and the hard floors they'd found beneath had been sanded down and were ready for stain. The large marble mantel stood majestically at the far end of the room. It was one of both Lindsey and Anne's favorite things in the entire house. An original piece that Lindsey had covered in sticky notes that read DO NOT TOUCH.

She'd left similar sticky notes on other pieces, too. The bookcases in the upstairs hallway, the original pocket doors that led to the dining room, the upper cabinets in the kitchen, and of course all of the trim work and hardware.

The house was over a hundred years old, which made it special and incredibly unique. Not that there weren't other old houses, but homes of this era were not prefab, mass-produced, or worst of all . . . modern. They were built with hard work, love, and attention to detail. Full of treasures that were worth preserving.

Lindsey was pretty certain that she and Derek didn't share this philosophy. This project wasn't the norm for the hotshot architect. He was used to building fancy office buildings with lots of metal and glass. *Boring.* Every time she came back to the house she was afraid he'd have approved the removal of one of the home's treasures and her sticky notes were her way to remind him that he was being watched.

The arrangement between the two of them, and of course their friends Anne and Mike, had been very clear. Being the general contractor, Derek would do the foundation work: structural, electric, plumbing, and so on. He was responsible for moving some walls, making everything safe, efficient, and sturdy. The crews he hired did the necessary work, then she'd come in and make it lovely.

Normally their two roles would be symbiotic, requiring lots of discussion and throwing ideas back and forth to come to a mutually agreeable plan of attack for the reno. However, that arrangement wasn't really ideal for Lindsey since she'd have preferred not to hear his voice again for as long as she lived. But so far it seemed the sticky notes and short-but-to-the-point e-mails were doing the trick. She was pleased. Along with getting her way, she was avoiding the man altogether.

Lindsey stepped into the kitchen, flipped on a light, and immediately grinned. The bottom cabinets were new and custom-made just for the space. They were currently unfinished, waiting to be painted and stained. But the uppers were the crowning jewels of the room. They were original to the home, and the white paint had aged and worn in just the right places to create a lovely patina. The same look that people scoured Pinterest to learn how to re-create on their eighties-era garage-sale finds. She appreciated that, heck she did it, too. Even sold pieces like that. But these cabinets were the real deal and she was in love with them. The juxtaposition of these originals with the newer lowers was going to be fabulous, especially when she reinstalled the bubbled glass doors. She could already imagine how Anne would fill them with beautiful dishes and glassware.

Running her hand along the roughened wood, Lindsey wondered about all the wonderful memories these cabinets had witnessed. The preparation of Christmas dinners, first-day-of-school breakfasts. Definitely days of sadness and despair. That was what she loved about old things, their stories. Knowing that these had been used for generations, served their owners well, made it her pleasure to give them a new life. A second chance. A light glaze would protect and polish the wood, hopefully helping it to last another hundred years.

Her eyes caught on a giant Ziploc bag resting on the cabinet shelf. She reached for it and read the sticky note at the top. DO NOT THROW THESE OUT!!!

It was one of hers, she'd left it on the original cabinet hardware. Written below it in a meticulous boxy hand-writing that she knew all too well, she read, YOUR BOSSY VOICE IS SEXY.

Lindsey sucked in a shallow breath. This was another one of the reasons she'd avoided Derek. It may have been eight years since she'd been in love with him—give or take. But as much as she hated to admit it, she was not immune to his charms. Derek was potent. Dangerous.

Gently laying the bag on the counter, Lindsey allowed herself a minute to collect her thoughts. He was just messing with her and she couldn't let it be a distraction. It was time to get some things done. She settled her cooler on the island, which was currently two saw-horses covered with a large piece of thin plywood. That was another project she was rather excited about because she had big plans to surprise Anne with a custom island.

Opening the cooler, Lindsey pulled out the small feast she'd prepared for herself. Hummus and carrots, chicken salad on a croissant, peanut butter cookies, and three bottles of raspberry wheat beer. She might not be on a Valentine's date but that didn't mean a girl couldn't treat herself. Munching on a carrot, she arranged the rest of her spread to her liking.

Plugging headphones into her cellphone, she popped the top on her first beer and then loaded up her favorite Aerosmith playlist. Tonight's goal was all about taking precise measurements. Things like backsplash tile, stain, paint, even window treatments needed to be ordered.

One of the most exciting parts of the renovation was that the entire process was being featured on the life-style blog Lindsey contributed to with her two best friends. My Perfect Little Life had originally been started by Anne, the future homeowner. The next to join was Callie. She owned an adorable—and incredibly successful—bakery in town. Nearly two years ago they'd invited Lindsey to post about repurposing and crafting. She loved every minute of it, and in the past few years the blog had become extremely popular. Their loyal followers were invested and excited to watch "Anne's Dream House Renovation" continue to unfold.

"Cryin'" blasted away in her ears as she pulled out her tape measure. She hated using the thing, with its cheap metal case and flimsy tape. But currently it was all she had. Fine for carrying in her purse, but as soon as she could Lindsey had plans to invest in some nice tools.

Setting to work, Lindsey focused on measuring the space between the upper and lower cabinets. A beautiful glass tile would be nice. Or maybe a beveled white subway tile. She smiled as she imagined all of the possibilities. This was what brought her joy, taking something

tired and worn, and making it beautiful. Hopefully this
job would lead to others like it. When she was finished
with this house, it was going to be spectacular. If she
couldn't have her own happily ever after, then the least
she could do was help her friends create theirs.

Derek Walsh wasn't in the habit of ambushing innocent
women, but Lindsey Morales had left him little choice.
She'd done everything short of seeking a restraining
order to keep them from encountering each other during
this project. After tonight that might be her next step,
but that was a chance he was willing to take.

He'd been using the barn at the back of his friend
Mike's property as his makeshift office while he over-
saw the renovation, and tonight he'd hung around to do
busywork.

Waiting.

Quietly he pulled the barn door shut and headed
through the yard toward the front door of the house.
He'd heard Lindsey pull up and go in about a half hour
ago and he wondered what she might be doing right
now. He was nearly aching to see her face, but more importantly the two of them needed to hash a few things
out. At the very least he had some things he needed to
say to her. Things he'd been too much of a coward to
say eight years ago, and as much as he knew she would
not want to listen, he was intent on them having a long
talk. They owed it to each other.

It didn't surprise him that she'd chosen a holiday—
and a Sunday night—to come out and work. She assumed that she'd have the place to herself. But when
Mike let the news slip-on-purpose that she'd be here,

Derek had quickly processed three thoughts. One, Mike was a really good friend. Two, why the hell didn't a gorgeous woman like Lindsey have plans on Valentine's Day? Third, thank God Lindsey didn't have plans on Valentine's Day. The thought of her out with another man . . . well, his feelings on that were not something Derek was ready to process just yet.

A snowflake fell in Derek's path, glowing in the moonlight, as he made his way up the porch steps. The wind had picked up in the past hour and the screen door pushed against his hand as he lifted his key to the lock. The door opened at his slight touch and he frowned. How could she leave the door unlocked while she worked alone? Did she not watch the news? Or horror movies?

He stepped lightly into the entryway, not wanting to scare her. He wondered if he should call out her name, but before he could consider his next move, he heard . . . singing.

A stupid grin spread across his face as he listened. Lindsey was no nightingale, but he was pretty damn sure she wasn't trying for great. Maybe a sweet voice lingered underneath there somewhere, but no, this was a woman who thought she was alone, trying to impress no one. He recognized the song instantly and it surprised him a little bit. Slowly he made his way down the long hallway, his body humming with the knowledge that she was near.

The first thing he saw when he peeked into the kitchen was her long brunette ponytail. He couldn't help remembering what it felt like between his fingers—so silky and thick. It was a living thing, her hair. He loved the way it complemented the warmth of her skin and her sparkling hazel eyes. Every inch of her was ingrained in his memory, always had been. That didn't say much for his ex-wife, but she'd never been Lindsey. No one had.

For a moment he stood watching her. Tight T-shirt, ass shifting in her jeans as she leaned across the countertop to hold her tape measure against the wall. He should look away, it would do him no good to remember all the ways he'd once wanted her. How beautiful that body looked bare. After many years of misery, he'd finally convinced himself that what he'd had with Lindsey was never meant to be. But goddamn, as he stood here drinking her in, he couldn't help imagining his hands on her body, the feel of backing her up firmly against him.

Derek ground his teeth down and forced the unwanted thoughts from his mind. He'd be lucky if Lindsey welcomed his offering of friendship, let alone his touch. So far she'd made it very clear that she was completely uninterested in speaking with him, but this avoidance business had to end. They were adults. Their best friends were getting married, so the least they could do was learn to be in the same room together.

The fact that he'd purposely spent more time on a job site than he ever did was the first sign that he was committed to seeing her. And yet she'd never showed, despite the fact that all of the aesthetic details were her job. They'd exchanged a couple of very curt e-mails in regard to her choices for lighting and trim pieces, but that was the only communication. Not good enough for him. That needed to end tonight.

Derek bit down hard on his bottom lip—holding in a laugh—as she belted out another line, doing her best Steven Tyler impersonation. He was going to have hell to pay when she realized he was standing here watching. *Worth it.*

Leaning against the door frame, he folded his arms across his chest as her humming echoed through the room and straight through his body. His lips quirked as she leaned down to scribble something onto a sticky note and then slapped it on the wall. Clearly she took as much pleasure in her little notes as he did.

His crew had gotten used to seeing little neon sticky notes all over the house with very brief, very bossy instructions. She used a lot of exclamation points. Things like DO NOT PAINT THIS!!!!!! or PLEASE MOVE THE ELECTRICAL OUTLET OVER HERE!!!!

He tilted his head and gazed at the makeshift island. She'd brought herself an entire meal. Beer included. Huh. Was she drunk? No, didn't seem to be drunk, just oblivious to the fact that she wasn't alone. He didn't like that thought, not at all.

Something in the air changed and he glanced up. Her body remained facing away from him, but she'd gone stone still. That's when he caught her stare reflected in the window over the sink. She'd seen him.

Lindsey jerked around, her hands ripping the earphones from her ears. "What are you doing here?" Her eyes were wide, panicked.

There were a couple of ways he could play this, but instinctively he went for the route she no doubt expected from him. He smiled before he spoke. "Enjoying the show."

The slight glare on her face didn't deter him. Pushing off from the door frame, he stepped into the kitchen. The temporary island separated them and she looked like a scared animal searching for an escape route. Then suddenly, smooth as silk, she pulled a mask over her emotions. What irritated him the most was that she seemed intent on not meeting his eyes.

Lindsey cleared her throat and set her pen down on the plywood. "How long have you been standing there?"

He shrugged. Her bad attitude pissed him off. And also reminded him of his earlier annoyance with her carelessness. "Long enough to know that had I been a stranger you'd be dead right now. Or worse."

"Well, had I asked for your opinion on the matter, I'd appreciate your concern. But since I didn't, then I don't."

Derek let out a hard breath. He needed to collect himself before he said something that sent her running. He'd already allowed this to get started on the wrong foot. "Fine. I'm just *saying,* next time, lock the damn door."

"Fine, you *said*. Now feel free to lock it for me on your way out." She turned away from him and reached for her headphones.

"Linds . . . please." He was shocked at the desperation in his voice. Apparently he wasn't the only one. Lindsey's hand stilled next to her side, but she didn't turn. They were both quiet for a moment, waiting for the other to make a move.

"I'm working, Derek," she finally said.

His eyes pinched shut at the sound of his name on her lips. It was the first time he'd heard it in eight years. If only it wasn't coated in such hatred.

"I see that. Measuring for backsplash tile?" he asked, stepping a little closer ever so slowly.

"Obviously." She lifted her cheap metal tape measure up to the wall again. It bent awkwardly where a crimp in the tape had formed. Derek instantly lifted his nice bulky one out of his jacket pocket and stepped around the island to lay it on the counter beside her.

"Here. Use mine."

"No, thanks." She didn't even look down. Leaning forward once more, this time she used two hands to hold the tape in place. Clearly the thing was such a piece of junk—or so old—that it didn't have a blade lock. In her frustrated state she accidentally let the right side go and it bent at the crimp once more before the tape began reeling itself back into the case.

Derek took the opportunity to scoot his tape measure farther in front of her. "Quit being stubborn and use this."

With a huff she slammed the old metal case down on the counter and picked his up. The chunky tool looked giant in her small hand.

"It's heavy," she said quietly. "Not sure how this will be any better."

Derek nearly rolled his eyes. She was hell-bent on being contrary. "Well, trust me, it will be. This one has a strong blade lock so you only have to use one hand. Keep it. I've got several more of those in my truck."

"Of course you do," she said with disdain.

Unbelievable. "So now you're even holding my tool collection against me? Perfect."

He watched as she turned the gadget over in her hands, feeling the heft, pulling the tape out a few inches to inspect it. He would give anything to know what was going on in her brain. But more than that, right now he wanted her eyes on his.

"You know . . . if you'd just look at me, we could have a real conversation." He forced himself to keep any bitterness out of his tone. The last thing she deserved was his anger, he knew that, but damn if her refusal to even glance in his direction didn't piss him the hell off.

Her body tightened in response but her head turned in his direction. She glanced at the ground between them and it was all he could do to keep from placing a finger under her chin and guiding her gaze to his. How he missed her eyes, the most beautiful color of green fading into brown he'd ever seen. Like a mix of grass, honey, and chocolate.

She gently set the tape measure down, her hands quickly grasping the counter in front of her, as if she needed the support to stay upright. He hated knowing this made her uncomfortable, but he was at a loss as to how to approach this woman. Make her trust him. Maybe he needed to accept that she probably never would.

If she'd just look into his eyes, let him explain, she would see how sorry he was for the way he'd let her go eight years ago. Just the thought of that night made his insides ache. Not one day had gone by that he didn't feel regret over the way things had ended between them.

There'd been no seeking her out over the years. Definitely not while he was married because he would not disrespect his vows like that, but not even after the divorce because he hadn't deserved to see Lindsey. But now that fate had brought them together again, he saw it as a gift. A chance to right his wrong in this woman's eyes, if just for an ounce of her understanding. If she'd only give him that.

"I never thought I'd see you again, Linds." Despite himself, his voice held too much emotion, too much longing, and immediately he knew it was a mistake to say the words out loud. She sucked in a shaky breath and began to fidget with the black and red tape measure on the counter.

Damn. He'd meant to keep emotions out of this. The plan was only to talk, not try and seduce her. No good would come of that because he would not allow himself to hurt this woman ever again.

"I *hoped* to never see you again." Her voice was cold.

That gutted him, but it wasn't a surprise. "I don't blame you," he said.

"Then why are you here?" she bit out, her head still facing the counter. "There is no reason for us to know each other anymore. It's just an unfortunate accident that our friends met and fell for each other. You have to stop doing this to me."

Okay, now that she mentioned it, maybe he was making a habit out of the ambush approach. Last fall, he had found a way to be at the right place at the right time, which happened to have been Anne's kitchen, in front of all Lindsey's friends. It had been stupid, but damn it, he hadn't known what else to do. At the time he'd just recently realized they were connected through friends and was desperate to see her. He'd wanted to explain, make her understand how sorry he was. Tell her that he'd thought of her nearly every day after he'd broken things off eight years ago.

And at night, God, at night, she'd haunted his dreams. He could never tell her that, but it might help if she knew that his feelings had been sincere. That although he'd never said it then, he had loved her very much. Had never stopped caring for her. She should know that all of it had been real.

"When Mike showed me the blog and I saw your face," he said, his voice strained. Now that she stood this close—within reach—he wasn't sure how to put it all into words. "I felt like I couldn't breathe."

Her eyelids fluttered for a moment, but she quickly turned and walked around the island in the opposite direction. She picked up her beer but didn't drink, only squeezed it, as if it were to keep her hands from shaking. "I wish you wouldn't say things like that."

"Linds—"

"Don't call me Linds," she snapped. "That's what my friends call me. We are not friends."

Derek felt tension take hold of his jaw and he moved it around to unlock it before he responded. "We used to be more than friends."

"I barely remember that," she said. They both knew the statement was false, especially considering her obvious reaction to his presence.

"You're a very bad liar, Linds." He cocked his head to the side, silently begging her to look up. And then she did.

He might have expected the hurt, even hate. But the cold disgust he found in the depths of her eyes could very well destroy him. Now that she'd locked on, she wasn't letting go, and they stared at each other as she spoke.

"Well, *you* are a very good liar, and that I *do* remember. So forgive me if I don't wish to speak to you anymore or ever again." Her voice was steady but he was almost certain there was a strain of raw, painful emotion simmering just beneath the surface. Still, she didn't look away, and as much as her words hurt him, they were also the truth. She had no idea what a good liar he'd been and he deserved every bit of her anger. But when he saw the sudden flash of pain in her eyes, he almost couldn't bear it.

With slow deliberation Derek put one foot in front of the other and stepped in front of Lindsey. This close he couldn't help himself. He gently touched beneath her chin with his finger, effectively tilting her face up to meet his. It was wrong and stupid, but God, it also felt so right. Her lips pursed but she didn't take her eyes off him. Her pupils were wide and full of warring emotions.

"I'm not trying to upset you, Lindsey." That was the truth. So why the hell was he pushing it like this? He knew better. And obviously so did she because she quickly pulled away.

"Then don't touch me."

"I'm sorry. I—that's what I'm trying to do. Tell you I'm sorry." He shoved his hands in his pockets to forcibly keep himself in check. "I just want a chance to show you—after all this time—that we could be friends."

Lindsey shook her head, slowly at first, but it quickly became frantic. "No. No, we can't be friends. Besides, you don't even know me anymore. I'm not the same person and I'm sure you aren't, either. It's been eight years, that's a long time."

"Clearly not long enough for you to forget how much you hate me."

A bitter laugh escaped her lips. "You're right on that score. I'm not sure I could ever forget what you did. You had no reason to hurt me the way you did beyond the fact that you're just a selfish asshole. So, no, we can't be friends. Please just stop now because you're wasting your time."

Derek sucked in a deep breath through his nose, then another. Every moment in this woman's presence was a reminder of how painful it had been to let her go. He could still picture the shock and devastation in her eyes as he'd lied to her face. Told her that he'd made a mistake—they shouldn't be together. That he still loved someone else. God, just thinking of it now made him angry with himself.

And then how he'd ached for her, even while awaiting the birth of his first child. All of it had been so messed up, and it had also been his fault. He'd been young, stupid, and seeking the approval of people who didn't matter. There was no way he could expect her forgiveness when he couldn't even forgive himself. She was right, he'd been an asshole. Selfish? That was debatable. At the time he'd been certain he was doing the right thing, just as he always did. The voice in his head had been that of his father. *Don't be a fuckup, be a man*.

She would have made him a *better* man, but it was too late to make the right choice now.

"You're right. I fucked up everything, it was my fault and I hate myself for it. But the only time wasted was all the years of my life you weren't mine. I think I can afford to waste a few more trying to make it up to you."

Surprise flashed through her eyes, but he was certain he could see her forcing any reaction below the surface, holding herself in check. She'd always been strong, but she was even more so now. He hated to think that he'd contributed to that through the pain he'd caused her. A woman—this woman—should find strength through a man's unyielding support and love. Not his betrayal. God, how he wished he'd been that man for her.

Derek stared into her eyes for a long moment, searching for the slightest hint that feelings lingered below the surface. The kind of feelings that might give him hope. All he could see was hatred.

"Good night, Lindsey," he whispered. He couldn't help it as he slowly ran the back of his knuckles down the length of her cheek. Derek clamped his eyes shut as he reveled in the softness of her skin, the hitch in her breathing.

Before she had the urge to slap him, he stepped away and left the kitchen. As he strode through the hallway fury overwhelmed him and he had a mind to throw something just for the pleasure of hearing it shatter. He was angry with himself for letting her go the first time, with her for being so beautiful and strong. He couldn't fault her for it, but damn it, he wouldn't mind her weakening just long enough to give him a chance.

Derek opened the front door, locked it, and shut it firmly behind him. He let out a string of muttered curses as he strode across the yard toward his truck that waited in the shadows of the barn.

Once inside he started the engine, blasted the heat, and then pulled down the driveway, forcing himself to ignore the lit-up kitchen window. Before heading out onto the state highway he sat for a minute, taking a deep breath.

What the hell had he thought was going to happen? He should have been charming. Sweet. Maybe he should have brought her a Valentine's gift.

God, no. That was all stupid thinking. Earning Lindsey's forgiveness would not come easy and he didn't blame her. He'd hurt this woman, badly. The entire thing had nearly killed him, too. That whole time in his life was a complete clusterfuck, but there was one thing she had completely wrong. He'd had a really damn good reason for doing what he did and that was his son. In that regard he knew he shouldn't have regrets. Tanner was everything to Derek, and although he'd broken the heart of the only woman he'd ever truly loved, he'd done the only thing he could. At least that's what he'd thought at the time. He just needed to make her understand.

Two

Lindsey pulled into the driveway of the farmhouse, a little surprised to see several cars already there, including a familiar—and unwelcome—black pickup. *Damn.* She'd intentionally scheduled this meeting early hoping to avoid another chance meeting with her nemesis. It had been three days since he'd crashed her Valentine's party for one and she wouldn't mind putting three months between then and their next meeting. No such luck apparently.

Lindsey parked alongside a dirty work van and got out of her vehicle. A woman's laugh rang out through the cool morning air, sending a tremor of self-doubt through Lindsey's body. It had to be Vanessa, the journalist Lindsey was here to meet. And she didn't need to actually see the woman talking to Derek to know that's exactly what she was doing.

She rounded the dirty van to find Derek leaning against a corner of the front porch, grinning down at a petite blonde clad in tight-as-hell jeans, tall boots, a cropped leather jacket, and an adorable knitted headband. So adorable Lindsey wanted to puke, especially when she considered her own outfit of black leggings, beat-up cowboy boots, and oversized bat-sleeve sweater.

It didn't matter. She wasn't here to flirt with Derek, that was for damn sure. Wasn't even here to speak to him, in fact. Mustering all of her confidence, Lindsey stepped right up to the two of them and smiled at the woman.

"Good morning, you must be Vanessa." Lindsey stuck out her hand.

"I am," Vanessa said with a grin as she took Lindsey's hand. "Lindsey?"

Lindsey nodded, trying hard to ignore the fact that Derek's eyes were on her. She wouldn't acknowledge him. Wouldn't look at him. But she could feel his gaze down into her bones. It had always been like that, the strength of his stare like a physical weight.

In college she'd sat through hours of class knowing full well he watched her every move, loving that when their eyes met he would give her a secret smile. As they'd gotten to know one another better his smile began to hold promises about how he would kiss her as soon as they could find an empty spot in the hallway. Sometimes his smile held memories, a reminder of how he'd touched her the night before, learning all the hidden spots on her body. Once upon a time, a lingering gaze from Derek could have her body liquid and needy in no time at all.

"Derek was just telling me all about Anne and Mike's story. How they met, then how she had her client's party here and fell in love with the place." Vanessa put a hand to her heart and made a pitiful face. "It's all so beautiful."

Lindsey fumed inside as the words sank in. She began to consider strangling Derek with Vanessa's stupid headband because *she'd* been looking forward to sharing all of Anne and Mike's story. This was *her* newspaper feature. Well, hers, Anne's, and Callie's. But definitely not Derek's.

Anne wrote a weekly column for the *Kansas City Star*, and the newspaper had asked if they could do a four-part feature in the Home and Hobby section on the remodeling of her old farmhouse. It was a boon for all of them: the blog, Anne's business, Callie's bakery. But most of all for Lindsey because her restoration, design, and craft business had yet to really take off. She'd been doing okay, but not well enough to support herself alone without a roommate, and she'd been counting on this to get her name out there. If something didn't happen before too long she'd have to get a job waiting tables.

Pasting on a forced smile, Lindsey responded. "How nice of him to share. It is a great story. I guess the only thing left is for me to give you a tour of the house."

Lindsey turned to head for the porch steps when she overheard Vanessa speak to Derek. "Are you joining us, Derek?"

"No." Lindsey turned hard and then realized she'd been a little too abrupt in her refusal. "He has so much work, I'm sure. It will be easier if we just do it together."

For the first time this morning, Lindsey really looked at Derek. That was a big mistake. Everything about him oozed testosterone, from his faded gray tee covered with a thick flannel shirt to his well-worn jeans. The sleeves

of his shirt were folded up to just below his elbows, revealing corded forearms covered in fine dark hairs. And
because he was a total jerk, he was even wearing a tool
belt, which she could not look at again. It was too much.

When she met his eyes she realized he'd been observing her quick perusal of him. His eyes were hooded
and assessing, his lips a tight line, as if he were on the
verge of saying, *I caught you*.

She'd done her best not to look at him the other night.
It had been a survival instinct and this was why. He was
too damn good-looking and his eyes were once again
making promises even though this time she wasn't quite
sure what they were. He wanted her to stare back, she
could feel it. The problem was that whatever Derek
wanted from her, she wasn't sure she was capable of
handling it.

After an awkward beat of silence, Derek pushed off
from the porch railing and turned to Vanessa with a
roguish smile that made Lindsey want to scream. "Lindsey's right. It's supposed to be a heavy snow tonight so
I need to help the guys get some things done. It was a
pleasure meeting you, Vanessa."

Lindsey didn't stick around to hear the woman's reply.
She couldn't, the interaction she'd witnessed between
them had already set her pulse to a boil. How long had
he stood there flirting with Vanessa before she'd arrived? Had they exchanged numbers? Made plans? Had
Derek complimented her? Was that all happening now
as she stormed away? A hundred scenarios ran through
Lindsey's head, each one making her angrier than the
last.

Stepping inside the front door of the house, she took

a deep breath. If she was going to keep encountering this man, she had to get a handle on her reactions. It wouldn't work if she appeared jealous and angry all the time. She didn't want to be that person—or give him the satisfaction.

They were going to be in a wedding together. He might bring a date. He might be inviting Vanessa at this very moment. It was suddenly obvious to Lindsey that she needed to get accustomed to seeing Derek around and that meant she also had to get used to seeing him flirt with women. Because that's what he did. Lindsey wished it didn't bother her so much. And why did it? She didn't want anything to do with the man so it was no skin off her back if he asked Vanessa out.

"Wow." The sound of Vanessa's heels on the wood floor behind her made Lindsey cringe. "That Mr. Walsh is incredibly good-looking. Did you see how that tool belt hung on his hips?"

Facing the other way, Lindsey rolled her eyes. "Ah darn. I didn't notice."

"You really need to put that man out of his misery. I wish I could do it for you."

Lindsey turned slowly and tried not to appear startled by the statement. "Misery? What do you mean?"

Vanessa grinned. "Please. That man is seriously hot for you. At first, the way he kept bragging about how talented you were, I thought maybe it was a big-brother kind of feeling. But the minute you pulled in the drive he went all hyperfocus on watching for you. There was no denying the way he looked at you when you walked up."

Sucking in a shaky breath, Lindsey shook her head.

She and Vanessa had exchanged a few e-mails and that was it. They didn't know one another. They weren't friends. But suddenly Lindsey had a deep urge to press her for more information, as if they were in the girls' bathroom in high school.

And yet, what an asshole. How dare he have the nerve to appear interested in her after what he'd done. "It may have appeared that way, but there is nothing going on between us. Honestly, we don't really get along that well."

"That's all just sexual tension. You need to release it. *Literally.*" Vanessa laughed. "But enough about that. None of my business. Let's look at this house."

"Yes," Lindsey said. Hating that Vanessa's comments had made her pulse speed up. The last thing she wanted was any attention from Derek. She'd been there done that. Clearly her physical reactions were like muscle memory. She had to show her body who was boss.

Vanessa dropped her purse near the front door and looked up at the two-story entryway. "This is so gorgeous. This morning I looked over the before photos Matt took in December once more. It's amazing what you all have done. You've managed to keep the original look and just make it sparkle."

Lindsey grinned, her discomfort over the previous ten minutes floating away with the pleasure she felt over a successful design job. "That was my exact goal. I love old houses. Love their charm, their quirks, their soul. But I like to find the perfect balance of new and old."

Vanessa nodded and held up her phone. "FYI, I'm recording you. Keep talking, I love what you're saying."

"Oh, okay," Lindsey said. The knowledge made her

a little nervous, but she knew it was necessary for the article.

Vanessa continued, running her hand along the wainscoting trim that lined the wall. "It's just lovely. What color will you stain the floors?"

That was all it took for Lindsey to share every detail that was to come. She walked Vanessa through the living room, the kitchen, and the entire upstairs. Lindsey described in detail the plans for the upper cabinets, the island, and the fireplace mantel she planned to construct with reclaimed wood. She answered questions about Anne and Mike, realizing that Derek had really only brushed the surface of their story, allowing Lindsey to elaborate on the proposal, Anne's blog, and how she planned to use the entire property for her special-event business.

They made their way back to the kitchen where Vanessa stood looking out the back window toward the currently barren wheat field.

"It's so beautiful here. The entire place just has the most romantic energy. I'm really excited to share the process through these articles."

"We're excited, too," Lindsey said. "As are our readers. Many of the design choices have been made using their input. We've let them vote on finishings, colors, even the color of the roof shingles going up now."

"Well, I think it's going to be a really popular series for the paper. So many great angles to work with here. The house, the wedding, the blog, the relationships. It will all coincide with Anne's articles where she will discuss how it ties into the wedding. People adore her and the blog. I just can't wait."

Lindsey smiled, so excited for the potential this held for all of them.

"Matt's stopping by Anne's this afternoon to take a photo of her and Mike together. Do you mind if I send him by here to get a few shots of the house? Readers love to see things at every stage."

"Great. And of course he can come by. I'm sure the guys will still be here so the front door will be unlocked."

Lindsey and Vanessa chatted a few more minutes on the porch and then finally the journalist got in her car and left. Feeling content with how the tour went and what Vanessa's plans for the feature was, Lindsey headed to her own vehicle on the other side of the van.

She stopped in her tracks when she found Derek waiting for her. His back rested against the driver side door and he was engrossed in texting someone. As soon as he heard her boots on the gravel he stood straight and turned toward her. And there went that muscle memory again, every cell in her body dialing into nervous tingling. Her body was a traitor.

"Hey," he said, shoving his phone in his pocket.

"I need to get going." Lindsey reached around him for the door to her SUV.

"Hold on, Linds." He reached for her arm but she pulled back and stared at him.

"What part of 'leave me alone' don't you understand?"

He smirked. "Trust me, I'm picking up your vibes loud and clear. How'd it go?" He folded his arms across his chest, pushing the muscles of his biceps into view.

She refused to notice them. Instead she gave a dramatic sigh and crossed her own arms.

"Uhh, fine. Why?"

He sighed and leveled her with a glare. "Well, maybe because this is my project too and I care how it's presented in the local newspaper."

"Well, you seemed to have no problem charming the pants off Vanessa before I got here so I wouldn't worry too much." For a moment they faced off, matching stances, both glaring at one another. But then slowly the corners of Derek's lips slid up until he was actively holding back a wide smile. He cleared his throat before he spoke.

"The pants off her, huh? Sorry I missed that." Derek chuckled. Lindsey's glare turned hostile. She couldn't help herself. How could he continue to joke around when she was so clearly irritated? "Good Lord, woman. I'm kidding. You need to lighten up."

"I will. As soon as you get out of my way."

Derek slid in closer to the door handle of her car, effectively blocking her entry. The only way she'd be getting in would be to shove him out of her path, which wasn't even physically possible. Before she could insist he move, his eyes turned warm and serious.

"I'm sorry about the other night."

She looked up at him but remained quiet. Truthfully she didn't know what to say. She was still angry with him for so many things. When it came to Derek, Lindsey's thoughts were so messed up she wasn't sure what she felt anymore. There was definitely a lot of anger and sadness. But there was also a little curiosity. And maybe a teensy bit of lust. Enough to make her angry with herself also. She finally gave a slight shrug in response.

"I shouldn't have surprised you the way I did." Derek ran a hand across the back of his neck, holding on to the tense muscles there. "I just . . . I really want a chance to talk to you. Without anger or hard feelings between us."

"Well, just so you're aware, not everything is about you and what you want. You're going to have to wait until I'm capable of that."

His eyes squinted a little. Contemplating, as if he hadn't even considered that she'd have to want their reconciliation. Finally he nodded and backed away from her car. Lindsey opened the door and pulled out her keys.

Derek's boots scuffed the gravel as he walked away and Lindsey's heart fluttered. Every time they parted she felt a deep sense of panic. A silly thing to feel considering she was always begging him to go. She turned, suddenly desperate to stop him. Look at him once more.

"Derek."

He turned immediately and took a step in her direction. Only one, not too close, his eyes wary. Soft. Too damn handsome and hopeful. Why did he keep pushing?

"You should know. I may never be capable of that."

The corner of his lips lifted before he spoke quietly. "Then I've got my work cut out for me, don't I?"

And with that he walked away.

Lindsey pushed "publish" on the blog post she'd finally finished and let out a deep sigh of relief. Through her bedroom wall she could hear her sister Mel and her husband Brett while they gave their three-month-old daughter a bath. Their goofy laughs and baby talk made her smile.

She clicked over to check comments on her previous post. These days all of her blog contributions revolved around the "Anne's Dream House Renovation" feature. But she was enjoying it. Once the house was done she would go back to posting DIY tutorials, antiques and flea market visits, and other crafting highlights. She enjoyed interacting with their readers, answering questions, garnering ideas, sharing a passion for repurposing and upcycling. The blogging community was fantastic and inspiring. She loved that Anne, Callie, and herself had bonded over the blog and built their own tiny empire. If said empire could provide her with enough income for an apartment soon, all the better.

Up until two months ago Lindsey had been living with a roommate, but then out of nowhere the roommate had decided to get married in Vegas, leaving Lindsey homeless when she couldn't afford to cover the entire rent on her own. Kind of a jerk move from someone she'd considered a friend, but what could she do? At that point her finances had already started to become precarious. The worst part was that she feared she was on the precipice of a downward spiral, because without a good place to create, there was nothing to sell. And without products, there was no money coming in.

Anne and Mike were paying her for her design work on the house, and they'd been very kind and generous, but it wasn't enough to get her a place of her own. Especially when she was getting paid in chunks. She needed to build a bigger cushion before she felt safe again. It would be really nice if her father paid her back what he'd borrowed, but something deep inside told her that money was long gone.

Lindsey closed her laptop and fell back on the bed as Mel's baby-talk voice seeped through the wall. "Look at you, little bean. You love your bath, don't you? Yes you do. Yes you do."

She was beginning to wonder if she'd ever have that. A family. A husband. Happiness and stability. But unfortunately that all required meeting someone. Dating, kissing, sex, marriage. And while guys liked her, asked her out even, she was always so hesitant to put herself out there. What happened when she realized they'd only been looking for a one-night stand?

And it had happened. A few times, so the struggle was real.

Lifting her leg, Lindsey pulled off her sock, then the other, and wiggled her body under the sheets. For a few moments she tried not to focus on the sounds of the condo beyond her door and walls.

Reaching up to the nightstand, Lindsey flipped off the lamp, closed her eyes, and nestled into her pillow. It was only eight-thirty but she had an early morning tomorrow. She was meeting Anne to go over some tile and stain choices. Sleep also had the benefit of keeping her mind from wandering.

And yet . . . wander it did. Because thoughts of the tile made her think about the house, which made her think about Derek once again. No surprise. The width of his shoulders, how his tool belt hung on his hips. He wasn't that old, only thirty, but he looked as though he'd spent a lot of time battling the elements. The roughened outdoorsy look worked for him. He basically had no business walking around everyday life like hunky calendar fodder. And of course she'd also spent way too much time overanalyzing every interaction. Every look, touch, even the things Vanessa had said. Lindsey didn't think Derek still had any feelings for her at all. Not really. It had been eight years. Certainly he had guilt and maybe regret. But those weren't the kind of feelings she was looking for from a man. His final words from the other day continued to ring in her ears.

I guess I have my work cut out for me.

Why did he care so much? And what exactly did he expect would happen? What could he possibly have to say that would make up for what he'd done? Because for the life of her, she could come up with no good excuse for starting something with one woman when you still had an inkling of feeling for another. She questioned it for months afterward. Years if she was being honest.

Their relationship had been short. But it had also been crazy, passionate, consuming. The happiest, most amazing few months of her life. Lindsey had fallen for him so hard and so fast she hadn't had time to process what they were doing before he'd ripped the rug out from under her.

She could still picture that night like it was yesterday. A few days before, they'd had the most amazing night together. They'd been seeing each other for a few months at that point and they'd driven into Kansas City from Lawrence and gotten a hotel room. The entire day had been perfect, with food, Christmas shopping, and then that evening he'd mapped out every single millimeter of her body with his mouth. It had been magical.

She'd known then that he was the one. Had been so sure of it she'd told Mel about him after they'd returned. And then she didn't hear from him for days which was so unusual. He didn't reply to her messages, answer her phone calls. Didn't show up to class. And then a few days later he'd knocked on her dorm room door, looking ragged.

At that point she was angry, but ready to hear him out. Forgive him for disappearing. Surely he'd had a good reason. But instead he'd walked in, his face twisted in pain, and then torn her entire world apart.

"Lindsey, I'm so sorry. I just . . . I didn't know how to tell you."

The minute the words had escaped his lips she'd known it was over. She'd stood there in sweatpants and T-shirt, hair in a ponytail, heart breaking, as he'd continued.

"This shouldn't have happened. I'm still . . . I'm still in love with someone else. And I'm so sorry. It just . . . It has to be this way."

As the years had ticked by she'd played that night over and over again in her mind. Considered what she should have said. Should have done. Sometimes she fantasized about slapping him. Or telling him it didn't matter, he'd been one of many guys she'd been sleeping with, which was far from the truth. Maybe she should have cried and demanded an explanation. Or refused to let him go. Because none of it could have been worse than what had really happened.

"I'm sorry, too," she'd simply said. And then he'd stepped into her, pushed her up against the wall, and kissed her. A long, slow kiss. He'd caressed her face, threaded his fingers through her hair, and groaned against her mouth as if it were all a mistake. For a moment that kiss had made her wonder if she'd only imagined his previous admission. But no. He'd pulled away and left her standing there all alone.

That kiss was what made her the angriest. He'd admitted to loving another woman and then kissed her anyway, like some cheap whore he'd used for a good time. And she'd let him. Kissed him back. And the fact that she still dreamed about it—wanted it again—meant she'd never forgive him.

Three

Derek pulled into his ex's driveway and tried to ignore the anxious knot in his gut. He loved his weekends with his son but they weren't nearly frequent enough. The hard part was seeing Lisa. That never got any easier. Throughout their separation several people had shared their unsolicited advice and a common saying was that "you see a person's true colors during a divorce." Derek hadn't worried much in the beginning because the Lisa he'd been married to was pretty damn hard to like. They'd both been unhappy so he was certain that putting them both out of their misery would make her kinder. Gentler. He never dreamed things could get worse. How wrong he'd been.

Lisa blamed him for her unhappiness, no doubt about it, and the divorce had been crazy ugly. She'd pulled lies out of her ass that almost would have been funny if they didn't threaten Derek's future with his son. She took everything he did or said as a threat against her character, her relationship with their son, and she lived in retaliation mode. It was as if the divorce were his final insult to her, despite the fact they'd grown to hate one another. Maybe she thought they should have lived unhappily ever after, but who in their right mind wanted that? Thank God he'd had a great attorney and a judge that could see through her bullshit, because she'd laid it on thick. Still did when it suited her purposes, which seemed to be every damn time he spoke with her.

Turning off his truck, Derek got out and headed for the front door. Thanks to nearly a week of snow, Kansas City and the surrounding area were covered in white. Derek had big plans for his weekend with Tanner that included sledding, hot chocolate, serious PS4 gaming, and maybe a snowman. He couldn't wait to tell him. He just needed to get them home on his own turf where they could relax and enjoy each other. Be guys. Derek needed some time with his son to remind him what his priorities were. For the past week his thoughts had been scattered, confused, and conflicted thanks to one particular green-eyed woman he'd not been able to stop focusing on.

He knocked on the door of the house he'd once lived in for five years and shoved his hands into his pockets, dreading the conversation that would follow. He really never knew what to expect from Lisa. One day she'd be over-the-top sweet, the next she might be spewing venom in his direction. The one thing he was grateful for was that she was sneaky and manipulative enough to keep Tanner oblivious to the drama. She made sure to appear to be the perfect mother in front of their son. Derek could only pray she would continue that practice.

He did everything he could to try and shield Tanner from the crazy conflict between his parents but he wasn't sure if he was successful at it.

Lisa opened the door and a hint of something cooking caught his attention. Was she planning to have company after they left? He sure as hell didn't care, the woman could do whatever she wanted as long she treated their son right and didn't try to take any of Derek's visitation rights away. But it was a little odd because she usually only flaunted other men in his face when she was mad about something he'd done. It was possible she'd invited a female friend over but she didn't have many, and on those nights they'd usually have dinner and drinks out. And it couldn't be her parents, they lived too far away and definitely wouldn't come on a weekend when Tanner wasn't going to be home.

"Hey, you," she said with a sheepish grin. Tight jeans and an even tighter sweater graced her petite form, only serving to annoy him further. Although Lisa had always been attractive, the sight of her did nothing to him now. Hadn't for years. But her outfit let him know she was up to something.

"You're going to be so annoyed with me," she continued. "I completely forgot it was Friday when I started making Tanner's favorite dinner—chicken strips and my homemade macaroni and cheese. He was so disappointed when he realized he wouldn't get to eat it. I told him I was sure you wouldn't mind just eating here before you go."

She was a piece of work. Derek stepped into the house, glanced around for his son, and when he didn't see him he gave Lisa a hard stare. He'd been looking forward to taking Tanner to the new pizza place in Preston. Sure, Tanner loved chicken strips but he also loved pizza. It wasn't like he'd never get another chance to eat her food, and he didn't buy her "I forgot" story. Nobody forgot it was Friday. Just as he was about to call her on it, Tanner came down the stairs. His floppy hair and Marvel hero T-shirt made Derek smile. God, he loved this kid so much.

"Hi, Dad," he said. "Sorry, Mom forgot. I hope you're not mad. She already made it, so . . ."

Derek let his rigid shoulders fall. Over the past few months he'd noticed that Tanner appeared more and more wary around his parents, as if he were trying to keep the peace. He could not allow his kid to feel that kind of burden. "Of course not, bud. No way I'd let you miss your Mom's mac and cheese."

Derek tried not to flinch when Lisa squeezed his arm and headed for the kitchen, her hips shifting as she spoke over her shoulder. "You're such a good sport, Derek."

He held in about a million nasty things he'd like to say in reply and followed her through the living room, ruffling his son's hair along the way. It had been a while since she'd pulled something like this, but it wasn't a shocker. She always had something up her sleeve. In the beginning he'd assumed she played these games to try and get them back together, but he soon realized she was taunting him. Daring him to be the bad guy. To hurt Tanner and give her justification to cut Derek from their lives. He would never give her the satisfaction. If it meant sitting through a meal with the woman, he'd do it. A million times if that's what it took.

They all stepped into the kitchen and Derek noticed she'd already set the table. For four. He sucked in a breath and then glanced at Lisa, who'd conveniently made herself busy. He hated having diabolical thoughts about the mother of his child, a woman he'd planned to spend the rest of his life with at one point, but he couldn't help it. She drove him to madness and she knew it.

"Where do you want me to sit?" he asked with all the politeness he could muster.

She glanced over her shoulder and smiled. "Right there is fine. I invited Lane over. Again, just not thinking."

"Sure," he said a little too dryly. He'd never even heard of this person and that pissed him off. Not out of jealousy, but because whatever she did affected their son. "I hope *Lane* doesn't mind me being here."

"Oh no, he's such a sweet guy. Laid-back, nothing ever fazes him. Such a nice change in my life. In fact I don't think I've ever been so happy."

Derek remained silent despite the fact that he was bursting to give her a piece of his mind. He would not allow her to manipulate his actions. He quickly decided that Lane might be a saint to put up with this woman. Or maybe this was all his fault. It could be that Lisa was a good woman—she had been once—and he'd damaged her with his terrible choices. Through high school they'd been inseparable. Happy. It had just been the natural course of things that led them to grow apart in college. It happened to young couples every day. And he'd seen their breakup coming for a while, he knew she had, too. But they'd held on to each other out of familiarity, comfort, fear . . . who knew what. And long after they'd both known that they wouldn't be with one another forever, they'd continued to have sex.

Tanner scooted his chair closer to the table and Derek instantly noticed that his son looked a little down. He hated anything that made his son uncomfortable—which he could tell this was—so Derek put on a fake smile, deciding to handle this like a pro.

"How was school this week, bud?"

Tanner shrugged. "Okay, I guess."

"Just okay? How'd you do on your spelling test today?"

"I only missed one."

"What word was that?"

"Situation. S-I-T-U-A-T-I-O-N."

"Well, looks you got it down now. But that is a tough one. Still proud of you." Derek gave Tanner a wink. Lisa placed a giant baking dish of steaming macaroni on the table before heading back into the attached kitchen. Derek looked back to his son and leaned in close. "Hey, I had an idea. I thought we could go sledding tomorrow."

Tanner's eyes flicked toward his mother for a beat before she turned and frowned, obviously overhearing the conversation.

"Oh shoot, Tanner just went sledding yesterday," Lisa said as she walked over and set a plate of chicken fingers down on the table. "Lane and I took him down the road to that hill behind the grocery store. I should have thought you'd have that idea. Sorry."

Derek worked his jaw back and forth as he collected his thoughts. He rested his forearms on the kitchen table and leaned forward a bit, steeling himself. *Do not react.* Derek glanced at his son who looked sad. And guilty. That served to settle Derek's frustration a little. The last thing he wanted was for Tanner to feel bad about what they'd done. Reaching out, Derek grabbed his son's hand and gave it a quick squeeze.

"Hey, bud, no big deal, I'm glad you had a good time." Derek forced a genuine smile.

"I still want to go with you, Dad. Your hill in Preston is the best."

"Darn right it is. And there's definitely no such thing as too much sledding, gotta pack it in when the snow hits."

Tanner grinned and that was enough to make Derek forget how much he wanted to strangle Lisa. She knew damn well that he'd always taken Tanner sledding when the weather permitted, had started the minute Tanner could fit into a toddler-sized snowsuit. In all those years Lisa had never accompanied them. Had never desired to stand out in the cold for any reason. Derek knew she'd purposely taken Tanner first yesterday just to try and rob him of that pleasure. It didn't matter. She and this *Lane* character—whoever the hell this moron was—could never replace him in Tanner's life. He was his father and that meant more than anything.

Five minutes later when Lane walked into the kitchen, Derek could tell by the shocked and awkward look on the man's face that he'd had no idea what he was in for when his girlfriend invited him over for dinner. Derek almost felt sorry for him as he stood and shook the man's hand. He introduced himself and apologized for the surprise.

"No problem at all. It's nice to finally meet you," Lane said with an awkward smile. Seemed Lisa had managed to make every male in the room uncomfortable. Classic. Why did she have to do that? She could be sweet and nurturing if she wanted to. He'd seen it before.

And "finally"? Lane's words settled into Derek's mind. How long had this guy been around? Derek wondered why Tanner had never mentioned him. Or maybe Lisa had kept the relationship from their son for a while. *Good luck, man,* Derek thought. *You're gonna need it.*

"I really think this one brings out the warm tones in the tile on the backsplash. Don't you agree?" Anne asked, her face scrunched up in indecision as she held a stained chip of wood next to a tile sample. It was early Saturday morning and they were choosing floor stain over coffee and doughnuts in Anne's current kitchen. In fact, they'd been at it for almost an hour and Lindsey was all decisioned out.

"I think you should go with your first instinct," Lindsey said, pulling another sample chip to the forefront. "This one is not as dark. That was a concern you had initially."

Anne shook her head. "You're right. I just can't help thinking that Mike said he liked this one." She pointed to a different stain sample.

Lindsey sat back in her chair with a sigh. "True, he did. But that was also after you'd forced him to choose even though he'd previously said he didn't care many times. And if I recall, he told you his favorite and then once again followed it up with a 'But do whatever you want, babe. I'm happy when you're happy.'" Lindsey had lowered her voice while imitating Anne fiancé. She now wanted to imitate a gagging gesture but she refrained. Good thing because Anne smiled, the happy, glowing smile of a woman well loved.

"You're right. He's said that through the whole process. I just keep trying to make him help me. He'll have to live there too, and I'd like him to tell me what he wants."

"I think all he wants is you," Lindsey said. "I'm pretty sure when he says he wants only what you want, you should believe him. Since you can't decide, how about we put this decision up for vote on the blog?"

Anne's eyes lit up. "Yes, let's do that. Take it out of my hands because I like them all and I just can't make a choice."

Lindsey nodded. "Okay. I'll post an updated photo of the kitchen and samples of each color. Let's allow them to vote for two days, see what we get."

"Readers will love that. Every time we have a vote they get so excited. But not nearly as excited as I am to go out and see the progress made on the house. I haven't made it out in a couple of weeks. Derek texted when the entryway was done but I told him not to send a picture. I want to see it in person."

Lindsey tried not to squirm when her friend mentioned enemy number one. Everything had been going great during the renovation until lately, and then boom, she just kept seeing him. Was that his plan, to just keep showing up and wearing her down? Lindsey wished she could be certain that plan wouldn't work.

"Why don't we head over there this afternoon and see how things are going?" Anne asked, interrupting

Lindsey's daydreams. "We can even take these stain chips and see what they look like in the afternoon light."

"That sounds like a good idea." Lindsey smiled.

"Perfect," Anne said. She then looked a little . . . wary. "How about this? I promised Claire we could go sledding for a little while. You could come with us and then we can stop and see it when we're finished. I'll even buy you lunch."

Lindsey narrowed her eyes, but gave a half smile before speaking. "Don't think I don't know what you're up to. You don't want to take Claire down the hill, do you?"

Anne sighed. "No. You know I don't love heights and I'm not quite comfortable letting Claire go by herself yet."

Lindsey considered it. It wasn't that she minded sledding but she didn't necessarily love heights, either. But how bad could it be? "Okay, that could be fun. Do you have some accessories I could borrow? I left my sledding gear at home."

Anne winked and stood up from the kitchen chair. "You're the best. I'll go get everything ready."

"I'm betting it already is if I know you," Lindsey called over her shoulder.

Twenty minutes later they were pulling into the parking lot of the elementary school at the edge of town. Lindsey didn't live in Preston—never had—but even she'd heard about the Hill. The town had cleverly named the long stretch of sloping grass that lined the elementary school property. People from surrounding small towns and even in the Kansas City suburbs drove out just to sled when it snowed, it was that impressive. And now that Lindsey was really looking at it, it was a little steep. A little tall. But she could handle it. Had to because at this point Claire was bouncing beneath her seat belt and there was no way she could let the little girl down.

Anne pulled into a parking spot and Claire squealed as she saw a couple of her school friends wave as they headed for the bustling sledding area. "Hurry, Mom. My friends are here."

"Claire, please quiet down. We'll get up there as soon as we can, no rush."

"It's busy today," Lindsey said as she got out of the car and shoved a red knitted cap over her thick hair. "Guess that's not a surprise since it might be the last big snow."

Lindsey adjusted the scarf Anne had loaned her, pulled on her gloves, and then helped unload everything else from the car. Claire, the sled, a thermos of cocoa, a bag of cups and extra snow gear. Anne was always prepared, and Lindsey smiled as she spotted the homemade marshmallows in a plastic bag. Only Anne.

"Okay, how about if you guys head up and I'll wait for you at the bottom?" Anne said.

"Come on, Lindsey," Claire yelled as she began to take off.

"Hey, little lady, you wait up. I can't run in these boots."

Lindsey tucked the big toboggan-style plastic sled under her arm and followed Claire through the snowy field and then up the incline. It wasn't long before she thought she might die, as the trek upward started to feel like climbing a mountain. With the wind blowing in her face, the cold biting at her nose, and the sun blinding her, she was exhausted by the time they made it to the top.

"Hang on, Bug. I need to . . . take . . . take a break," Lindsey said, stepping over to the side and dropping the sled in the snow. Several groups of teenagers pushed by, laughing and roughhousing. Lindsey blew out a long breath and loosened her scarf. Funny how her cheeks were frozen but she was pretty darn sure that sweat was pooling beneath her clothing. She needed to join a gym. Fast.

"Hi, Mr. Derek," Claire called from behind Lindsey. "Hi, Tanner."

Lindsey stilled. As if her heart weren't already working overtime. She didn't want to turn around but had little choice. And there he was, the object of her ire. He looked just as shocked to see her. Even a little panicked. He quickly looked her over and then stepped closer.

"You okay, Linds?" Derek asked.

Lindsey shifted her boots in the snow in order to face them. His deep voice held a hint of concern.

"I'm fine," she said, retying her scarf and hating how short of breath she was. "Just not used to climbing hills."

"Understandable." Derek gave her a halfhearted smile, and although Lindsey couldn't see through his sunglasses, she could imagine his bright blue eyes staring back at her. He was in jeans, a puffy navy coat, gloves, and a bright orange knitted cap that appeared to be made for hunters. He looked ridiculous. And adorable. She suddenly felt like an abominable snowman in the coat she had on.

Lindsey's eyes flicked to the young boy standing

beside Derek, her heart doing a flip in her chest. She looked back at Derek and he noticeably swallowed.

"Lindsey, this is my son, Tanner," he said.

The boy gave a shy smile and just like that Lindsey felt dizzy. This boy was . . . older than she expected. Courtesy of Callie, she'd known Derek had a son, known he'd been married and was now divorced. Her brain quickly tried to process how old he appeared to be. Definitely older than five as he was fairly tall. But certainly not a teen.

She bit the inside of her cheek and looked up at Derek. The confidence she'd grown to expect from him was wiped clean from his face. For once Derek looked nervous. Incredibly so.

Laying an arm across his son's back, he pulled him in close and then cleared his throat before continuing. "Tanner, this is Lindsey. An old friend of mine."

"It's nice to meet you, Tanner." Lindsey focused on the handsome little boy staring up at her. He had Derek's blue eyes, full lips, and a mop of dark blond hair on his head that peeked from under his knit Spiderman cap. He looked so much like his dad it made her heart ache.

"Nice to meet you, too," he said in a little-man voice.

"You couldn't drag your mom up here, Claire?" Derek teased, clearly trying to change the subject.

"She's scared of being high up," Claire said.

Lindsey tuned out of the conversation between Derek and Claire for a moment, instead turning her focus on Derek's son who stood quietly near his dad. Tanner was nearly a foot taller than Claire. Definitely older than Claire's six. So Tanner had to be at least seven. *Or eight.*

Lindsey suddenly felt sick to her stomach because so many things began to make sense.

I'm still in love with someone else. This shouldn't have happened. She'd never forget his words for as long as she lived. They had ripped her in two.

"So, you ready to go down?" Derek asked.

Lindsey jerked her head up to catch him staring at her. There was no missing the tight line of his lips. He knew exactly what she'd been thinking. This was obviously what he'd wanted to explain to her. Silly her. Derek hadn't wanted something to spark up again between the two of them. He'd just wanted to ease the burden of his guilt. Probably wanted to explain it before she had a chance to figure it out on her own.

But why bother, really? Their past was just that. The past. Whatever his reasons for leaving her, it was no longer her problem. She had a plan to keep her distance while they worked on the farmhouse project, and if she stayed strong she would be fine. Just fine. She was always fine. She'd been fine for years. Fine. Fine. Fine.

Don't cry, Lindsey.

"Of course we're ready. Come on, Claire." Picking up their sled, Lindsey walked toward the line of people waiting their turn. Claire stood beside her, peeking around the milling bodies, watching people descend.

Lindsey knew Derek and his son stood behind them, but she didn't dare turn around. She knew it was rude, she'd just been introduced to the boy, but she could not look at them anymore. It was bad enough hearing their conversation behind her.

"Dude, was that your stomach growling?" Derek asked in an amused tone.

The mini-Derek laughed. A full-out little-boy giggle. Lindsey clamped her eyes shut. Why was it always her listening in on the laughter of other families? Never part of it. Never for her.

"We'll go get some pizza after we leave here," Derek told his son.

Finally they were up and Lindsey looked down the hill with a twinge of unease. It was much steeper than it appeared from the base. And higher. She let her eyes roam until she made out Anne's red coat in the distance. She looked pretty darn small way down there, and now it was apparent why she'd chosen to stay at the bottom. Lindsey swallowed.

Behind her Derek spoke quietly. "You okay?"

"I'm fine," she said without turning. "Ready, Bug?"

"Uhhh." Great. Claire was scared also. Was a fear of heights genetic? Either way, neither of them were running in fear. Of the man behind them or the drop ahead.

Lindsey bent over and dropped the sled in front of them. "We can do it, Claire. It's gonna be so much fun."

Debating the best way to gracefully plop down on the sled, Lindsey straddled the purple plastic. When it began to slide, a big booted foot came out to stop it.

"I got it. Sit down," Derek said. She chose not to give him the satisfaction of looking up into his eyes. Instead she leaned down, rested one glove in the snow and eased herself into the back of the plastic. Her butt instantly froze. She adjusted her legs and patted the space between them.

"Okay, sweetie. Climb in," she said to Claire.

Claire hesitated. She glanced from Lindsey down to

where her mother waited. She was at the bottom of the run waving her encouragement.

"I'm scared," Claire whispered, her glove making a scratching noise as it brushed Lindsey's shoulder.

"It's okay, Claire. It will be fun. Promise." Lindsey couldn't very well admit to the six-year-old that she was a little intimidated, too. She patted the space between her legs again, sensing the restlessness of the line growing behind them. "Your mom will love watching you. And the sooner we get down there the faster you can have some of that hot cocoa."

Claire paused, glanced over Lindsey's head, presumably at Derek and Tanner.

"I promise you'll love it, Claire," Derek said. "How about I take a video of you on my phone and we can send it to Mike? He'll be so proud of you."

Lindsey's insides twisted at the paternal way Derek spoke to Claire. There was absolutely no doubt in her mind that Derek was a wonderful father. And his idea to film it for Mike was good. Claire adored Mike and would be thrilled to send him the video.

Claire grinned. "Yes, please."

But of course now Derek was going to do the honors, meaning he would have footage of her, Lindsey, in this ginormous Michelin-man ski jacket she'd borrowed from Anne. Oh well, she'd have to suck it up. Claire climbed in and snuggled between Lindsey's bent legs. No going back now.

"Okay, hold on," Derek said. Lindsey could feel the toe of his boot resting against her backside. "Ready, ladies?"

"Ready," Claire called.

Lindsey felt Derek's foot shove the back of the sled and she instinctively gripped the little person in front of her as they flew down the hill. Through the piercing cry that broke free from Claire's mouth Lindsey briefly registered the rumble of Derek's laugh. But it didn't last as they sailed down, Claire's screams turning into giggles. Lindsey felt the snow bump under her rear, at some point they seemed to catch air, and then all too quickly they were coasting along the flat base of the hill. Lindsey put her legs out to the side to stop them—frigid snow rushing up her pant legs. As soon as she was able Claire rocketed out of her seat, running to Anne, laughing and screaming.

Lindsey realized she'd been grinning like an idiot the whole way down. She stood up and turned to look up to the top of the hill. She found Derek quickly with that atrocious hat on, even though many bodies dotted the area in front of the trees. He gave her a small wave before he and Tanner sat down on their own sleds.

Lindsey's smile vanished, the reality of what had just transpired finally sinking in. He truly hadn't been in love with her. All that time he'd been with someone else and that someone had given birth to his child. This handsome little boy. None of it had been what she'd thought it was. Those feelings she was certain he'd revealed in his touch, his kiss, his looks . . . clearly she'd dreamed them up.

The only time wasted was all the years you weren't mine.

What did all of this mean? Had he made a mistake? Well, regret was a hard pill to swallow and it was too little too late with her. Not that he'd implied he wanted anything more than for her to understand. She was clearly a piece of his guilty conscience because he'd made her fall in love with him. And then he'd abandoned her.

Well, she'd just have to convince him that she was in no need of his apology or pity. These days she decided what happened to her and she was determined to be stronger. She'd done her fair share of being a pushover. Sometimes out of love like with her father. But sometimes out of fear, which she couldn't allow to happen. No longer.

She would use Derek's return into her sphere to mark the beginning of a new Lindsey. She knew if she didn't learn to stand up for herself, Derek Walsh had the power to destroy her heart all over again.

Four

She knew.

He'd seen it in her eyes, the way she'd glanced between Tanner and Claire, trying to assess his age, work out the time line. Obviously Derek had planned to tell her when the time was right, and this had most definitely not been that time.

He'd wanted the right setting, the perfect lead-in. Wasn't gonna happen.

Damn it.

He should have just said it the last time he'd seen her. To hell with her not being ready. He'd never dreamed they would run into Lindsey at the Hill. She didn't even live in Preston. Although Derek couldn't deny that a tiny part of him was relieved, okay, maybe a big part. Now maybe they could finally have the conversation that needed to be had. Say the things that should have been said years ago. He hoped that he could finally make Lindsey see why things had happened the way they did. Surely she would give him that now. But if he were to be honest, he was still a little fearful she wouldn't be willing.

He couldn't accept that. He would beg her to hear him out if he had to. He wanted Lindsey's forgiveness. Wanted them to move past what had happened.

From a distance Derek watched as Lindsey trudged up the hill once more, Claire yapping along beside her. Lindsey looked exhausted, her legs dragging and her shoulders slumped. This was trip six up the hill for them. Actually eight for Claire. She and another little girl had gone together a few times and Lindsey had waited for Claire at the top. Not that he'd kept tabs on her the whole time. Okay, he'd definitely been watching her all morning. Couldn't help himself.

How she managed to look sexy in that damn puffy coat he couldn't say, but she did. Maybe it was because he'd seen enough of her in the past to know what was concealed beneath. Lindsey's body had always been breathtaking, but the years had been good to her. Full hips and thighs, round ass. Her breasts used to fit perfectly in his hand but he could tell that even those were fuller. He imagined the weight of them, the satiny feel of her nipples against his lips.

Derek clamped his teeth together, lifted his stocking cap to scratch at his hair and then pulled it back down on his head. He really had to stop having thoughts about her like that. Starting things back up with Lindsey was not only slim to none in the chances department, but also a bad idea. He wasn't in a place to have a serious relationship and the last thing he could ever allow himself to do was hurt Lindsey again.

As they ascended the summit Derek and Tanner headed toward the ever-growing line. All the while he watched as Claire, Lindsey, and what appeared to be Mike's niece Bailey spoke a little farther down the hill. He hadn't yet seen Mike's sister here, but obviously she'd brought her daughter. Derek knew the two little girls were best friends from school. In fact, it was that friendship that had brought Mike and Anne together in the first place.

Derek continued to watch them as Lindsey pulled something out of her pocket. It was blue and egg shaped. She twisted it apart and rubbed it on her lips. He angled his body away—concealed by a group of kids—but continued to watch her through his dark sunglasses, her lips rubbing against one another as she shoved what had to have been lip gloss back into her coat pocket. Her head turned in his direction then, and he looked away.

After a few minutes it was nearly their turn to go down when Tanner patted Derek's arm.

"Look, they're going to the big drop."

"Damn," Derek muttered under his breath. For just a moment he considered how interesting it was that his son had apparently caught on that the girls were to be watched, but he didn't have time to analyze whether he was being too obvious in his interest. He motioned for Tanner to step out of line and follow him.

"Dad. What are you doing? Are we almost done?"

With a quick hush, Derek led them over to where the girls had gone. The big drop was the tallest, steepest section of the Hill. It was frequented by teenage boys and snowboarders looking for a little more of a thrill. Kids were known to use it too occasionally, but it certainly wasn't as popular with them. Derek suspected many parents prohibited their kids from going down it, although there wasn't anything truly unsafe about it. He and Tanner usually saved it for last, since you always wiped out at the end and left with snow shoved into every available crevice.

He wasn't really certain why Lindsey was taking the girls over there. Didn't really seem like their kind of gig considering she and Claire had both started out a little fearful.

Derek and Tanner followed them and came up behind where they stood watching a few boys do tricks on their snowboards.

"You gonna try it?" he asked.

Lindsey jumped and jerked her head around. "I need to put a bell around your neck."

Derek couldn't help chuckling. He stepped around to face her. "That would take all the fun out of things."

Lindsey gave him a sidelong glance before finally dropping her shoulders. "Claire and Bailey want to go down this hill. Claire on her own sled. Is it safe?"

"I go all the time. Uncle Mike took me when I was three." Bailey put a hand on her hip. Lindsey and Derek looked at each other, and for just a moment he thought they might almost laugh together. But she collected herself.

"I don't doubt Mike did that," Derek said. He knew his friend well.

"He did!" Bailey continued. "Claire and me can go by ourselves. It will be so fun."

"Please, Lindsey," Claire whined before turning to

look up at Derek. "Will you record it again and send it to Mike? I want him to see me do it, too."

The girls nearly bounced in their boots with anticipation. Not for the first tim, Derek was a little grateful he didn't have girls. They were a handful, and he was certain that Claire was a little jealous because Bailey had gone down the steep hill with her soon-to-be-stepdad and she hadn't.

"I'm gonna have to leave this one up to Lindsey," he said in response to Claire.

Lindsey eyed him for a moment and then glanced around him to look at the drop.

"I just don't know . . ." she said, her voice hesitant.

"Please, Lindsey?" Claire begged.

"I'm gonna call your mom and ask her." Lindsey quickly pulled her phone from a zipped pocket inside her coat, stepped to the side and briefly spoke to Anne. After a second she came back, her face twisted in uncertainty.

"Okay, she said yes, but you have to wait till she can get to the bottom on this end before you go," Lindsey said. She put up a finger and wagged it as she spoke. "And you have to stop yourself at the end otherwise you'll coast toward the creek."

"I will," Claire said.

"No worries there," Derek couldn't help interjecting. "They probably won't even make it that far. Not heavy enough. Even Tanner and I usually wipe out after that bottom run."

Lindsey's head tilted to the side as she looked at him wide-eyed. "Are you trying to make me change my mind?"

Derek grinned. "Just giving you all the facts. They'll be fine."

They all watched in silence as Anne—along with Mike's sister Erin—made their way across the field below and stood toward the bottom of the hill in front of them. Anne gave a wave and then Lindsey looked down at Claire.

"All right, please be careful." Lindsey dropped the sled onto the snow. While she got the girls situated, Derek quietly motioned for his son to go ahead and descend also. Tanner nodded and sat down on his disc sled. If he and Lindsey were here together he was going to use this situation to his advantage. There was no way he was going to walk away from her today without some kind of conversation taking place between them.

"Why don't you watch Tanner go first?" Derek suggested. At his words, Tanner took off down the hill. They all watched as he disappeared over the steep slope, reappeared and then bumped a few times, and finally wiped out about eight feet from Anne and Erin. Tanner waved as soon as he got up.

"That doesn't look too bad, does it?" Lindsey asked aloud, although Derek had a feeling she was trying to convince herself. "Okay, on three."

She began to count and on her mark, Lindsey pushed the sled over the crest and the girls instantly began to scream. The sound of Lindsey's laughter sent an ache through Derek's body. God, she had the most beautiful laugh. He hadn't heard that sound in years, but it felt like yesterday.

Derek stepped beside Lindsey. She was focused intently on Claire and Anne at the bottom of the hill, a faint smile teasing her lips. Her face was reddened from the cold wind, highlighting her cheekbones and drawing his attention to her eyes. She had the longest eyelashes. When she caught him staring her expression fell. Clearly she would be happier anywhere else but standing at the top of the hill alone with him.

"You look pretty today," he said. Instantly he regretted opening with such a line. It was ridiculous considering their current state of affairs, but he definitely meant it. She always looked beautiful and he wanted her to know he thought so.

She gave him a quick look of surprise that blurred into annoyance, but she said nothing.

"Okay, no compliments. Noted." Derek shook his head. "So, we going to talk? I think we both know it's necessary."

"Absolutely not." She didn't even bother looking at him.

Derek's shoulders dropped. "Lindse—"

"Stop." She turned hard, pointing a finger into his chest. He could barely feel it through the bulk of his coat, but the fury in her eyes entranced him. "Don't do it. I'm telling you now, you better stop talking."

He sucked in a breath, a little shocked at her outburst. "Okay. Fine." Her hand dropped and Derek angled his head toward the woods at their back. "So you gonna grab a log to slide down on?"

"I'll just wait for Claire to come back up."

"Oh please, that'll take ten minutes," he said.

Just then her phone rang. As she looked down and then answered it, he happened to notice Anne at the base of the hill, her phone to her ear.

"Hey," Lindsey said, her voice turning friendly as she stepped toward the trees. "No, everything's fine." A pause. "He what? Oh crap. Okay, bye."

"What's wrong?" Derek asked.

"Apparently your son informed Anne that we were probably up here fighting."

"Damn." Derek put his hands on his hips and glanced back down the hill. Anne had led the kids away and was filling cups out of a thermos. He caught Tanner glancing up at him and Lindsey before he turned back to the group. His kid was obviously a lot more intuitive than he ever suspected.

"How old is he?" Her question sliced through Derek's thoughts like a knife. He'd known the conversation was coming. Had wanted it. But the reality of facing her, telling her the truth, was going to kill him.

Here we go.

Derek blew out a breath and stood straight. He looked directly into Lindsey's eyes. She deserved that. "Tanner will be eight in June."

Her lips twisted to the side and she began to shake her head. As if she were still working through the information.

Or trying not to cry. She turned away once more but he ducked in front of her, effectively cutting her off.

"Lindsey, talk to me. Don't pull away. I want to make things right."

She choked out a bitter laugh. "Make things right? Are you serious? There is no making anything right. There is only moving on, which I keep trying to do but you're making it very difficult." Her voice broke on the last few words and he was certain he could feel her pain in his chest.

He took a tentative step closer. So close that he had to tilt his head down to look at her face. She stared right at his chest, lips pursed. "There are so many things I want to say to you. Obviously . . . I wasn't honest with you. Not always, but that day. That day I lied to you and I owe you an explanation."

She scoffed and then met his eyes, her expression indignant. Her teeth clamped down, her emotions turned to fury as she spoke. "God, you're an ass. *An explanation?* You have an eight-year-old son, Derek. With that knowledge I'm pretty sure I don't give a damn what you have to say to me."

Anger churned in his chest, but there really was no arguing with her. She was right. He was an ass and she didn't owe him a damn thing.

"This is humiliating, us fighting up here and your son witnessing it." Lindsey's gloves formed fat fists, her body nearly vibrating with her anger. "And he knew. Your son knew we weren't getting along and called it. How do you think that makes me feel?"

"Linds, he's just a very perceptive kid," he said. And it was true, much to Derek's chagrin. Tanner had years of experience picking up on the subtle nuances that were exchanged between adults. He hated to think of what ran through his son's innocent young mind when it came to him and Lisa. He'd tried so hard to protect him from all of it.

"Perceptive? Is that supposed to make me feel better? I'm a nice person, Derek. A good person, but you make me bitter and ugly."

Derek swallowed hard. The glistening of her beautiful eyes made him want to howl in frustration. "You could never be ugly, Lindsey. No part of you. My son was sensing something from me. Not you. So let's prove him wrong. I'll tell him we were just discussing something. Better yet, go down the hill with me."

Her eyes went wide. "You must be crazy."

Derek forced out a tight grin. "Something like that."

"You have a one-person sled."

He tilted his head to the side, watching her shiny lips. "I'm sure we could work it out."

Lindsey stepped around him and headed back toward the trail. Derek blew out a breath, defeated and irritated. "You going to run, then? Is that it, you're just going to keep hating me forever?"

She suddenly stopped in her tracks. Before he could respond she trudged back over to the edge of the embankment. "Put the damn sled down."

Surprised, Derek immediately followed and dropped the sled down at her feet. Then he waited for her instructions because clearly she was in charge. No problem. He'd give her whatever she wanted.

"Sit down," she ordered.

He sat down on the disc and let his legs hang off the front.

"Cross your legs."

Without a sound he followed instructions. Matter of fact, he kind of liked this bossy side of her. If she needed to be nasty to him he would take it. Deserved it. This was sticky-note Lindsey in the flesh.

With an annoyed sigh she began to ease down into

his lap. He grasped her hips with his hands to guide her but she slapped them away. "Don't touch."

"Linds, come on. We're two adults cramming our bodies onto a sled made for one. I have to hold on to you."

"No you don't."

Derek shook his head but sat still as her body pressed down against his.

And then he was officially in hell. Pleasure hell. And it was torture. Even through the many bulky layers, she felt amazing in his lap. Surely if she hated him as much as she acted like, she wouldn't have just sat down. Lindsey shifted her ass in an attempt to lock herself into place and Derek squeezed his eyes shut.

"You comfortable yet?" he inquired. Because he was in blissful agony.

"No, I'm not comfortable. I'm afraid I'll fall off." The sound of their coats scratching together muffled her voice.

"I hate to bring it up again, but I could hold on to you. Or maybe you should straddle me. Both options sound good," he said with a laugh.

She stilled. And then began to push up out of his lap. "That's—"

Derek wrapped his arms around her waist and pulled her back down. "I'm sorry, that was uncalled-for under the circumstances." He pushed her mass of hair out of his face and shoved his chin onto her shoulder. She smelled like lemons and mint. And because he might never have Lindsey in his arms again, he became reckless for a moment and spoke quietly next to her ear. "I wouldn't have minded, though."

She angled her head, giving him a hard glare. "Get your hands off me, Walsh."

"Oh-kay." He held his arms out and then dropped them to his sides.

"Let's get this over with," she said. Her legs were now crisscrossed on top of his and her arms carefully looped over his thighs so she could grasp the rim of the sled.

"If you won't let me hold on to you, than at least hold on to me. Your fingers might get pinched."

"I'm fine," she bit out. "Just go."

"If you say so. Here we go."

He used his feet to inch them over the edge of the hill and within a second they tilted forward and just as quickly the air was rushing into his face. Lindsey pressed back into his chest, her forearms clenching tightly against his thighs. He couldn't help himself at that point. With the momentum it felt as if she might lose her balance and he took the opportunity to wrap his arms around her waist and pull her against him.

She remained silent but he could feel the tension in her body as they hit a small bump. Her ass bounced in his lap and he grabbed onto her ankle, pulling her body against his to keep her on board. Unable to hold it in, Derek laughed against her and he could have sworn he felt her do the same, her body vibrating against his chest.

They hit the last bump and began to career into the final stretch, and before he knew it they crashed and rolled. He could feel Lindsey turn onto her side beneath him, and as soon as they came to a complete stop he worked to quickly get off her.

"Everybody okay?" Anne called.

Derek turned to find everyone rushing over. He leaned down to shake the snow out of his jeans.

"Uh . . . Dad," Tanner said. Derek glanced down to where Tanner was looking. *Lindsey.* She was still down on all fours, her back heaving up and down as if she were having trouble breathing, her head limp. Instantly Derek felt as if he would be sick.

"Linds." Derek's heart thumped in his chest as he fell to his knees beside her. From this angle he could see the way she held her left arm close to her chest, putting no weight on it. She was wearing gloves but they weren't very thick.

"Lindsey, are you hurt? Did you scrape your fingers?"

"Oh no." Anne rushed to Lindsey's other side. "Lindsey, are you okay?"

Lindsey's head shook quickly back and forth and he wasn't sure whose question she was responding to. Derek pulled back the hair that was concealing her face and found her eyes red and pinched in pain.

He instantly leaned forward close to her face, his lips brushing her temple. "Babe, talk to me. What happened?"

"I'm okay," she whispered.

Clearly she was not okay. "You hurt your fingers, didn't you?"

"No. My wrist." Her voice weakened on the last word and he knew she wanted to cry. It nearly undid him, and he couldn't help himself. Instinct took over.

He instantly stood up and went behind Lindsey, wrapping his arms around her waist. "Brace yourself." He felt her stiffen and he immediately pulled her upright into a standing position.

"Derek, is her arm broken?" Anne said, her voice sounding panicky as she saw the way Lindsey favored the limb.

"I don't know. Lindsey, let me take a look."

Thankfully she turned to face him, and the pain etched into her face worried everyone. He could tell when he heard Claire gasp. A set of teenaged snowboarders nearly collided only a few feet from them and Derek turned to his son.

"Tanner, get all the sleds and let's get everyone back to the parking lot," Derek said, thankful when his son immediately obeyed. Anne began to gather everyone up, and without waiting Derek began to guide Lindsey through the field, cutting across to the lot where he could assess the damage. He felt sick to his stomach knowing that she was in pain, especially when he heard her sniffle through her nose. She was still trying to hold herself together.

As if she could read his thoughts and they'd annoyed her, she spoke up.

"I'll be fine," she said. She cleared her throat, trying to sound the part. He knew better. She kept it up anyway, frustrating woman. "Really, I think I just need to take some pain medicine. Maybe an ice pack. Or a heating pad. It's not a big deal. If you could just let go of me, everything would be better."

There was no way in hell he was letting her go without checking things out. He had a bad feeling she might need a doctor. Derek stepped over a large fallen tree limb and helped her do the same, never once releasing his hold of her right hand.

"I mean it, Derek. It's fine. *I'm* fine. It doesn't even hurt that bad anymore. The only—ssss!" She hissed as her body moved against a bit of cold wind.

"Lindsey," Derek said in warning.

"What?"

"Stop talking."

Surprisingly she did as he said and as soon as they hit the pavement he led her to his truck.

"What are you doing? Anne's car is over there." She began to pull away and Derek tightened his grip on her coat. *"Derek."*

He ignored her protests and unlocked the doors, opened the driver side and gently shoved her into the space between the seat and the door. "Now let me look at your wrist."

She bit her bottom lip and lifted her left arm about waist high. Derek pulled off his gloves and tossed them into the front seat of the truck. He gently steadied her arm with one hand and then began to slowly pull off her glove. As soon as he gave the slightest tug she yelped, sliding it away from him.

"Babe, this isn't good. It might be broken."

"Will you please stop calling me that? And Anne is perfectly capable of helping me figure this out."

Derek glared down at her and then looked back toward the tailgate of his truck where Anne, Claire, and Tanner stood waiting. Bailey and Erin had apparently taken off. "Anne, how about you take the kids to your place? I'm taking Lindsey to the hospital."

"What? No!" Lindsey protested. She looked pleadingly at her friend. "Anne, don't you dare leave me with him."

Anne's eyes widened and she nonchalantly nodded down to Tanner. The look must have done something to Lindsey because she quickly changed her tune. "I mean, can't you just take me? Please? I'd hate to inconvenience Derek and Tanner."

Anne looked sympathetic. "Sweetie, it might be easier if the kids just came home with me. Claire hasn't had lunch yet and who knows how long it will take in the ER. I could feed them both and we can wait for you without exposing them to hospital germs. It's still flu season."

Lindsey stood a little taller, her body sending off all kinds of signals. Derek knew she was freaking out right now at the thought of spending so much time alone with him. He could feel it. But he also knew that Lindsey was an insanely sensible woman and there really was no arguing with Anne's logic. He had her. This wasn't necessarily how he wanted her, but he knew better than to be choosy.

"Get in the truck," he whispered. Her eyes met his.

"I don't like you right now," she whispered back before pulling herself in with her good hand.

"I'll have to live with that. After I make sure your wrist is not broken." Derek pushed her hip in a little farther and shut the door before she had a chance to respond. He went around back, had a few quick words with Tanner—who seemed fine once Anne mentioned grilled cheese, potato chips, and chocolate chip cookies—and then got in the driver's seat.

Derek felt awful for causing Lindsey to get hurt. He should have made her hold on to him and not the sled, but trying to force Lindsey Morales to do anything didn't feel like a smart move. Until now. He was definitely forcing her to the hospital.

After turning on the ignition Derek looked over to see her fumbling with her seat belt, obviously unable to use her left hand to buckle it or even pull off her right glove. Derek leaned over, removed it from her grasp and locked it in place for her.

"Thank you," she said. But he could tell it was difficult for her to mutter the words.

"You're welcome." Derek sighed and took in the sight of Lindsey sitting in his truck. Her cheeks were still flushed, her eyes glassy, and her long hair a little messy under that ridiculous red stocking cap. She was chewing on her bottom lip and very purposely not turning toward him. It was kind of cute, her trying to be a hardass. He'd still much rather see her smiling.

"I *can* be a nice guy, you know?"

She didn't respond. The only way he knew she'd heard him was the way her lashes fluttered and her teeth worked at her lip with a little more intensity. Fine, he'd just have to keep trying to prove it to her.

Five

Lindsey stared straight ahead as they made their way down the highway. Dirty snow was piled along the ditch and watching it fly past through the windshield made her nauseous. She clamped her eyes closed and let herself fall back to the headrest. The throbbing in her wrist probably wasn't helping her state of mind, but she was doing her best to think of anything but the fact that she was sitting in the enemy's truck.

It was torturous in so many ways. On top of her pain, the scent of Derek overwhelmed her. A heady mix of his familiar musk and . . . wood shavings? That was new, he'd never smelled like that before, but it made sense given his job. She could also smell leather but figured that was coming from the huge tool belt that rested between them on the center console. A pile of rolled-up papers cluttered the floor at her feet. Obviously building plans. This was definitely a workingman's vehicle and she hated that it was so . . . *him*.

He'd cranked up the heater, the warm air blowing on her chilled cheeks. That felt nice, but warming her skin did nothing for the intense agony radiating through her arm and the roiling of her stomach.

She should have listened to him when he'd warned her against holding on to the plastic. At the time, pinched fingers seemed preferable to hooking her hands around Derek's thighs. When they'd flipped into the snow she hadn't let go, her fingers tight on the plastic rim as they tumbled and rolled.

In the midst of their wipeout, her wrist had hyperextended and twisted. Their combined body weight landing on top of it was the final straw. When the searing pain had shot through her arm she'd nearly cried out.

Please don't let it be broken.

She didn't have time for a broken arm, but more than anything she couldn't afford it. An X-ray alone was going to do her in. But it was probably going to be necessary. Her wrist was definitely damaged and she had to know how bad. What if it was broken and she didn't find out? As much as she hated to admit it, she knew Derek was right about going to the hospital. She just hated that he was the one driving her.

"You okay?" Derek's deep voice filled the truck's small cab. "You didn't hit your head when we wiped out, did you?"

"No, I'm fine," she said quietly. Again. If she kept saying those words would they eventually be true? She opened her eyes but didn't turn to look at him. Thankfully they were already pulling into the hospital parking lot. Derek went around back to the emergency room entrance and drove under the portico that covered the entryway. He came to a stop outside the sliding glass doors.

"Thanks for—" she began, but he cut her off.

"You go in and get your name down. I'll meet you in there."

"No, I'm good alone for now." She finally turned to him. "You go and I'll call my sister to come get me when I'm done."

Derek glared at her. "Lindsey, I'm not about to drop you off and leave."

"But I don't want you here." She stared, urging him to see that she was serious. The look in his too hand-some face told her he cared nothing for what she had to say at the moment.

"Tough, babe. Now get out of the truck so I can park."

Lindsey ground her teeth together as she used her right hand to try and unlock her seat belt. Her coat was so big and her gloves so slippery that she couldn't man-age it—she'd known that before she'd even started try-ing. Once again Derek reached over and handled it for her. She didn't bother thanking him, just opened the door, slid off the seat, and slammed the door.

He pulled away and she walked into the waiting area. Thankfully it wasn't incredibly busy—only a woman with a small child sleeping in her arms and a couple of men. One of them was holding a bloody towel to his forehead. Yikes. She turned and walked over to the check-in desk. Another woman with a sick child was fin-ishing up in front of her. Finally she stepped up to the counter.

"Fill out the clipboard and I'll be right with you," the woman sitting behind the desk said.

Lindsey glanced down at her uninjured gloved hand and hesitated. She had to free her fingers in order to write, so she didn't have a lot of options. "I'm sorry to bother you," she said. The woman looked up and Lindsey held out her hand. "Any way you could—"

A large arm reached out from beside her and grabbed her arm.

"I got it." Derek's warm fingers grasped her right wrist while he gently pulled the glove off. She told herself that the sight of his hands did nothing to her, but that would be a lie. She'd dreamed of Derek's hands. The sprinkling of dark hair on the back of his palms, his blunt fingers topped with trimmed nails. She couldn't help noticing that they looked a little rougher than they had in college. Without comment, Lindsey filled out the paperwork, and then they headed into the waiting area.

Derek sat down right beside her, bringing his warmth and his scent with him. He'd removed his big coat and stocking cap before coming in, trading it for a light but rugged work coat. His hair was mussed, as if he'd run his hands through it, leaving it in sexy disarray. So typical.

"This could take a while. You really don't need to stay." Lindsey carefully rested her left hand on her thigh.

"I thought we'd already discussed this. How are you feeling?" he asked. "Hopefully they'll give you something for the pain."

Clearly he was staying no matter what, and she hated that a little part of her was glad. If for no other reason than the fact that no one wanted to be in an ER alone. "I'll be okay."

The plastic window at the check-in counter slid open and banged on the frame. "Lindsey Morales."

Lindsey stood up and walked over, answered a few questions about why she was visiting, if she'd taken any medication, and if she'd been out of the country recently. Right, she could just barely afford to fill up with gas most days, she certainly wasn't vacationing.

When they were done she was instructed to sit once more and wait for the triage nurse. She went back to where Derek was seated and this time—out of spite and the desire to keep some distance between them—chose a chair across the aisle from him.

"Really?" he asked, shaking his head. He leaned forward and rested his elbows on his knees. His words were a harsh whisper. "You can't even sit by me?"

"What do you want me to say?" she asked. "We aren't even friends."

"Yeah, because of you."

Lindsey gasped. "Because of me? You have a lot of nerve saying that."

Derek sighed and let his head fall forward in defeat. After a second he looked up at her, his expression soft. "You're right. I'm sorry. It's absolutely because of me. But we *could* be friends if you allowed us to try."

She shrugged. "It doesn't really seem necessary."

"Oh come on, Linds. One of my very good friends is getting married to your very good friend. We are both in their wedding and we are also working on their house together. The least we could do is learn to be pleasant."

"I'm not unpleasant!" she said indignantly.

He raised his eyebrows and had the audacity to chuckle. "So you're going for sweetness when you leave all those snotty little Post-its all over the work site?"

"Those aren't snotty, they're informative. I'm not trying to kiss anyone's butt. I'm trying to get my point across."

"Oh, you're getting your point across, all right." He leaned back and glanced out the window, a smile working at the corner of his mouth. "The guys even have a name for your little notes."

She gasped, shocked at what he was saying. "What is it?"

Derek laughed and shook his head. "Nah, I don't want to betray their confidence."

"That's not fair. I'm a really nice person." It was true. Her sister was always telling her she was too nice. Too agreeable. It actually hurt her feelings that his crew talked about her this way behind her back. She'd only gone on-site while they were working a couple of times. Had they been thinking bad things about her then?

"I know you're a really nice person," Derek continued. "I remember it. But these days you're only nice to everyone else. Not me."

Lindsey took a deep breath and looked into Derek's face. "I don't know how to feel right now. I was mad at you before. But now . . . after today . . . Now I know it was even worse than I'd always thought. Knowing that you'd truly never lo—"

"Lindsey Morales," a voice called from across the room. And thank God it had stopped her from saying something she'd regret. Obviously she was in an altered state due to the pain.

Lindsey stood up and when Derek rose also she glanced at him, ready to tell him to sit down. He beat her to it.

"I'm going with you, and if you argue with me I'll make a scene. Also, this conversation is far from over."

Derek was fuming as he followed Lindsey back into the triage area of the ER. He knew what she'd been about to say. She still believed he'd never loved her. And why wouldn't she? That was basically what he'd led her to think all those years ago. At the time it had seemed the easier way out, because how did you explain to the woman you loved that you weren't choosing her? That instead you were doing the right thing, what was expected of you, despite the fact that it hurt her. It still sounded wrong to his ears and yet he owed her the truth, as messed up as it was.

The nurse led them to a curtained-off triage area and Derek stood while Lindsey sat in a chair. Immediately the woman asked what exactly had happened and guilt overwhelmed Derek as he listened to Lindsey explain how she'd felt her wrist twist and then smash beneath the weight of both their bodies. He was no lightweight and it was eating him up inside to know that if he'd just let her go down the hill alone as she'd first suggested, she wouldn't be here in tremendous pain.

"Well, let's get this coat off of you," the nurse said. "Then we'll get all of your vitals."

"I can't take the glove off," Lindsey said. "It has elastic around my wrist and it hurts."

The woman's brows knitted together and then she turned to a drawer. "I'll have to cut it then."

Lindsey looked hesitant so Derek spoke up. "We'll buy you some new ones. Let her cut it off."

"They're Anne's gloves," she said.

"Anne will understand." He glanced at the nurse. "Cut it."

She did, and a moment later Lindsey's swollen and purple wrist came into view. Derek felt dizzy at the sight of it. Not because he was squeamish, but because it was Lindsey. His Lindsey, and she was hurt. Obviously so. And he'd played a part in it.

"Wow," Lindsey said, her lip quivering. "It looks worse than I thought."

"What is your pain on a scale of one to ten? One being no pain at all," the nurse asked.

Derek didn't miss the way Lindsey glanced at him quickly. "If I hold it still . . . maybe a three. If I bump it or move it, more like a six and a half."

Derek had to hold back a laugh at her choice. "A half?"

"Seven just seemed too high, okay?" she snapped.

The nurse's eyes darted between the two of them as she typed something into her laptop. She continued with the examination, taking Lindsey's blood pressure, temperature, and pulse. Luckily they were taken to a room immediately after. The nurse left them with a promise that someone would be in soon.

Derek had been in the emergency room with his son enough times to know that "soon" could mean anywhere from five minutes to an hour.

"Well, get comfortable," he said, sitting down in a hard-as-hell rocking chair. "You were right. We're gonna be here a while."

"Yes, so you might as well go." Lindsey sat perched on the side of the bed, bracing her bad arm with her good one.

Derek picked up the remote and flipped on the television that hung from the ceiling. SpongeBob came on. "Can't leave now. This is my favorite episode."

Lindsey rolled her eyes, but he was relieved when she pulled her legs up on the bed and leaned back on the reclined top half. Under the harsh lights of the hospital room her normally warm-toned skin looked noticeably paler.

After about ten minutes a woman wheeled in a cart with a laptop and announced herself as the admissions person. Derek noticed how Lindsey looked uncomfortable, her eyes darting between him and the woman, who was busy typing.

As soon as the personal information questions started, Derek realized what was wrong. Lindsey didn't want him in the room—even more than usual. He stood up and her eyes found his. "I'm just gonna hang out here for a minute."

Lindsey's body visibly relaxed and she nodded. Derek stepped around the curtain and into the hall, leaning against the wall. It wasn't really busy today—or at least didn't appear to be. A few nurses glanced at him from their station and he smiled. That was when he heard Lindsey's voice.

"Um, I actually don't have insurance at the moment. And I don't have payment today. Can I just give you my address and be billed?"

Derek let out a breath and looked down at his feet. No wonder she hadn't wanted to come. He'd forced her here and she was stressing about paying for it. He stepped away from the wall and sauntered down the hall, feeling like an ass for eavesdropping. After a few moments the woman pulled back the curtain and wheeled out her cart.

Derek followed her down the hall a ways before getting her attention. "Hi, uh, what do I need to do in order to have her bill sent to me?"

The lady looked a little taken aback. "Are you a family member?"

"No. I'm not. But I am a close friend."

"Well, I'm afraid I can't send just anyone her bill," she said.

"Okay, fine. Who do I need to call to take care of this? Or can I just give you my card now?" Derek reached for his wallet. He held out a card to the woman. "Here, just . . . charge it to this."

"We don't require payment up front at this facility."

"Fine. But you also can't send me her bill, correct?"

"Correct."

"Surely a hospital isn't going to turn down money. I don't need to know anything about her account or what you do here. I just want to pay." He raised an eyebrow, shaking the card.

She took it reluctantly. "I'll bring this back in a moment then."

"Don't bring it into the room. I'll come find you in a little bit."

"My office is right down the hall to the left." She pointed.

Derek nodded. "Okay, thanks. Now put all of it on there. Anything they do today. Got it?"

After she walked away he headed back to the room to find Lindsey resting, her eyes closed. The chair made a noise against the floor as he sat down and her eyes shot open.

"How ya feeling?" he asked.

"I can feel my heart pounding in my wrist," she said. She laid her head back again.

He was about to flag somebody down a few moments later for some pain meds when a young nurse pulled the curtain open. Derek nearly had a heart attack when he realized he knew her.

"Knock, knock," she said. As soon as she turned and caught sight of Derek her eyes widened. "Oh . . . well hi, Derek."

"Hey, Beth, how are you?" And please keep it brief, he thought.

"Good. Well . . . I'm Beth, your nurse." She put a smile on her face and turned to Lindsey who looked incredibly uncomfortable. And annoyed. "I've brought you some relief."

She had pills and a small cup of water which she immediately handed to Lindsey. "This is just ibuprofen for pain and swelling but it should make a good dent in that pain pretty soon."

Turning to the cabinet behind her, Beth pulled out a cold pack and then helped Lindsey arrange her arm comfortably on a pillow. After that she found a blanket and covered Lindsey's legs. Had she been cold? Why hadn't he thought of that?

"So tell me what happened," the nurse said. Lindsey repeated it again, a lot more quickly this time, and Beth gave an appropriate "Poor thing. You aren't the first sledding accident we've seen in here this week."

After asking Lindsey about her pain level and touching her arm in various places, Beth informed them the doctor would see Lindsey next. Derek gave her a slight nod as she left with an awkward smile.

He assumed Lindsey would comment, but she only laid her head back on the crinkly paper sheet and closed her eyes once more. He shouldn't be surprised, Lindsey had always been the type to bite her tongue. Part of what made him crazy when he'd broken things off was that she'd barely said a thing. She didn't scream or yell, call him names or hit him. He didn't know if it would have made a difference, but he'd wanted . . . *something*. Tears had welled in her eyes that day, and it had killed him. Then he'd kissed her. Big mistake, but he hadn't been able to stop himself and he swore he could still feel it on his lips.

Derek threaded his fingers in his lap, watching her face as she rested. Her lips were still full and lush. Beautiful. But his Lindsey was different now. The same girl . . . woman, rather . . . but with a new edge. A stronger version of herself. At least when it came to him. It made him proud and furious at the same time. He wished they could talk about a few things now, but he hadn't envisioned discussing the past with Lindsey in pain and lying in a hospital bed.

Her eyes remained shut but Derek knew after the awkward nurse visit her mind was going a mile a minute. The least he could do was explain. The last thing he needed was another reason for her to hate him.

"If you're wondering, that wasn't . . . whatever it seemed like it was." He'd met Beth at Smokey's—the bar in Preston—one night last summer. They'd flirted and then gone out once. End of story. No overnights, not even a second date. It just hadn't been a match for whatever reason. He wasn't against hookups and had even dated one woman for a while after his divorce, but he didn't have a lot of free time, so if he wasn't feeling it why go much further? He was pretty sure Beth had felt the same. He hoped she did anyway since he'd never called and asked her out again. The previous ten minutes had felt a little uncomfortable. Oh well.

Lindsey didn't bother to open her eyes or lift her head. "Well, I *wasn't* wondering and I really don't care what it seemed like." The venom in her voice betrayed her words.

That was it. Derek pushed out of the rocking chair, stalked over to the hospital bed, and rested his fists on each side of her hips. Lindsey's eyes flew open, full of panic, as he leaned over her. Good, he wanted her to have some emotion besides bitchy and angry.

"Can you throw me a fucking bone or something? I've done everything I can to be nice to you and you're making this very difficult."

"I'm making this difficult?" she hissed. "I've done everything I can to stay out of your way. I don't come to the house when you're around, I don't call you when something comes up, and I don't go to Anne's when I think you might be there. You're the one who keeps forcing yourself on me and I'm tired of it."

"What if I *want* you to come to the house when I'm there? Do you think a contractor usually spends so much time on a job, especially if he has other properties being built in the city? What if I want you to call me when things come up? Have you thought about that?"

"Have you thought about me? For once, can things be about me and not you? What I want and what I need? I just met your eight-year-old son and you want me to throw *you* a fucking bone?"

Derek was silent for a moment, his jaw tightening. They stared at each other, he still hovering over her as she reclined on the hospital bed. All he'd done was think about her and her needs, but he knew that's not what she meant. And she was right. He'd been selfish. Now *and* then. But he couldn't help wanting a glimpse of the old Lindsey. The one that smiled at him, laughed at his jokes, and whimpered when he kissed her. He wanted it bad, even that last part, he suddenly realized, and that was a shame. It was a bad idea on so many levels.

After a moment he sighed deeply and let his head fall forward. This close he could smell the scent of her skin, her hair, and see her chest rising with each breath. God, how he just wanted to touch her right then. Have the *right* to. But he didn't have that right and probably never would if she had her way.

He lifted his head once again. "I'm sorry. God, I keep saying it. And you're right. I keep pushing you and it's not fair. But please believe me when I say . . . I just wanna talk. I messed a lot of things up between us and I just want us to get to a place where we can . . . smile at each other. I miss your smile. So damn much. I dream about it. See it when I close my eyes."

For one moment he was sure he saw something in her eyes. Something that wasn't anger or hatred. Something that he remembered from another time . . . when he was almost certain she'd been deeply in love with him.

Derek watched her throat work as she swallowed. He

leaned forward once more and let his lips rest on her forehead. He inhaled deeply, his eyes sliding closed as he soaked all of her in. This woman had tied him in knots since the moment he'd met her.

She didn't move for a long moment. He lifted his mouth just enough to press his lips lightly against her skin once more in the barest hint of a kiss. When he felt her right hand latch onto his wrist he waited for her to push him off.

She didn't. It must be the pain or the shock of her injury. Surely she wasn't holding him against her, as much as he wished that to be true. Either way, he took it, and turning his head to the side he nuzzled her temple.

"Lindsey . . . please," he whispered. "Stop pushing me away."

The curtain rings shook behind him as they were pulled aside. Her body gave a small jerk beneath him and he stood upright as the doctor walked in. Touching her that way—having his lips on her soft skin—had only made things a million times worse. He wanted more.

Six

Nearly three hours later Lindsey walked out of the emergency room doors sporting an arm splint due to a grade 2 wrist sprain. Thank goodness it wasn't broken or required much more than that or she'd have been in real trouble. Already she was stressing the hospital bill, wondering how long it would take for them to process everything and send it to her house. How long she might be able to put it off before they turned it over to collections. God, she wanted to lie down and cry.

Lindsey glanced around the circle drive. Derek had run out ahead of her and pulled his truck up to the curb to wait. As soon as he saw her he got out and came around to open her door.

"Thank you," she said quietly. A gentle hand touched her hip as she stepped onto the running board and hoisted herself in with her good hand. She was already feeling the need for more pain pills and she was exhausted.

Before she could reach for her seat belt Derek was leaning over her and latching it. Lindsey let her head fall back so as not to have her face smashed into his chest. She'd just about had enough of being close to this man. She didn't like that he was starting to feel familiar. His scent, his voice. His presence. This was exactly what she'd been trying to avoid and here he'd gone and gotten her acclimated to him. Damn the man.

Shutting her door, he headed around the front end of the truck and got into the driver's seat. If she didn't count the few moments he'd thankfully stepped into the hallway, he hadn't left her side in the hospital. He'd walked beside her hospital bed into radiology. Stood behind the glass, arms folded against his chest, as they'd taken X-rays. She'd protested every move he made at first, but finally she'd given up arguing with him.

He'd even spoken to the doctor and the nurse, inquired about things she hadn't thought to ask. It was irritating how caring he was being. He was feeling guilty. That had to be it. But it was also working because she was finding that she lacked the energy to stay mad at him. Surely it was just the events of the day. Tomorrow, after this mess was behind her and he was back doing his own thing, she'd be able to refocus on all the ways he was a selfish ass. How he'd lied to her. Cheated on her. And with that sobering thought her anger came rushing back.

"You hungry?" Derek asked.

She hadn't realized how quiet it was until he'd spoken. Lindsey shrugged. "Not really."

"You'll feel better if you eat. It's dinnertime."

She didn't respond, only looked out her window at the Kansas City skyline as they crossed over the Missouri River. He'd insisted on taking her home. Also insisted on letting him deal with her car, which was still at Anne's. Absolutely maddening.

After a while she realized he was pulling into a shopping center parking lot. "What are we doing?"

He pulled into a spot and put the truck in park. "I'll be back," he said.

Lindsey sighed when he got out, happy to finally have a few minutes alone. Her head had begun to pound along with her wrist. The sound of the heater blowing lulled her into a drowsy trance and she let her eyes close once more.

The sound of the driver's door opening startled Lindsey awake and she turned to see Derek getting back into his seat with two bags. The scent of greasy food entered with him and suddenly her mouth watered.

"Sit up," he commanded. She did, wiping at her eyes. The sun was already setting, making it feel a lot later then it really was. He messed with some things in his seat and then faced her.

"First this." Derek passed her a pill. She took it and then he held out a bottle of water. "Now this. Eat."

He held out a paper wrapper opened up to reveal a cheeseburger and French fries. Lindsey took it, laid it in her lap, and automatically lifted the top of the bun. Cheese and pickles. Nothing else. The exact way she'd eaten cheeseburgers her entire life. The way she'd ordered them at the Grill counter at the campus food court. They'd eaten there so many times together.

"Everything okay?" Derek asked. He'd already taken a bite of his own burger.

"Yeah. Thank you." Lindsey's stomach growled then. "Guess I was hungrier than I thought."

"Figured. I knew I was hungry as hell after sitting in that hospital all afternoon."

"You didn't have to do it," she snapped.

Derek let out a sigh. "Well, I wanted to, Lindsey. Got it? There was nowhere else I wanted to be."

Lindsey looked down on the center console at the second bag between them. He'd taken her prescription in and gotten it filled. Why was he being this guy? The one that did all the right things? It was overwhelming, and this show of chivalry was starting to make her feel like a complete bitch. Which wasn't at all fair. He was the one in the wrong and today's developments made that even more apparent.

Suddenly the reality of his son was too much for Lindsey to bear. She was strong, damn it, and she could handle knowing everything. Needed to know everything. He owed her that.

"You knew that day. Didn't you?" she asked. For a long moment the only sound was the city noises from outside the truck and the warm air blowing on her legs. "Why didn't you tell me?"

Finally Derek took a deep breath and let it out through his nose.

"I don't know, Lindsey. At that time . . . I was ashamed."

"Ashamed?"

Lindsey turned to look at him. He stared out the windshield, the lights of the store beyond highlighting his chiseled face. His lips worked back and forth.

"I didn't want you to know the truth. It was easier if I just ended things between us. Lisa was pregnant— which shocked the hell out of me. And my father . . ."

She'd never really known much about his family. The truth was, their relationship had been all surface. All emotions, passion, and excitement. They'd never even said the word "love"—although she'd felt it and assumed it would come in due time. It had never reached that stage where you show each other your vulnerabilities, and she suddenly wondered if there was more Derek had kept from her. Not because they'd not got around to it, but on purpose.

"What about your father?"

He shook his head. "Nothing. I had to do what I did, Lindsey. Were there other options? Yeah, of course. But at that time, I had to be with Lisa. I had to be my son's father." Finally he turned to look at her. "But what I want you to know is that I was in fucking hell losing you."

Lindsey swallowed hard. She bit down on her bottom lip to keep any unwanted emotion from slipping past. She breathed deeply once. Twice. There were so many questions floating through her mind, but she couldn't speak. And she wasn't sure if she wanted the answers.

"I didn't cheat on you, Linds," he said. Why did he always seem to know what she was thinking? "Lisa and I had split as soon as I knew that I was attracted to you. Her pregnancy was completely unexpected."

"I don't understand."

"She was my girlfriend through high school. Then college. We'd started to grow apart and I knew we'd break up, we didn't go through with it. We both just kept . . . God. We continued to have sex. We shouldn't have, but we did. During that time I first saw you . . . and God, I was so attracted to you."

Lindsey looked away, unable to focus on the intensity of his eyes.

"I broke up with her the day before I left you that first note. We didn't know then that she was pregnant. But she was."

Things became a little clearer now. The way their breakup had come out of nowhere. How he'd closed his feelings off from her so suddenly her head had spun. It had all been so confusing and painful. But none of what he was saying changed the past. He'd made his choice. There really wasn't much more to say.

"You told me you loved someone else," she said quietly.

"I lied, Linds. I was stupid as hell. I thought . . . I don't know what I thought. That it was what I should be thinking. If I was going to stay with Lisa, surely I should have loved her. But I didn't. I didn't want you to love me back because then I'd want to stay with you. Maybe I wanted the whole world to be as miserable as I was. But I had to let you know it was over."

Lindsey let out a bitter laugh. "I knew it all right." Suddenly the truck felt like it was closing in on her. "Can you please take me home now?" she said quietly.

Derek stared at her for a long moment but she couldn't look him in the eye any longer. Finally he shifted in his seat, put the truck in drive, and pulled out of the parking lot with one hand on the wheel and one on his dinner.

It was possible she might get to a place where she

could accept what had happened. Maybe she could even try and understand. Even forgive. But she would never forget, which meant there was no way they could ever be romantically involved again. Friends?

Maybe.

Derek headed down the road chewing on the last bite of his burger. He wasn't even tasting it any longer because he was just sick over every single thing that had happened today.

Sitting in a parking lot with a wounded Lindsey was not the way he'd always imagined having that conversation. She'd listened. And hadn't yelled or cried. But she also hadn't said much in response. There had been no resolution and he didn't feel any better than before. The stupid thing was, he wasn't really sure what he'd wanted.

Her understanding? Definitely. Hopefully her forgiveness. But damn it, he realized that even against his better judgment, he also wanted her. Yeah, he knew they would never return to what they'd had eight years ago, but he saw this as a second chance.

Sure, they could be just friends. But there were moments when looking at her was so close to torture he questioned why he kept putting himself through it. He realized with clarity that all of his adult life he'd been waiting for something equal to what they'd had to come along. It never would, because there was only one Lindsey. Only one woman that could make him feel whole. Like he was good enough just as he was.

Obviously she wasn't throwing out those vibes these

days, but he knew that she was still the same loving, compassionate, gentle girl that he'd fallen for eight years ago.

Trying to focus on where he was going, he began reading street signs.

"Tell me again which street your sister lives on," he said. He listened as she explained to him how to get to the building and they continued on in silence.

Gripping the wheel, he forced himself not to demand a response from her. He desperately wanted to know what she was thinking and it was by iron will that he didn't continually turn to glance at her so he could try and figure it out on his own. She'd always been easy to read, worn her heart on her sleeve. No more.

Looking at her these days drove him insane. She was still so beautiful. Her full wide mouth with bow-shaped lips, the thick lashes that would brush the top of her cheeks when she laughed so hard her eyes shut. He might never see that again but it was ingrained in his memory. He hadn't lied in that hospital room. He was desperate to see her smile at him again.

After a few moments Derek pulled into the parking lot and followed her directions up to the sidewalk. He put the truck in park and reached over to unlock her seat belt. "Hang on, I'll help you out," he said as he jumped out.

By the time he got there she was easing her way off the seat. "I got it," she said.

He was really tired of her being so stubborn. "Haven't you realized that I like helping you?" he asked.

She didn't respond, and he assumed the only thing

that kept her from making a snotty comeback was how physically exhausted she was. He could see it in the way her head hung to the side.

"Can I walk you up?" he asked.

Her eyes went wide and she shook her head. "No. Please . . . I'm fine."

He gave a small nod, not surprised. Derek reached into the truck and handed her the bag of medicine.

She took it and then looked up at him. "Thank you for taking me to the hospital."

Derek shoved his hands in his pockets. "It shouldn't have been necessary. I'm sorry you got hurt. Truly."

She shrugged. "I'll be okay. I always am." And with that she turned and headed toward the building and then up the stairs and out of sight.

Derek cursed under his breath and then got back into the truck. What a horrible day. He was starting to think that she was right, they needed to stay far away from one another. But no, he couldn't stomach that. Now more than ever he was determined to do something right by this woman. There was a lot of baggage between them, but damn it, there was a lot of good, too. Really good. He just needed to remind her how things used to be before everything had gone to hell.

At that time his personal life had been shit. He'd chosen to pursue a degree in architecture just to make his father happy, which had meant giving up his dream of being a comic book artist. It had been his lifelong passion and his father had robbed him of it by constantly reminding Derek how he'd never make it. Looking back, it was probably a childish thing to hope for, chances are it would have led to nothing. But now as a father himself, he couldn't imagine looking into his son's eyes and telling him his dreams were stupid.

Derek's relationship with Lisa, which had started in high school, had also been a constant source of frustration in college. About the time the school year had started, he'd been in denial about them for almost a year, just putting off the inevitable. Actually, he'd kept hoping she'd do it for him, but they'd both stayed together for their own stupid reasons, none of which had anything to do with love.

And then along came Lindsey.

The first time Derek ever laid eyes on Lindsey she'd been a freshman sitting in the front row of Professor Robert's Principles of Modern Architecture class. A lot of students took it as an art elective and at the time Derek was Roberts's undergrad teacher's assistant. He'd been late that day, sneaked in through the office at the front of the class and sat down quietly at the desk reserved for him off to the side.

It had taken him less than a second to notice her. The first thing that had caught his attention was her lips as they chewed on a pencil. She'd watched Roberts intently, soaking up everything he said and taking copious notes.

Derek hadn't taken his eyes off her, knowing that any minute she would notice and he'd have to look away. Finally she did. But it wasn't the instant flicker of someone who accidentally catches your gaze. It was the slow glance and stare of someone that said *I feel you watching me, cut it out.* It had made him smile instantly, and she'd tried as hard as she could not to reciprocate as she turned her focus back to the professor.

She'd failed.

He'd seen her lips quirk and her palm rest on her chin so she could cover the evidence with her fist. That was all it had taken. He'd become obsessed. For two weeks he'd watched her in class and every day she'd shoot out of her chair and through the door as soon as the class ended.

Finally he'd gotten fed up with her avoiding him after class, so one day he'd arrived early and left a piece of paper on her desk. It was a two-paneled cartoon. It featured a male and a female in each panel, and it just so happened the female looked a lot like her, with sexy lips, big eyes, and even bigger hair. In the first panel the male said "Hi, I'm Derek." In the second panel he'd left the female's speech bubble empty.

Thinking back on it now, he realized it was probably the corniest thing he could have done. He'd been twenty-two years old, for God's sake, not twelve. But he'd watched as she looked at his work, and a huge grin spread across her face. Immediately she'd taken a pencil and filled it in.

Once again after class she'd bolted, but sure enough she'd left the comic strip on her desk and he'd retrieved it immediately. He still remembered what it said.

"Hi, Derek. I'm Lindsey."

Seven

Lindsey woke to a baby crying. She glanced at the clock. It was seven in the morning and way too early to be up. A sharp ache zinged through her wrist, reminding her that she was injured and hadn't taken pain medicine in almost twelve hours.

Immediately her thoughts traveled back to yesterday. Sledding, wiping out, going to the hospital. *Derek*. Lindsey squeezed her eyes shut once more. She could feel her resolve chipping away where that man was concerned because he just wouldn't give up. Apparently that was his superpower: persistence. Always had been.

It was still hard for her to process the reality of what she'd learned. What he'd said. She should have asked more questions, but it was still hard for her to even accept that he'd left her because his previous girlfriend had been pregnant. That he'd *lied*.

One thing that kept nagging at her was the what-ifs. If he had told her the truth then, what would she have wanted? Could she have stayed with a man that was having a baby with another woman? Would their passion for one another even lasted? It was possible that eventually one of them would have lost interest in the other. What would it have been like to continue dating a man with a small child? Was it possible that he'd done her a favor? Maybe he had made the right decision.

The part that hurt was that she would never know because he hadn't given her the option to decide or even share her feelings on the matter. Hadn't trusted her enough. Even if he had felt the need to leave her, he should have said why. She'd deserved to know then, not eight years later.

Now that she was fully awake, Lindsey's wrist throbbed all the harder. Her sister and brother-in-law hadn't been home yet when she'd gotten back last night so she'd gone right to bed, exhausted from the hill climbing and pain. For a moment she considered pulling the pillow over her head and sleeping in, but then the crying down the hall reached a crescendo. Trembling wails punctuated by long pauses of silence, meaning that three-month-old Eden Marie Miller was screaming so hard she literally lost her breath.

With a groan Lindsey carefully rolled out of bed, grabbed some sweats off the floor, and tugged them on with one hand. Once she hit the hallway she nearly ran into her sister's husband, Brett.

"Oh, thank goodness, Linds. Would you mind?" He nodded toward his bedroom as he adjusted his tie. Brett was a restaurant manager so he often left early on the weekends. "I'm running late. Eden was up all night."

Lindsey gave him the most sympathetic smile that she had to offer this early. "No problem. Where's Mel?"

"Shower," he said over his shoulder, already heading down the stairs. He hadn't even noticed her arm brace. Just as well, since she wasn't in the mood to explain to him. "Thanks, Linds. Later."

"Later." Lindsey sighed and went into the master bedroom. Eden was young enough that Melanie still had her sleeping next to the bed in a bassinet.

"Baby girl," Lindsey cooed. For a moment she considered how she would pick the tiny infant up and then finally decided on leaning over and scooping her up football style. It wasn't graceful but it worked. Although Lindsey was right-handed she was surprised to realize how often she used her left hand for normal tasks.

Eden's little head rooted around, searching for the nearest food source. "Not gonna find anything to eat here, little lady. Mommy will be done soon."

Lindsey glanced into the bassinet to search for the pacifier. It must be under the blankets. Groaning, she gently laid Eden down on her sister's king-sized bed, retrieved the necessary equipment, and then nuzzled the rubber nipple past Eden's puffy little lips.

"Here you go, sweet pea." Finally Eden caught hold of it, sucking furiously. It wouldn't be long before she realized the plastic wasn't filling her tummy. Lindsey heard the shower turn off in the bathroom.

"Mel, hurry it up," Lindsey yelled.

"Almost done," her sister called from beyond the closed door.

Lindsey sat and bounced on the bed, trying to soothe Eden. She smiled down at her beautiful niece. Becoming an aunt was one of the best things that had ever happened to her. Someday Lindsey hoped to have a child of her own. Maybe. But in the meantime, spoiling Eden was the next best thing.

Living with her family was a temporary arrangement, and Lindsey was grateful for their generosity since they weren't charging her rent. If things could just pick up she hoped to earn enough for a down payment on a new place of her own. Maybe a studio in one of downtown Preston's old buildings. She'd be closer to her friends there. Or a two-bedroom apartment so she could have some space to work. Something was bound to come along. Had to, because Lindsey just knew her business was never going to become what she dreamed it could be if she didn't find a way to make it happen. She wanted nothing more than to run a thriving design and restoration company.

She currently still had her online shop where she sold small items like restored light fixtures and accessories, and she consigned her larger items in a booth down in the West Bottoms at an antiques store. But she wanted more. She dreamed of having a studio of her own. Maybe even a small storefront where design clients could meet with her. Another reason why this feature in the Kansas City newspaper was so important for her. She hoped it might help her business to take off.

The bathroom door opened and a cloud of steam followed Melanie out. Her wet hair was wrapped in a towel and her robe was gaping open. "Mommy's here, bean," Melanie said in her baby voice as she lay down on the bed to feed her child.

It was certainly something special to watch your sister become a mother. Sometimes Lindsey felt a twinge of jealousy, but mostly she felt pride. All of her life Mel had lived what appeared to be a charmed life. She was an exotic beauty with almond skin and dark eyes, and lustrous mahogany hair courtesy of her mother, Geri.

Lindsey's thick dark hair and unibrow had been parting gifts from her own mother. A full-blooded Italian who up and left when Lindsey was three. Wax and tweezers had fixed her eyebrow situation, but she'd never seen her mother again. Instead she was left with a mess of a father whom she'd spent more time mothering than he spent looking after her. A father Lindsey loved more than anything. Thanks to him she'd inherited some of Mel's features, the dark hair and healthy curves, but she'd still sometimes envied her big sister.

As sad as it sounded, Lindsey's childhood hadn't been completely devoid of a woman's influence. Geri had sometimes invited Lindsey back home with Mel for weekend stays. Treated her like a stepdaughter. Lindsey cherished those visits, learning what it truly meant to be a proud Mexican woman. A strong woman in general. She was still trying to put those lessons into practice.

Mel's voice pulled Lindsey's thoughts back into focus.

"I didn't even see you yesterday. I was surprised to find you already in bed when we got home from dinner," Melanie said. She glanced past Eden's head and her eyes went wide. "Oh my God, what happened to your arm?"

Lindsey gave a weak smile. "Just a sprain."

"Are you sure? With that big old brace? What were you doing?"

"Sledding."

"*Linds*. Does it hurt?"

"Yeah, it does. I have some pain meds, so it's not too bad."

"I didn't even know you were going sledding," Mel said.

"It wasn't planned. I went with Anne and Claire." Lindsey lifted her wrapped wrist and turned it, wincing in pain.

"Did you go to the hospital?" Mel asked, her voice full of concern.

"I did. They took an X-ray, but it's fine. I just have to keep it in this brace for a while."

"How will you work on Anne's house like that?" Lindsey stroked Eden's fuzzy head as she nursed.

"Well, it will be tricky, that's certain. I'm sure I can manage," Lindsey said. But what she was thinking about was how Derek had offered to help her with her projects last night before he'd arrived at their building. She'd said thanks but had been noncommittal. Surely there had to be another option. The thought of working in his presence for hours sounded like the fastest way to make herself crazy.

Mel shook her head. "You should have called me, sis. I can't believe you were at the hospital and I didn't even know."

"It's not a big deal, and I was just fine. Promise." Lindsey debated telling her sister about Derek. She knew it would bother Mel, considering eight years ago she'd been ready to key his car, egg his house, and sell his identity to the first e-mailing prince offering a reward. Mel was not going to be happy when she found out Derek was back in the picture, in any capacity. Melanie was strong, had never let a man decide anything for her, and didn't allow anyone to push her around. Lindsey had always admired that about her sister. If somebody hurt Mel—or even tried to—they'd never live it down.

When Derek had ended things Melanie had been the first person Lindsey told. Looking back, it might have been a mistake. "Screw him," she'd said. "He's an asshole and he doesn't deserve to breathe your air." But even though Mel was on Lindsey's side, she'd never understood why she was so devastated when the guy clearly didn't deserve Lindsey's tears. That was easy for strong-as-steel Melanie to say, but it had hurt Lindsey, made her feel weak.

"Is something going on?" ever-intuitive Melanie asked as she picked Eden up, sat, and then leaned in the opposite direction. Eden let out a wail and Melanie shushed her as she adjusted her breast so Eden could get back to her breakfast. Lindsey hoped that during the interruption of switching sides, Melanie would let her question drop.

"Okay, so tell me what's wrong," Melanie said as she got situated. All right, so she wasn't dropping it. Lindsey could handle this. And honestly, if she was interested in being strong, standing up for herself, then it had to start with her very own sister. She didn't need to apologize or explain anything about her life.

"Nothing's . . . *wrong*. Exactly," Lindsey said, not making eye contact. So apparently being strong was easier said than done. There was always the option of lying and not telling Mel. But Lindsey couldn't imagine how that would work. Mel and Brett were invited to Anne's wedding, so she was bound to recognize Derek. And then Lindsey really needed her sister's advice.

"Sis, I can see something is up with you. Spill."

Lindsey sighed. Might as well rip it off like a Band-Aid. "So . . . I didn't tell you, but last fall, I ran into Derek Walsh again."

Melanie was quiet for a moment, then her eyes narrowed. "Do you mean frat-boy asshole Derek Walsh?"

"The one and only."

"And by ran into, you mean . . ."

"You know Mike, Anne's fiancé? Well, it just so happens that he and Derek are best friends."

"And you're just now telling me this?" Surprisingly she didn't sound too annoyed. "Have you spoken with him?"

Lindsey hesitated.

"You have." Melanie sighed. "I can't believe you didn't tell me."

"I know, Mel. It's just . . . I was kind of hoping to treat it like a nonissue. I've been trying to avoid him, but it's tough. He's working on the house also. He's the contractor."

Mel's mouth dropped open. "Linds . . ."

"I know, I know. He was there yesterday when we were sledding. He's actually the one who took me to the emergency room."

"What?" Mel said in exasperation. "I can't believe this. All of this happening and I had no idea?"

"I'm sorry, Mel." Lindsey shrugged her good side. "When I first saw him last fall you were pregnant, everything was about the baby, and then Eden was born and everything was still about her. I'm not complaining . . . I'm just saying, it didn't seem important. I figured dwelling on it would just make it a bigger deal. I wanted—and I still want—the whole thing to be nothing at all."

"Jesus, Lindsey. I think I could have handled making things about you for five minutes. I mean, this guy had you in the fetal position for weeks," Melanie said, a bit of hurt in her voice.

Lindsey cringed at the reminder of that horrible time in her life. Of course, that was the part Mel would remember best. Who wouldn't, she'd been a complete wreck. "I guess I just really didn't want to discuss it. But that has become impossible since I keep running into him everywhere."

Melanie sighed and looked down at Eden, who had nearly drifted back to sleep, then lifted her eyes back up to Lindsey. "Has he been nice?"

"Well . . . yeah." And he had been. Too nice. Even considering that yesterday she'd discovered that he was not only the jerk that dumped her, but also a liar. Lindsey chose to keep the news about Tanner to herself. Mel would flip, tell Lindsey how she should react. She couldn't handle that right now. She needed to figure this out on her own.

"Is he still hot? I can see him being one of those guys that actually gets hotter as the years go by."

Lindsey smiled. These were the conversations she enjoyed having with her sister. And of course Derek was still hot, but she didn't even want to admit it out loud. The man had been gorgeous when she'd met him, and Mel was right, age only seemed to favor him. The small lines that creased the corners of his eyes were sexy, his shoulders were broader, and his legs fuller. Derek had put on manly bulk in all the right places.

"I'm gonna take that look as a yes. Dick," Melanie said, sitting up on the bed. She tightened the robe around her waist, crossed her legs, and rested a satisfied Eden on the comforter in front of her. Without having to be told, Lindsey stood up and grabbed a diaper and wipes off the nightstand to hand over to her sister.

"What kind of car does he drive?" Melanie asked as she unsnapped Eden's onesie.

Lindsey knew her answer would annoy her sister. "Well, he has a big-ass work truck, and when I first saw him again he was driving a Mercedes. Clearly being an architect is working out for him."

Mel's arms drooped and she rolled her eyes. "So typical. Well, you keep him in check. He does one thing to hurt you and I'll lose it. I'm not kidding. I got a dozen eggs and a crowbar with Derek's Mercedes written all over it."

"I can handle this, Mel."

Her sister's eyes softened. "I know you can. But I'm a reactor. You're always so levelheaded and understanding. Maybe it's good. Now you can erase the fantasy of him from your mind. He's just a man, like all the others. He doesn't have a hold on your emotions any longer."

After a while Lindsey stood up and headed back to her room. She was thankful for her sister's love and support. Needed it. But she wished she felt as levelheaded as Mel seemed to think she was. Lindsey wanted to be that woman, but it was almost as if Derek's return to her life reminded her of how bad being low could feel. And Mel was also wrong, because Lindsey's emotions about her and Derek's breakup did still feel like they were holding her hostage.

She was so fearful of losing herself the way she had back then. Hated that for so many years she'd been naïve, allowing people to treat her as a pushover. The new Lindsey deserved—and would demand—more. She'd just have to fake it till she made it.

Later that morning Lindsey headed north into Preston. After dropping off a few smaller items at Sweet Opal for consignment, she walked down to Callie's Confections. The bakery was owned by her friend and fellow blogger Callie. Lindsey was in the mood for some of the baker's perfect coffee and Callie's amazing cinnamon rolls.

A bell jingled over Lindsey's head as she stepped in the door. Instantly she was met with the scent of cinnamon and sugar. She inhaled deeply and sat down at a table off to the side. Callie gave her a wave as she helped the next person in line.

After a few minutes Callie joined her at the table, setting a cinnamon roll and a to-go coffee cup in front of Lindsey.

"I hate to be presumptuous but . . . ." Callie said with a grin.

"Nope, you're right, I definitely wanted that." Lindsey picked up the cup and made to get up before Callie stopped her.

"I totally forgot you were one-armed." Callie stood up and snatched the cup back. "I got you, girl."

Lindsey smiled as she watched Callie saunter over to the little blue buffet she used as a coffee station.

"Vanilla or cinnamon?" Callie called over her shoulder.

"Vanilla sounds good."

A moment later Callie walked back and set the steaming cup in front of Lindsey. "So Anne told me all about it. God, what a crock. And with Derek of all people. Anne said he looked completely devastated."

Lindsey shook her head a little. "I don't know about devastated but he definitely felt bad. It was an accident." The conversation reminded Lindsey that she should return Anne's call. They had spoken briefly after Derek had dropped her off. Anne had wanted to make sure everything was okay but Lindsey barely remembered the conversation she'd been so tired.

"So how's this gonna go with you working on the house?" Callie asked. There was no irritation in her voice, even though Lindsey felt so guilty for being injured and unable to do her part of the work the way she'd planned. "I'm happy to help when you need it. Basketball season is over so there aren't as many performances for the girls."

In addition to owning the bakery and blogging, Callie also coached the local high school's dance team. She was a workaholic and Lindsey wasn't exactly sure how she managed to do it all and spend time with her boyfriend. There was no way she could ask Callie for help.

"No, I'll figure this out."

"Linds, you are down to one arm," Callie said, emphasizing the last two words. She then gave Lindsey the Callie look. The one that said *Are we seriously having this conversation right now?* "You're gonna need help."

Lindsey smiled and shook her head. "You have like eighteen jobs, and Bennett to think about."

Callie grinned at her boyfriend's name. "That boy does keep me very busy."

Holding up a hand Lindsey went on. "No details please. Anyway, you're busy, Anne's busy planning a wedding and running the blog."

"Sometimes life gets crazy. But we take care of each other." Callie picked up Lindsey's coffee and took a drink. Lindsey appreciated Callie's words more than she'd ever know, but there was another option.

"Would you think *I'm* crazy if I accepted an offer of help from Derek?"

Almost spitting the hot coffee on Lindsey, Callie swallowed and then grinned before she answered. "I think you'd be crazy not to. And I knew it. That broken arm is your kismet."

"Well, it's not broken so—"

Callie waved that information away like it was completely inconsequential. "You're in a cast for goodness' sake."

"It's technically a brace but—"

Callie groaned. "Lindsey. Stop fighting this. Definitely accept Derek's offer to help you. I mean not because I don't want to help. I'm totally your girl if you need me. But . . . this could be good. If nothing else it could be closure or something. Anne and Mike would be so happy to know that you guys had come to some sort of understanding. Anne hates for you to be uncomfortable."

Lindsey sighed. She'd known two things before she'd stepped into Callie's bakery. One, that she was going to accept Derek's offer. And two, that Callie would say exactly what she'd just said. And that was what Lindsey had needed to hear. But there was also something she needed to share with her friend.

"You know, he broke up with me because of his son. His—now ex-wife—was pregnant."

Callie's eyes went wide and she leaned forward. "Oh my God. Did you just now find out? I thought you knew he had a son. Didn't we discuss that?"

"Oh yes, I did know. But . . . I just assumed he'd broken up with me and eventually had a baby. I never dreamed it was part of the equation."

Callie sagged into her chair. "Damn. So he was seeing you and someone else?"

Lindsey shook her head. "No. I mean, he says he wasn't. I guess he'd broken up with his longtime girlfriend when he met me."

"Do you believe him?"

Did she? The first answer to come to mind was yes. She couldn't explain why. Whether it was just hope or blind trust. She wasn't sure but the answer was the same. "Yes. I do."

Callie nodded, obviously thinking. "Derek doesn't strike me as a cheater but sometimes they can surprise you. If you believe him then I do too."

Lindsey nodded and then Callie went on. "So when he found out she was pregnant he broke things off with you because he thought it was the right thing to do? Marrying her."

"Yep. I still wish he would have just told me that then."

Callie gave Lindsey a sincere look. "Sweetie, would that really have made it any better?"

"No. It wouldn't have. But I still deserved the truth." Lindsey took a drink of the now communal cup of coffee.

"Well, I won't argue with you there. But people do stupid things when they're overwhelmed by emotional situations. And sometimes it requires us to forgive them. Trust me, I know."

Lindsey smiled in understanding. "I know. I'm not looking for a relationship with him. Definitely not. But it would be nice to not have to hate him. Especially with the wedding coming up. I bet after that—and the house being done—we really won't see each other too much."

Callie didn't look convinced. She gave Lindsey a teasing smile. "I guess only time will tell."

Eight

Derek held the phone away from his mouth and sighed. He listened as Lisa went on about how inconvenient it was for her to have to rearrange her plans so Derek could have Tanner the weekend of Anne and Mike's wedding.

At this point her arguments were getting ridiculous. She'd just tried to tell him that Tanner would be traumatized by walking down the aisle. This was what happened when Lisa started to feel out of control. Desperate. She was willing to try any tactic. It would be helpful if he could figure out what she was so afraid of, because he'd never given her any reason to believe he would take Tanner from *her*. That wasn't his style. He knew his son needed his mother. He only wished she'd acknowledge that their son also needed his father.

"Lisa, listen." Derek sat up straight in his chair. "I don't ever make demands of you, but my best friend is getting married and he would like my son to be his ring bearer. I will be damned if I have to tell him my ex-wife will not allow that to happen."

Getting nasty with Lisa was a risky move. In fact, he was pretty damn sure he was going to pay for this.

"Fine," she finally replied. "I guess you'll owe me then when it's time for *my* wedding."

Derek's stomach dropped as he listened to the silence stretching between them on the phone line. Finally he spoke calmly. "And when should I expect this blessed occasion to take place?"

"I don't know." Her haughty tone pissed him off. "Possibly this summer. I deserve that, Derek. You may not think so, but I do. I deserve to marry someone that loves me. Someone who isn't emotionally abusive."

Derek steeled himself. He'd agreed with her statement until that last bit. But flying off the handle was exactly what she wanted him to do. If he knew Lisa, she'd probably just hit record on their phone call, hoping he'd sound like a controlling and vengeful asshole.

He wasn't sure why the news made him so angry. It wasn't jealousy, he felt none of that when it came to his ex. It was mostly fear. Fear that somehow she would use this change in her life to pull Tanner away from him. Fear that another man might take his place. The idea of another man living with his son . . . it tied his stomach in knots.

"Lisa, I was never emotionally abusive to you and you know it." He could hear the huff of her breath on the other line. "But you're right. You absolutely deserve to marry someone that loves you. And since you're willing to let Tanner spend that weekend with me, I will be happy to make concessions when the time comes for us to discuss the arrangements of your wedding."

A quiet knock pulled Derek's gaze to the doorway. Lindsey stood there, the most beautiful woman he'd ever known. How much had she just heard? His ex continued to speak in his ear.

"Lane will be good for Tanner, you know. He's smart and patient. He loves us both." Derek froze at her words. That. That right there was his worst nightmare. He looked up once more to find Lindsey staring at a painting on the wall a little too intently. Seeing her in his office while listening to Lisa's voice on the line made him cringe.

Derek worked his jaw back and forth before he finally responded. "I hope so. Our son can only benefit from having *another* positive influence in his life. We can discuss all of this good news further at another time."

"Of course," Lisa said. Too easy. Things were going to get ugly soon, he could feel it.

"Bye, Lisa." Derek ended the call and stood up from his desk, staring at Lindsey. He almost didn't believe she was really standing there in his office. Her dark hair was loose and flowing against her red sweater and her faded jeans hugged her in a way that made his body tense.

"This is a surprise," he said. He nodded at her left side. "How are you feeling?"

"Oh, good. As long as I keep the brace on it's not too bad," she said, glancing down at her arm. Her eyes flicked around the room, obviously taking everything in. "I'm sorry to bother you."

"Don't apologize, you are always welcome here." And he meant it.

"Is everything . . . okay?" she asked, her tone wary.

He knew she'd heard enough of his call to know whom he'd been speaking with.

"Yes, absolutely," he said, ignoring his desire to share with her. It had been so long since he'd had someone to really talk to. He had Mike, and knew that his best friend would be there for him at any moment, but guys usually only opened up so much to one another. And he'd stopped relying on his parents for anything a long time ago.

Derek leaned against his desk and rested his palms beside him. "What brings you in here?"

"Well . . . I guess I just wanted to thank you."

She was nervous, unsure of herself. The urge to get closer to her was strong, but he would control himself. Earn her trust. If nothing else, they could become friends. That would make him happy. Mostly.

"You're wearing a suit," she said. Her eyes roamed up and down his body. And damn, she really shouldn't do that.

Derek laughed, glancing down at the dark gray slacks covering his legs. "Yeah. I am. I do that about three times a week on average. Depends on what's going on."

"So you build a lot of buildings around Kansas City?" She touched a lock of hair that rested on her chest and Derek's eyes wandered to her slim fingers. Her nails were short but well manicured, painted in a soft pink polish. Everything about her was so astoundingly beautiful.

"Somewhat. I'm still establishing my business, but we just broke ground on my eleventh major project. A six-story multiunit. Mainly doctors' offices."

"Wow. That's impressive."

The normality of the conversation was making him uneasy. "Why are you here, Linds?"

"If you want me to go—"

"I definitely don't want you to go. I just know I'm not your favorite person and that makes me wonder why you're here."

"Well, you had offered to help me."

He was more than a little shocked at her admission. Yes, he'd definitely mentioned that she should let him help her. More than once actually, but he'd never dreamed that she'd take him up on his offer.

"I did." He pushed off the desk and took a hesitant step toward her. "Are you saying that you want my help?"

Her eyes flicked to his for a moment. " 'Want' is a rather strong word. I'd probably say 'need' is more appropriate. No . . . I don't like 'need,' either. I would say, resigned myself to the fact that I require help since I'm not functioning at a hundred percent and the house is on a deadline."

"I don't know. I kind of like the words 'want' and 'need.' " Derek couldn't help the grin that broke out on his face, especially when Lindsey gave him her best *you're an asshole* look. She didn't mean it. She wouldn't be standing there in his office if that's what she thought of him. All of which had his mood on a considerable upswing since his call with Lisa.

"If you're still willing I guess I would like to have some help."

"I'm definitely willing."

"There have to be some rules," Lindsey said.

This should be interesting. "Okay. And what would those be?"

She cleared her throat quickly and then continued. "First, no flirting with me."

"Uh, we may have different ideas of what flirting means. That could be a problem."

"I'm sure flirting is your default mode when it comes to women. But not with me. I'm not interested."

Ouch. "Okay. So no talking. Next rule?"

Lindsey rolled her eyes and then went on. "No touching."

"Isn't that a given based on rule one?"

"I'm just covering my bases."

"No pun intended, right?" He gave her a wink but she most definitely did not look amused. Derek swiped a hand over his mouth and dramatically put a frown on his face. "Sorry. Forgot about rule one."

"Three, we don't discuss the past again."

Okay, now that one he had a problem with. "Linds, we can't move forw—"

She put her hand up. "Please. Things are fine right now. See? We're talking. We're going to work together for a short time. Rehashing anything further will not do any good."

He blew out a hard breath and scratched at the back of his neck. He didn't like these rules. At all. But he'd take what he could get for now because it was probably as good as it was gonna get for a while. "Okay, fine. You've given me your three rules. Now I'm gonna give you mine."

She quirked an eyebrow at him. "Yours?"

"Yeah, mine." Derek crossed his arms over his chest. "Rule number one. No flirting with me."

"Psshh." Lindsey put her good hand on her hip. "What are you doing?"

"I'm giving you my rules. Pay attention because I'm serious about this. Two, no touching me." She looked completely perplexed. He had to force a straight face.

"Seriously, Derek?"

"And three. I get to say one thing about the past."

Her lips locked tight, her eyes became wary as she stared back at him. Derek wasn't going to touch her, although the urge was suddenly very strong. But he did step a little closer. Close enough that he had to dip his head to continue looking into her eyes.

"I'm sorry, Lindsey. Sorry I hurt you. Sorry I didn't trust you enough to be honest. I'm just so damn sorry."

Derek took in every facet of her expression. There was no mistaking the slight glassiness of her eyes or the way she bit the inside of her mouth. It was always something she tended to do when she was nervous or uncomfortable and he could see the slight indent of her cheek. After a few seconds she let go and pulled herself together.

"Okay. Thank you." She took a step back and angled her body toward the door. "I guess now we can get to work. Should I meet you at the house tomorrow?"

He should have known she wouldn't have much to say in response. And he wasn't even sure what he'd expected, but something more would have been nice. He kind of wished she'd stay here and discuss their plans, but instead Derek gave her a tight smile. "Okay. I'll see you there about nine?"

"Yeah. Nine is good. Not too early, not too late. Good."

Their eyes met one more time as if there were something on her mind. Derek raised an eyebrow, inviting her to say more.

"Okay, well. Bye, Derek."

"Bye, Lindsey."

His chest ached as he watched her leave his office. Part of him wanted to stop her, request a little more negotiation. But no, he needed to be grateful that she'd shown up today. It was a big step. For now.

In that moment, Derek knew for certain that just being her friend was not going to be enough for him. He suddenly wanted to say to hell with her rules, they deserved another chance. But the smarter, calmer side of him was proud of her for standing up for herself. Either way he was happy. Spending time with Lindsey was good news for now, no matter the rules. He might just have to be a little creative in order to convince her they were worth breaking.

The next morning Derek showed up at the farmhouse at eight. His plan was to get there and set them up, figure out what needed to be done, and inspect a few things in the process. He got out, chatted with the plumbing crew, and then went back to his truck to grab his tool belt. As he attached it around his waist he watched as Lindsey's little SUV pulled in beside his truck. Derek glanced at his watch. It was ten after eight, which amused and annoyed him.

He walked around to her driver's side and waited for her to open the door. As soon as she did, he spoke. "You're early."

"As are you."

"Yeah, well, I'm the contractor. You're a one-armed crew of one. You hadn't planned to come out here and work, alone, had you?" The more he thought about it, the more it irritated him, which he was pretty sure was evident in his tone. Especially when she reared back in annoyance. *Way to go, asshole.*

"Are you serious right now? First of all, you don't employ me so I don't answer to you. Second of all, what I planned to do is really none of your damn business." She reached into her vehicle and emerged with a Styrofoam cup of coffee he recognized was from Callie's Confections. She held it out to him. "Here's some coffee, asshole."

And just like that he felt like a complete dick. He took the cup and grabbed her hand before she could turn away. "Hey, I'm sorry. That was uncalled-for. You're just here almost an hour early and so I assumed you were going to try and work without me. You heard the doctor, if you do more than you should you could really damage that wrist."

She slid her fingers from his grasp and he waited for her to call foul on account of rule number two. She didn't. "I'm not a child, Derek. I heard the doctor and I don't need you hovering. I was up anyway so I just decided to come early. Although I don't owe you an explanation. You're really making me question my sanity in asking for your help."

Derek let out a low growl and then glanced up toward

the house to see a couple of guys quickly look away. "You're right, I'm overstepping. I'm just worried about you, okay? You're going to have to accept that."

"Well, then you need to accept that you don't have the right to get testy with me. I do what I want. If I want to go play baseball with this injury I'll damn well do it. We clear?"

Derek was stunned to silence. But obviously there was only one thing to say. "We're clear."

Lindsey reached back into her car and came up with a second cup of coffee. She carefully placed it in the fingers on her braced hand and then reached for a bag on the center console. Derek stepped forward.

"Let me get that for you," he said, grabbing it from her hand. Thankfully she let him and they walked together toward the house. "Thanks for the coffee."

"You're welcome." She still sounded annoyed and Derek inwardly cursed himself for starting things off on such a negative note. She'd been up early, gotten him coffee. All after asking him for help, and he'd had to go and fuck it up.

He glanced over at her as they cut through the yard. Her long hair was pulled up in a ponytail, showing off her slim neck. God, how he loved her neck.

And her face.

And her body.

She was wearing a tight forest-green Henley unbuttoned at the top, showing a white tank and a modest amount of cleavage. Derek fell back and allowed her to walk ahead of him as they went up the porch steps. He caught her scent as he followed and it made him wish that he could just reach out, touch her. Pull her against him and forget about anything that stood between them.

He held open the screen as Lindsey opened the main door and led them inside. Once they were in the kitchen, she set down her coffee on the makeshift island and turned to face him. Derek held her bag out and she plucked it from his grasp without comment.

"What's first on the agenda today?" he asked.

"I'd like to get the cabinets stained. I sanded them a week or so ago. Before my injury. The lowers will be the same stain as the floor and the uppers just have a light glaze. I have all the paint and stain in the backseat of my car. Would you mind?"

"Of course not. Is it unlocked?"

She nodded and he headed back toward the front door and across the yard. When he opened the door to her backseat he stopped short. A car seat. For a fairly small child. Something bright on the floor caught his attention. Toys. A pacifier. He knew this look, this was a mom backseat. And just like that his body went rigid. Surely someone would have mentioned it if Lindsey had a kid. Surely *she* would have mentioned it. It certainly would be the most twisted kind of irony if she'd withheld that kind of information.

Derek grabbed the box loaded with supplies, pushed the door shut with his shoulder, and headed back inside. Lindsey was already wiping down the cabinets with a rag. She glanced over when he entered the kitchen but quickly went back to her task.

"Do you have a child?" He couldn't help himself. It just came out. He had to know.

She let out an awkward laugh and then stood facing him. "Uh, no."

"Why is there a car seat in your backseat?"

"That's Eden's. My niece."

Relief surged through him and he set the box down on the floor. He wasn't sure why the idea had upset him so much, but damn, it had. A lot. It wasn't the idea of a child that upset him, but the idea that she'd have been that close to someone else. Experienced something so important with another man. It wasn't lost on him that that was exactly what she'd had to feel about him. It was like a deep gnawing ache in his chest to think of Lindsey with anyone but him.

"I didn't know you had a niece."

"Well, how would you? I didn't tell you." Lindsey went back to wiping down the nearest cabinet.

"How old is she?" Derek asked. He began to unload the cans of stain and lay them out. Lindsey definitely had good quality stuff. Clearly she'd done this before and knew what she was doing.

"She's almost four months old. She's also the reason I was up so early. Last night was her first night in her big-girl crib. Her room is right next to mine and she was up every few hours wailing."

Lindsey was still facing away from him but Derek smiled at the way her voice softened when she spoke of her niece.

"New babies are hard. I remember when Tanner was first born, I thought I'd never get a full six hours again. He took quite a few months to start sleeping through the night."

"Yeah, Mel thought she was ready. I guess she'd slept without waking up to eat for two nights, but I'm not so sure."

"It's like they know you're not near. Tanner was the same way when we moved him into his own room. He'd cry and I'd go get him, change his diaper, and then bring him to Lisa to feed. A lot of nights we were so tired we'd let him fall back asleep between us."

Lindsey stopped moving, her hand frozen on the cabinet in front of her.

Shit. "I'm sorry, that was—"

"Don't apologize." She quickly got back to work. "Of course you'd have wonderful memories of that time in your life."

He needed to put a muzzle on. Not that he regretted what he'd said. Tanner's birth truly was one of the most magical things that had ever happened to him, but he could have kept those comments to himself for now. She was probably imagining that he'd left her only to get married and become blissfully happy with Lisa.

That couldn't be further from the truth. Sure, he'd tried. In the beginning he'd committed himself fully to trying to make Lisa happy. When Tanner was a couple of years old they'd even attempted to have another child. He'd hoped maybe a planned pregnancy—one that hadn't turned their world upside down—would make them feel complete. Happy. But the truth was, he and Lisa just hadn't been compatible and no child could fix that. Toward the end they hadn't even shared a bed and even their brittle friendship had slowly crumbled, turning into anger and resentment.

"So how long have you been living with your sister?" he asked, trying to change the subject.

"A month or so. It's just temporary." Lindsey moved on to another section of the cabinet.

"Until what?"

"Until I find another place." Her voice held a note of annoyance so he decided it was probably best if he let it drop. He could more than likely get more info about Lindsey from Mike.

"Okay. So what should I do?"

Finally she put her cloth down and turned to him.

"There's another cloth in my bag. We wipe everything down and then clean it up with a vacuum attachment." She nodded to the vacuum in the corner. "Then we stain."

"Easy enough."

Derek walked over to her bag, grabbed a small towel and wet it in the sink. He walked to the other end of the cabinet and began to scrub. After a few minutes he glanced over at Lindsey to find her watching him. When their eyes met she gave a hesitant smile and then turned away.

It reminded him so much of their stolen glances from the beginning. For so long he'd suppressed thoughts of this woman, basically because they were useless. He'd lost her and everything they'd found in one another. The easy laughs, the stolen kisses, and eventually the consuming passion that he'd never known up to that point or any time after. Even to this day. They might not get back there—probably wouldn't because they were no longer those people. But he'd take what he could get.

Nine

Monday morning, the sky was a brilliant blue and the air was inviting. It wasn't unusual in the Midwest to need snow boots one week and flip-flops the next. This was one of those rare and beautiful late February days that made you want to go outside and soak up the warmth of the sun, which was exactly what Lindsey planned to do.

Derek had to visit a job site in the city so Lindsey considered it a work-from-home kind of day. She pulled Eden's bouncy seat out onto the deck, placed her inside of it, and then ran back into the kitchen to grab her coffee. After turning on a musical toy to keep her niece appeased for a while, she finally settled into one of the comfortable patio chairs. The brace on her arm itched like crazy so she undid the straps and rested her arm on the cool glass tabletop before tilting her face up to the sky.

It was heavenly, the heat on her skin and just the slightest hint of a breeze. Birds sang along with the toy's happy jingle and Lindsey smiled. She needed this. The entire weekend she'd been overwhelmed and confused about the previous week. Overwhelmed with all of the work that still needed to be done on the house and confused by her unsettled feelings about Derek.

They'd now worked together for most of the week. Tuesday they'd finished the lower cabinets, Thursday glazed the uppers, and Friday they'd prepped the floors. Tomorrow they planned to stain them. The most annoying part was that she was beginning to look forward to seeing him. That was a dangerous feeling. She'd been down that road before. The one where he made her feel good about herself. Flirted with her just a little, then a lot. Then made her fall hard for him. That road had ended in heartbreak, which was exactly what she never wanted to experience again. And yeah, he'd slowly started to break rule one, but she'd let him get away with it. Definitely unwise, but she couldn't seem to help herself.

Deciding she had more important things to dwell on, Lindsey sat up, took a sip of her coffee, and then opened her newest crafting magazine. She loved to look through and get ideas for projects, find out what was becoming trendy. If it wasn't for her art she would go crazy. If things were different financially, her work could resume being her source of peace instead of another stressor.

She flipped through the pages, making mental notes to herself. Between her Etsy shop, consigned custom furniture pieces, and occasional design clients, she was doing okay. But her inventory would soon run out and she required money to make money. Supplies weren't free, and as much as she loved a good Dumpster dive, she often had to scour antiques and garage sales to find good items worthy of repurposing. She needed to do better. If her father was able to pay her back the money he'd borrowed over the past year, she'd be in a lot better shape, but she wasn't going to hold her breath on that front. Her dad didn't have anyone else so she didn't regret helping him. He knew better then to ask Mel for money. It was time for Lindsey to start making a plan.

Eden began to fuss so Lindsey leaned down. "Hey, pretty girl, did you lose your paci?" Lindsey pushed the rubber back between Eden's tiny lips and then started the musical toy once more. She hummed along, smiling to herself when she realized she knew every note of the baby toy.

Lindsey's phone rang and she glanced at the caller ID. She smiled to herself when she read Callie's number before answering. "Hey!"

"Hay is for horses," Callie said.

"Ha ha." Lindsey loved how her friend always sounded happy. Several months back, Callie had started dating Preston High's football coach and was madly in love.

"I'm headed downtown to the restaurant supply shop to get some things and wondered if you wanted to meet for lunch after."

"I'd love to, but I'm watching Eden for Mel," Lindsey said.

"Ooh, even better. Bring her with. I thought we could discuss Anne's bachelorette party."

"Okay, that sounds good. Oh, but wait . . ." Lindsey gave a pause, glanced down at her sleeping niece, and continued. "Eden just said she can only agree if we do Thai."

Callie laughed. "Four months and she's already so bossy. She's my type of girl. Want me to come by and pick you up?"

"How about we meet you? I've got the car seat already hooked up in my car. Eleven?"

"Sounds good, see you soon."

Two hours later Lindsey walked into Lulu's Noodle Shop, Eden in her car seat slung over her good arm. Callie waved from a booth near the back and Lindsey made her way toward the table. The hostess brought a holder for Eden's carrier and then Lindsey slid into the booth.

"Look at her. She's still so tiny." Callie smiled as she peered into the car seat. "Soooo. Tell me how it's been going with Mr. Walsh."

Lindsey just shook her head and smiled. "It's fine. It's nice to have the help and things are coming along nicely."

"Coming along, huh? So have you kissed him?"

"Oh my goodness, no way!"

Callie laughed. "Okay, okay. You just never know. You guys create a lot of energy when you're in the same room. If you're not too careful it's going to combust."

Lindsey didn't have much time to process that thought because their server greeted them. They ordered crab rangoon, chicken pad thai with extra heat, and two green teas.

"Okay, so continue with your story," Callie said.

"I don't recall telling a story."

"Well, you were just getting started."

"Oh no I wasn't," Lindsey said with a laugh. "There's really nothing to tell. We've kind of come to an understanding, I guess. We're friendly and working well together for now."

"You know he wishes it were more," Callie said.

Lindsey's stomach dropped at the comment. "You can't be certain of that. And I don't think he does. He feels bad for the way things ended, that's all. He needs to know I'm over it and maybe someday I can give him that. I don't know."

"Have you guys talked about it?"

"A little. But I think we both realize that there is nothing to be gained by going over it again and again."

"I can see your point, I guess. But have you forgiven him?"

Lindsey blew out a hard breath, considering her answer. "I don't know. I'm just not sure how I feel about any of it anymore. It still hurts but . . . I don't know. Maybe I've realized it was long ago and it doesn't do me any good to hold on to the anger."

Callie gave her a weak smile. "I'm sorry that happened to you. I wish I'd been your friend then. You better believe I'd have beaten that boy's ass for you."

Lindsey smiled. "I do believe it."

Eden began to stir in her seat, probably ready for her own lunch. Lindsey pulled a pumped bottle out of the diaper bag and began to unbuckle her from the car seat.

"Can I feed her?" Callie asked, eyes wide with excitement.

"Of course." Lindsey lifted Eden and then placed her in Callie's arms.

"Oh my goodness, she's so tiny. I want to take you home with me." Callie spoke in a baby voice down at

Eden and then kissed her fuzzy little head. Eden responded by squirming, her face twisting into a cry.

Lindsey handed Callie the bottle and then sat down to her own lunch. "Okay, I've dished my dirt. When are you and Coach gonna start making babies?"

"Hush your mouth," Callie whispered, as if her voice might disturb Eden's meal. "I'm nowhere near ready for babies. Although this cutie could maybe change my mind."

Lindsey chuckled. She knew what Callie meant. Holding Eden was magical. The difference was, Callie had a partner. One that Lindsey was pretty darn sure her friend planned to be with forever. She didn't know Bennett real well yet, but she could tell just by the way he looked at Callie that they were it for one another. And Lindsey could totally see Bennett as a family guy. He probably wanted three boys and a baby sister. The thought of Callie with multiple kids made Lindsey giggle.

"What?" Callie asked.

"Just imagining you with a brood of children."

"Oh, no way, Linds. Don't let Bennett hear you say that. He's already informed me his first son will be named Robert after one of his first coaches."

"Robert?" Lindsey cried, her eyes widening. "He is so going to knock you up soon. But a little boy nicknamed Bobby would be so cute. Little Bobby Clark."

"Right? Isn't it the cutest thing you've ever heard?" Callie crooned. They both laughed and then began to discuss Anne's party while Eden ate her lunch. They'd thrown Anne a bridal shower in January that had been a success. Quite a feat considering Callie and Lindsey had both been nervous about planning a party for the woman who did that for a living. But Anne had loved every minute of it.

"So I feel like her shower was our special girl time and this should just be crazy, grown-up fun. You know what I mean?" Callie asked.

"Okay," Lindsey said. She was a little apprehensive about hearing what Callie's ideas were. She had been known to really love a good time. Lindsey wasn't so much the nightclub type. But this wasn't about her, either. "What did you have in mind?"

"Welll . . . don't freak out. But what would you think about doing a coed bachelor and bachelorette party?"

"That sounds fun." But immediately Lindsey felt panicked. Bachelorette party meant a night out. Coed meant with boys. So Derek would definitely be there. "Where were you thinking we would do this?"

"Well, one of my best customers at the bakery is the head of PR for that big new casino in Mayville. I was going to ask her about getting a few rooms. See if she could get us a deal. What do you think? It would be close, all-inclusive, so we could drink and not worry. There is a club inside, gambling, food, swimming pools." Callie's grin was wide and hopeful.

"It does sound fun. Who were you thinking of inviting?" Lindsey picked at a piece of tofu on her plate.

"Well. Obviously Mike and Anne, me and Bennett. Maybe Brooke and Alex. Of course Eric and whoever he's dating. Maybe Emma if she's free. Oh and of course, uh, Derek. And you."

"So instead of coed bachelorette party, you really mean couples."

"No! I said Emma. You and Derek don't have to hang out if you don't want to," Callie said. She tilted her head to the side. "Although it kind of sounds like you might not mind. You know, since you've gotten used to being around one another."

"Even if we were fine hanging out, you guys will go back to your rooms for the night and then it will be awkward." And Lindsey didn't want to admit it, but she couldn't afford to get herself a room on her own.

"It will not be awkward. If you want, Derek and Mike can get a room and we girls can get our own."

"Oh yeah, that will go over like a lead balloon with your horny boyfriends," Lindsey said.

"True." Callie scrunched up her lips. "But if they have to take a cold shower for one night then that's what they'll do. Lindsey, I don't want you to worry about this. We'll all be there."

She had to go along with the plan. How could she not? The scariest part was that she was mostly afraid she might enjoy herself. And if at the end of the night she had to drive herself home then she'd do it. "You're right, it's fine. It *is* a good idea."

Callie grinned. "Yeah? I promise the party will be fun."

"I know it will be. I'm excited."

"Yay! Me, too." Callie pulled out her phone and opened the calendar app. "Might as well get it down."

Lindsey pulled her planner out of her bag. She was a paper-and-pen kind of girl. They settled on a date and each jotted down a few planning notes.

"Perfect. Why don't I check in with everyone else and make sure that date is good, although I can't imagine there would be any problems. If Anne has Claire . . . or Derek has Tanner, we can just help them figure something out."

Lindsey nodded, taking a sip of her tea. She was just going to have to accept it. Derek was once again a part of her life. It was up to her to make sure that she was in control this time.

Lindsey sat up straight and swept a lock of hair from her eyes with the back of her arm. Her hands were covered in stain, and her body ached, but the kitchen floor was done. She suddenly felt giddy about the progress they'd made over the past week and a half of working together.

Glancing across the room, she laughed when she caught sight of Derek. There was stain on his face, his forearms, and in his hair.

"What?" he asked.

"You're just a little dirty. That's all."

"I was hoping you might like me a little dirty," he said with a wink.

She rolled her eyes. "Rule one."

"Ah please." He laughed. "That's all in good fun. When I flirt with you, babe, you'll know it."

Lindsey shook her head. He'd been doing that more often the past few days. Slowly unleashing his powerful charm on her.

Occasional conversation had started up between them but mainly on safe topics. Anne and Mike, movies, the house. A few times she'd caught herself before saying something that began with the phrase "remember that one time when." She definitely didn't need them traveling down memory lane together. In fact, she'd straight-out made it a rule that it was forbidden between them.

Lindsey laid down her paintbrush and reached for her bottle of water before taking a long drink. It was nearly five o'clock, which meant they should probably start cleaning up. She wasn't sure what his plans were this evening—and she wasn't going to ask—but she was certain he wouldn't want to work through the evening.

Derek headed for the hall and then she heard him call out from the bathroom. "Jesus, you weren't kidding. I'm a mess."

She chuckled to herself and then glanced around at the now fully stained kitchen floor. They had worked hard today. Especially Derek. Her ability to paint wood floors was a little ineffectual considering she couldn't bend over and hold her weight up with her bad arm. She'd had to sit on her knees and lean to the side, doing small little strokes with her paintbrush

Derek on the other hand had strapped on giant knee pads and gone at it like a madman. She might have stolen a few glances at his butt when he was facing away from her. Any woman in her position would have done the same.

The doorbell rang, surprising Lindsey. She figured it might possibly be Anne and Mike coming out to see how things were going. It would be exciting for them to get a glimpse of all the progress they'd made during the past week.

"I got it," Derek called over his shoulder. She could hear his work boots clomping down the hallway, his

voice low as he spoke with another male. When he didn't
return right away she began to grow suspicious. Slowly
Lindsey grabbed onto a window ledge and hauled herself up to a standing position. She backed herself into
the dining area so as not to step on the wet stain and
nearly collided with Derek holding a pizza box and a
case of beer.

"You hungry?" he asked with an eyebrow raised. "I
hope so because it's already a done deal."

"You didn't have to do that. It's nearly five and I figured you'd want to get home. Or that you'd have plans."

He looked wary and stepped back a little. "Right now
you are my plans. Did you have somewhere to go tonight?"

"No." She shook her head, feeling guilty for assuming he'd want to rush off and relieved that he didn't.
Why was she always determined to assume the worst
about him? She eyed the pizza box. "Is that from Pie
Mia's?"

"It is." Derek grinned. He walked over and set the
pizza and beer down on the floor next to what appeared
to be a folded-up blanket that she'd never noticed before.
"Hope you don't mind eating picnic style. I figured
we've been on the floor all day. Why stop now?"

Lindsey couldn't hold back the smile on her face as
she walked over to where he stood fluffing out the blanket and laying it on the dining room floor. Once he had
it arranged he held out a hand to her. She took it, allowing him to hold some of her weight as she lowered herself to the floor. He sat down beside her.

"What kind of pizza did you get?" she inquired. "Did
you plan this?"

"You ask too many questions. But I will answer the first one. Someone might have informed me that you have a particular favorite flavor at Mia's." He gave her a crooked smile as he opened the box and turned it to face her.

Lindsey gasped in delight when she saw the goat cheese, chicken, and caramelized onion pizza she and her friends loved. "That is definitely my favorite!"

Derek chuckled. "I'm glad you're happy. I have to admit, never in a million years did I think I'd be ordering pizza with goat cheese on it."

"Oh, it's so good. You'll have to try it."

"Eh, I don't know about that," he said on a laugh.

"I see your favorite pizza is the heart attack special." One half of the pie was her favorite and the other was a concoction of every meat available and topped with strips of bacon.

"At least I'll go down happy. Good pizza, good company, and a good day's work."

He handed her an opened beer and then held his own out toward her. She clinked her bottle against his. "To sore backs tomorrow," she said.

"No kidding. And sore knees."

"You had knee pads on," she said as she grabbed her first slice of pizza.

"Babe, nothing is gonna stop the pain of being on your knees for six hours. Not at my age."

She stopped short for a moment, partly because he'd used that endearment again, and partly because she suddenly felt bad. He'd worked incredibly hard the past few days when he didn't have to. None of this was his responsibility. Contractors hired crews to do these kinds of tasks. On top of that, it was taking him away from his more important jobs in the city.

He must have sensed her worry. Derek leaned forward and looked her square in the eye. "Linds, I'd do it all again. For you. Understand me?"

She nodded. "Thank you."

"Now eat up."

They ate in silence for a while until he finally swiped the crumbs from his hands and leaned back to rest on his palms. "So tell me how you got involved with this blog."

Lindsey swallowed. "Well, Anne created it, as I'm sure you know. Started it years ago. After a while she added Callie. She posts recipes and such. At some point Anne and I met at the opening of a little craft shop downtown. I was there because . . . obviously I like crafty things. She was there because she likes crafty things. We started talking, e-mailing, I followed the blog, she followed my Etsy shop, and eventually she asked me to be a contributor."

"Etsy shop?"

"It's an online retail space where people can sell handmade items. I repurpose found objects, unusable antiques. And then I sell them."

"Repurpose. So, like, a trash-to-treasure kind of thing."

"Well . . . sort of. And I am impressed to hear you say that phrase. But more of . . . finding a new way for something to be useful. Like taking an old broken ladder and turning it into a lamp base."

"You've done that?"

"Yeah, I do that kind of stuff all the time." Lindsey

pulled her phone out of her pocket and opened her Etsy app. She'd become pretty good at one-handed phone typing. She scooted closer to Derek and showed him the screen. "These are a few of the items I have up now."

He leaned in toward her, their heads close, and looked at the screen. Reaching out, he began to scroll through a few photos. "What's that? A jewelry holder?"

She laughed at his confusion. "Basically. It's made from reclaimed barn wood, chicken wire, and found wrought-iron brackets. I've sold twenty just like it this year. I also do some custom work in addition to interior design, but repurposed art is sort of my thing."

"So you're one of those people that pull over and take things off peoples' curbs on trash day?"

She laughed. "I've been known to do that, yes."

Derek laughed. "Nice. Lindsey Morales, professional trash digger."

"Shush," she said with a smile as he continued to look at her phone.

"Wow. Fireplace mantel, bookshelves, light fixtures." He scrolled further down the page in silence and then looked over at her. "I'm really impressed, Linds. And not at all surprised."

His words pleased her way more than they should. In fact, she was feeling so warm and fuzzy at the moment she scooted away from him before she did something stupid. She was certain that she caught disappointment flash over his expression.

"Thank you."

"Where do you make all of this at?"

"Um, here or there. Right now I don't really have a place since I'm staying with Mel and Brett. Condos aren't really conducive to major craft projects. But I do small projects on their porch. It's been kind of a bummer not being able to have the space to work how I want." And why was she opening up to him like this?

"What kind of space would you like to work in?"

"Big, lots of fresh air. Room for storage. A space to spray paint."

He nodded. "You need a studio."

"Yeah, well, studio space doesn't come cheap. Plus, larger pieces like furniture can't be hauled up and down stairs or inside easily. That's why the garage at my last place was awesome."

"You do furniture also?" He looked surprised.

"I do. In fact, I'm about to get started on a piece for the island. It's kind of a surprise for Anne."

"I wondered what your plan was for that."

"Well, for the past few weeks I've been on the hunt for the perfect piece of furniture. Something old I can paint to match our color palette. Maybe a distressed cranberry or teal. Then I plan to install a thick butcher-block countertop."

"That's quite a project."

"Yeah, but I've done it before. I have a little booth down in the West Bottoms. In fact, this coming weekend is a First Friday so I thought I'd head down and search for something while I checked out my space."

Every first weekend of the month, her favorite area to look for deals—the West Bottoms in downtown Kansas City—was filled with antiques booths and shops. There was such an amazing creative energy down there and she never missed a first weekend. Her booth there was located in a bigger retail space that allowed artisans to rent. Lindsey had a good feeling that's where she'd find just the right piece for Anne's island.

Derek reached for his beer and then hesitated. "So this Friday, huh? You want some company? I'd love to see some more of your work."

Lindsey froze, uncertain what to say. She couldn't ignore the little voice inside of her saying, *Too much too fast.* This was supposed to be a no-big-deal friendship. But another part of her—the one that needed a firm talking-to—was thrilled by the thought of spending a day with Derek in one her favorite places. Showing off her work. She knew they had different tastes—he always preferred a more modern style and clean lines—but he'd just said really nice things about her small projects.

He could obviously sense her hesitation. "I've got a truck, you know?"

Lindsey laughed. "You might have me there. I usually have to hire someone to haul things for me." Something she couldn't afford in her build budget right now if it could be helped. Anne had paid her a good chunk of her fee up front but it wouldn't last long. And while Anne and Mike also paid for all the supplies, Lindsey wanted this one to be a secret until it was completely done.

Derek grinned. "See how useful I can be?"

"Okay, fine. You can come with me. But I warn you, I go early."

He shrugged. "Not a problem. I'll pick you up. We can grab some breakfast."

"Breakfast? What for?" They were already having a picnic dinner. Doing another meal in just a few days time could put them into dangerous territory. "We shouldn't try and make this into . . . a *thing*."

"I'm not making this into a thing. What does that even mean . . . a *thing*?"

"You know, more than it is."

He leveled her with an irritated yet amused glare. "Lindsey, this is nothing. Two people working on a project together and eating in the general vicinity of one another at a table. There might possibly—hopefully—be conversation involved. But that is definitely not a thing."

She considered his words for a moment, picking at the wrapper on her beer bottle. "Okay. Friday morning pick me up at seven."

Derek was noticeably pleased with her answer, his easy smile teasing her. "See how easy this is?"

"How easy what is?" All she could think was how easy it was to find him adorable even when she'd sworn to herself they wouldn't even get this far with each other.

"Being friends with me," Derek said. He gave her a wink before picking up another piece of pizza.

Lindsey just needed to keep reminding herself that friends was all it would ever be.

Ten

Derek pulled into the parking lot of Lindsey's condo a few days later. Or her sister's condo, who he assumed was also the woman currently coming down the stairs with Lindsey and a small baby in tow.

Derek parked his truck and exited the vehicle. The sun was warm but the air still held a winter chill. He stepped onto the sidewalk. "Good morning. You must be Melanie," he said.

She took his hand but he didn't miss the slight skepticism in her expression. He had a really good feeling this woman knew everything about his history with Lindsey. Not a surprise, they were sisters. Even looked a hell of a lot alike. Melanie wasn't as pretty as Lindsey, but she was still attractive, albeit a little rough looking with her hair in a messy bun and oversized sweatpants. He assumed it was the early morning look of a woman with a new baby. Not that any man in his right mind would ever mention anything like that out loud.

"Nice to finally meet you," she said with a hint of warning.

"Likewise." He turned to the adorable baby in her arms and touched her chubby outstretched hand. "And this must be Eden."

"It is," Lindsey finally chimed in. He turned and smiled at her over Eden's head as the tiny little fist clamped onto his finger.

He chuckled. "She's strong. Must run in the family." He met Lindsey's eyes once more.

Eden jerked his finger and Derek looked back at her just in time to be rewarded with a big toothless smile. He could definitely see hints of Lindsey in her little round face and large eyes. For a fleeting second he imagined what it would have been like to have a child with Lindsey.

"She likes you," Mel said. "I guess I'll defer to her judgment for now. But I'm watching you."

"Melanie," Lindsey said with a gasp, clearly embarrassed by her sister's verbal warning.

Derek cleared his throat and untangled his finger from Eden's grasp. "I'll consider myself warned, then."

"Let's get going," Lindsey said. She leaned over and kissed Eden's head of dark hair. "Bye, bean."

Derek smiled at the exchange and looked once more at Melanie, who apparently hadn't taken her eyes off him. "It was nice to meet you."

"Mmm-hmm," she said. He could only give a silent laugh as he turned and headed back to his truck. He could hear the two sisters having a whispered exchange behind him, but he just went and opened Lindsey's door, willing to wait. It was nice to know that Lindsey had a sister that cared so much, but it was also a reminder of all the roadblocks between them. Also of how bad it had been when he'd left her. The fallout must have been severe for a sister to be so overly protective. That thought sobered him a little.

After a moment he watched as Lindsey made her way over to him. She looked beautiful today in tight pink jeans that highlighted her generous and sexy lower half, white Chucks, and a worn denim shirt. Her hair was loose and flowing, his favorite, and she slipped a pair of sunglasses onto her face. It really didn't matter what Lindsey wore, she always looked gorgeous.

"Thank you," she said quietly as she ducked under his arm and climbed into the truck. Without waiting for her to try he pulled himself up and buckled in her seat belt. She smelled good with that hint of citrus, and something else feminine. He wondered what perfume she wore.

Once in the driver's seat he headed north toward the West Bottoms. They were quiet for a few moments. Every time they were together it still felt a little like two steps forward one back.

"So is there somewhere we can eat down there?"

"There's a diner on Eighth."

"Okay, diner it is." After another minute of silence he glanced at her. "Everything okay?"

"Yeah." Her answer came too quickly and without his prompting for more she continued. "It's just . . . this is a little weird. Isn't it?"

He shrugged. "Not for me. I like being with you."

He didn't look over but from the corner of his eye he caught her turn away toward her window. Derek held in a sigh. He felt like she was constantly warring with herself about being his friend. He wondered how much of today's hesitation stemmed from that final chat with her sister.

Ten minutes later Derek pulled down into the West Bottoms. The now hip antiques shopping area had once been the thriving stockyards and trade epicenter of Kansas City in the late 1800s and early 1900s. Being an architect, Derek had gone through a period of learning everything he could about the planning and development of Kansas City. The giant warehouse buildings were now home to shops, a few restaurants, and some of the largest haunted houses in the United States during the fall. He hadn't been down here in years but clearly it was the place to be on the first weekend of the month. There were cars and people everywhere.

He turned onto Eighth Street and Lindsey pointed. "There it is, just ahead on the right."

Derek found a parking spot and then reached over to unlatch her seat belt before getting out. They walked up to the door in silence, but Derek nearly groaned aloud when he held the door open for Lindsey and was hit with one of his favorite smells ever: coffee and bacon.

The diner was a cute place. Probably could use an update, but he figured that was the look they were going for. Or, more likely, they just didn't give a damn.

A server passing by pointed to a booth along the back wall where they could sit. Derek followed Lindsey through the dining area and he couldn't help but get a good look at the backside of her pink jeans. *Good Lord*. He was getting tired of admiring her from a distance. He wanted to touch her.

They sat down across from each other and she immediately picked up her menu. He chose instead to lean on the table and watch her. After a moment she peeked over the top of the laminated sheet.

"I suggest you decide," she urged. "These servers here are busy and they want you to be ready when they come over."

He smiled at her. "You think I can't charm a server? I guarantee you I can."

She rolled her eyes but he could see the way her lips creased at the corners. "There is no doubt of that."

He still did as she suggested, quickly deciding on the Ranch Hand Platter. He immediately went back to observing her, the way her eyes narrowed as she contemplated. Her fingers, perfect dark gray nail polish this time. The natural highlights in her hair that framed her face. Even the tiny freckle just below her left eye. He could analyze the finer details of Lindsey Morales all day long.

From the corner of his eye he saw a middle-aged woman approaching their table. He whispered, "Oh my God, she's coming. You better be ready, she already looks pissed."

Lindsey set down her menu. She was trying and failing to hide her smile.

"Morning, folks," the server said. She instantly grabbed Lindsey's coffee mug. "Coffee?"

"Please," Lindsey replied. She looked at Derek and he give her a wink.

"Coffee for the gentleman?"

"Absolutely." Derek handed her his mug and glanced at the woman's name tag.

"Thank you, Lynn," he said when she put down his mug. Lynn noticeably preened a little at his words. Derek smirked at Lindsey who just rolled her eyes.

"What can I get you two for breakfast?" Lynn asked, her smile more genuine this time.

He nodded to Lindsey to go first. When she was finished, Derek gave his order and immediately the woman smiled at him. "I guessed you to be a Ranch Hand kind of guy."

"Uh-oh, I hate to be predictable." Derek smiled in Lindsey's direction.

"Uh-uh," the server said as she picked up their menus. "This one is a compliment. You two let me know if you need anything, ya here?"

"Thank you so much, Lynn," Derek said, before taking a sip of his coffee.

When they were alone once again, he grinned at Lindsey.

She was shaking her head. "That really wasn't so impressive. She's a middle-aged woman, you're a handsome younger man. I don't think there was much skill involved."

Derek huffed out a laugh and without thinking blurted out, "Okay, I can agree with that. So is that what it takes? Do I need to wait until you're middle-aged for my *handsomeness* to work on you? Or should I maybe just try a little harder."

Her eyelids fluttered down, her fingers began fidgeting against the wooden tabletop. "Stop. This is supposed to be just breakfast. Remember?"

Derek leaned a little farther across the table. "You still afraid we're stepping over the line here?"

She shrugged. "Maybe."

Derek sat up straight but continued staring at her. Her sister had definitely gotten into her head. "Lindsey, I've enjoyed working with you. A lot. It feels good to be with you like this. You can't tell me it doesn't feel good to you, too."

She relaxed, her shoulders dropping just a little. She put her hands on the table, chunky brace and all, and folded her fingers together. "Of course it does. Better than being angry. I don't like to feel angry at anyone."

"It's more than that. I'm not just anyone."

Her eyes darted to his and he could tell he was on the verge of going too far. But it felt as if she were so close to giving him a hint of her feelings. "Derek. Please," she whispered.

Derek leaned forward once more, his hands resting near hers. He lowered his voice. "Please what, Lindsey? Tell me."

He took a gamble and slid his middle finger very slowly across the side of her hand, down the length of her little finger, all the way to the tip of her painted nail. Rule two, officially broken. He wanted to obliterate that rule. Touch her so thoroughly that there was no going back. She didn't move, her eyes staring at his fingers. Did she want him to touch her again? Only one way to find out.

This time he picked up her pinky and gently caressed it. It was a seemingly innocent touch, but it almost felt wicked as the pad of his thumb slowly massaged her knuckle.

Just as he was contemplating his next move, Lindsey pulled her fingers away under the guise of grabbing her coffee mug and sliding it closer. Derek pulled his hands back and watched quietly as she picked through the little bowl of individual creamer cups. She frowned.

"What?" he asked. "Not see what you want?"

"Usually they have hazelnut. None today." She picked up a couple of vanillas.

"Well, hold on," He glanced around the room for Lynn.

"No, it's fine. I'll just use something else," she protested quietly. "She's busy."

"Linds, stop. I want you to have exactly what you want."

A moment later the server came out from the kitchen and Derek gave her a subtle signal. She walked right over.

"Lynn, could you do us a big favor and get us some hazelnut creamers?"

"Sure thing, I'll be right back, sweetie." Lynn headed for a side station.

Derek turned to Lindsey and gave her a wink. "See, if I can't flirt with you I'll just flirt with Lynn."

Lindsey's eyes dropped and she let out the most beautiful laugh. He was in trouble.

Lindsey stepped out of the diner and into the warmth of the morning. The sun was shining and birds were chirping. She hoped spring was here to stay, but it had been known to snow in March so one was never sure. Not that it mattered now because her insides were like an inferno after breakfast with Derek. The way he'd spoken to her, looked at her. Touched her. She couldn't decide if this had all been a mistake or exactly what she wanted.

Derek came up behind her, having just finished paying their bill at the counter.

"You really didn't need to pay," she said.

"Lindsey, if you bring that up again, I'm going to be insulted. Friends take each other out to breakfast sometimes."

She turned to look at him. He was moving a mint-flavored toothpick around between his lips. Lucky toothpick.

Ugh, stupid Lindsey. Before they'd left this morning she and Mel had had a very frustrating conversation. Lindsey was now confused about all of her conflicting emotions and desires for this man. Mel couldn't understand and had argued that it was impossible for two people that had once been intimate the way she and Derek had to remain *just friends*. The worst part was that down deep inside Lindsey was afraid her sister might be right. The fact that she couldn't stop thinking about how sexy Derek looked was *proving* her to be a little bit right. Lindsey's argument had been that she was strong enough to deal with him. But she hadn't anticipated how turned on she could be by just the slightest touch.

Derek had been the enemy for so long she wasn't sure how to process this sudden change. She still felt immense pain when she thought about how things had gone down, but could she eventually move past it? Was she being fair putting all these protective walls between them? Was she acting out of smarts or fear?

Definitely a little of both.

They left the truck parked on a side street and headed down the road to the official shopping district. It was now bustling with people searching for a good deal, that perfect piece for their home, the latest trend in home decorating. Building after building, floor after floor, filled with things to purchase. Even though it was still early, many local food trucks were pulling in and setting up. One of the buildings even had large speakers blasting jazz music from the rooftop. Just being here made her feel happy and inspired.

"First let's go there," Lindsey said, pointing to a building ahead. "That's where I consign and I want to check in with Becky, the owner."

Derek nodded. "You're in charge today." After a moment he spoke again. "How long have you sold stuff down here?"

"Oh, a few years now."

"What kind of items? Same as on your Etsy site?"

Lindsey stepped out of the way for a woman carrying a painted end table and then continued their conversation. "Yes, a little of everything, but here I can sell bigger items that aren't easy to sell online. I hit antiques stores, thrift shops, garage sales . . . curbs. Try and find stuff supercheap then repurpose it."

"So this is more Dumpster diving. Sometime I'm gonna have to go on *that* field trip with you."

"Stop it." But she couldn't help laughing along with him as they walked up the big stone steps into the building that housed several shops, including the Pink Pearl.

Derek stopped and glanced at the hanging sign.

"Seriously? Between you and me," Derek whispered, "the name of this place is indecent."

She looked at him, one eyebrow up.

"The *Pink Pearl*? Come on now," he said with a grin.

"You are so disgusting." She gave him a little shove in the stomach and pretended to be offended.

"I'm a guy," he said. As she opened the big glass door he leaned in behind her and whispered, "I didn't say I don't like the name. It definitely brings a few nice things to mind."

She turned and gave him a playful glare. "Quiet."

Lindsey was in so much trouble spending the day with Derek. He was incapable of not embarrassing her. He was also funny and charming, not to mention so handsome it should be a crime. No less than five women had eyeballed him on their walk down the street. He was hot. It was that simple, and although she told herself over and over that nothing was going to happen between them—because it just couldn't—it was going to be hard to hang on to that resolve if she started to . . . *like* being with him.

Lindsey led them up a narrow flight of stairs to the second floor, which belonged to the Pink Pearl boutique. It was a busy First Friday, which she was glad to see. Not even ten in the morning and the place was packed. She could feel Derek right behind her as she made her way through the bodies—made up mostly of women—to the counter.

"Lindsey," a feminine voice called over the line waiting to check out. Lindsey waved at Becky.

"Wow, what a crowd," Lindsey said as Becky walked up to them.

"I know, right? I think everyone's tired of being cooped up this winter and took the day off. It's such a beautiful day." The entire time she spoke, Becky's eyes kept landing on Derek. Lindsey angled her body so he could step up beside her.

"Becky, this is my friend Derek. He's the contractor in charge at Anne's house."

The woman's eyes lit up while simultaneously running up and down Derek's form. She put out a hand. "Oh my, it's so nice to meet you. Lindsey has told me all about the house, even shown me pictures. It's so amazing."

There was a somewhat flirty tone to Becky's little speech and Lindsey found herself having to force a smile. Becky was divorced, a mother of two little girls. She was a little older than Derek, but she was attractive, her hair trendy, her makeup perfect. They'd probably have a lot in common. If nothing else they'd probably both enjoy a random hookup.

Suddenly irritated, Lindsey looked up at Derek. He was smiling as he shook the woman's hand and thanked her. Becky's wrist full of bangles rattled with the motion. Lindsey decided she hated those bracelets. Becky was a grown woman, not a teenager. How many damn bracelets did a woman in her thirties need to wear?

"Well, we just came by to check out my booth real quick. Remember, I told you I couldn't come in and stay this weekend because of all the work that needs to be done. But next month I will be here," Lindsey said. She was trying to end the conversation and separate them from the woman. "Today we're looking for a base for Anne's center island. So we better get to it."

"Oh, fun!" Becky exclaimed with a little too much enthusiasm. "Let me think if we have anything here."

"That's okay," Lindsey said, nodding toward the huge line at the counter. There were several women working, but it didn't matter. "You're so busy today. We'll just take a look around."

"Sounds good, you two. Let me know if you need any help." Becky gave Derek's arm a quick touch. It was innocent enough, but hardly necessary, and it made Lindsey's blood boil in her veins. She purposely didn't meet Derek's eyes, heading immediately to the back where her items were displayed.

"Is she the owner?" Derek laughed over Lindsey's shoulder. "Makes you wonder about a woman who names her store the Pink Pearl."

That was it. Lindsey turned on her heels, eyes wide. He looked shocked and abruptly halted, almost running into her. Lindsey lowered her voice and whispered. "If you're curious, why don't you go ask her? She seemed eager to talk with you."

Derek's wide eyes slowly turned into a naughty grin. His lips pursed for a moment as his gaze traveled over her face. Lindsey swallowed hard, knowing that she was not fooling him. She was all talk, and by the look in his eyes, he was so on to her. And he was pleased, darn it.

He lifted his hand and nudged her chin like she was a child. "You know damn well I have no desire to speak with her. But you getting agitated is awfully cute."

"I wasn't agitated, just . . . frustrated." She tried to pull herself together, but she knew it was futile.

Granting her mercy, he didn't respond, only stepped around her and began to look at an old record player on a tabletop. Lindsey glanced over her shoulder toward the front of the shop, just in time to see Becky look away. She'd been watching, seen the whole thing unfold. Lindsey and Derek standing so close, him looking down into her eyes and then touching her face.

Good. Let Becky think he was off limits. Even though he wasn't. Not at all.

Eleven

Derek was officially in trouble. Every interaction with Lindsey was a balance of doing the right thing and wanting to tease a response out of her. He couldn't shake the newfound knowledge that she was fighting her attraction to him just as he was to her. She'd made it official just now. He'd been pretty certain that she was still attracted to him at the very least, and the look on Lindsey's face when that woman had checked him out was the final proof he needed. It had been pure jealousy.

They wanted each other. And the truth of it made him feel smug as hell on the inside. He also knew he'd ruin things if he didn't play it cool.

He spoke over her shoulder. "So, where's your repurposed trash?"

Lindsey gave a dramatic sigh. "Against the wall. Here."

The entire place was clearly arranged into booths separated by using larger pieces of furniture, shelving, and other big items in order to give it a cohesive look. Derek walked up to where Lindsey stopped and took in her space. He'd been prepared to fake enthusiasm, certain that what he found would not appeal to him. He was wrong.

Her little section of the room was lit from above by several vintage light fixtures, some with crystals, some beads, some painted bright yet distressed colors of yellow, turquoise, or even black-and-white. They looked old . . . but fresh, somehow. Girly but beautiful and classy.

The entire space couldn't be more then twelve-by-twelve feet, but it was loaded. He had to turn sideways to walk through. There were several pieces of furniture, an old bureau painted and distressed in a shade of taupe gray, several end tables, and even an old warehouse cart on wrought-iron casters used as a coffee table. Small decorative pieces were scattered throughout the area. Random items, like antlers and glass vases, wooden bowls, old tool chests, and even a few antique dolls. It was quite a mash-up of stuff, but it had an overall feel to it he couldn't quite describe.

Feminine, subtle, and beautiful. Warm and safe. It was completely Lindsey. If she had a place of her own this was what it would look like. *Feel* like.

She needed a studio to create these beautiful things that clearly brought her so much joy. An overwhelming desire to give that to her washed over him.

He turned back to her. She bit at her upper lip, clearly nervous. Her eyes rose to his and then she spoke. "Anyway, this is it. Looks like I've sold an old desk. So that's good." She nodded to an empty spot toward the back.

"Linds, this stuff is really nice. I'm impressed once again."

She looked surprised. And pleased. "Yes, I can imagine your modern office with one of my pieces in it," she said sarcastically.

"Just because it's not my style doesn't mean I can't appreciate it. This is the kind of stuff that high-end stores sell remakes of, and you're making the real deal. You've always been creative, had an eye for design. I've seen plenty of your drawings, remember?"

A slow smile emerged. "Yes, of course I remember. Although if I recall, you did most of the drawing."

"Maybe so, but the point is . . . you're very talented."

"Thank you." They stared at each other for a moment, until two women came along and needed to get by. Lindsey stepped out of the way as the women walked into her booth.

It was a little awkward to watch, see them whispering to one another as they picked things up and looked at prices. They had no clue that the owner and creator of these pieces was within earshot.

"Let's get out of here so we can find what we need," Lindsey said, stepping away.

Derek followed her through the convoluted space, knowing full well that he'd already found exactly what he needed.

Tired and frustrated, Lindsey stepped up to the fifth floor of the old building. It was nearly two in the afternoon and they'd found nothing despite the fact that they'd been through almost five buildings. All of which they'd covered thoroughly.

Despite not finding what she'd come for, they'd still had a lot of fun. Shopping on First Friday, you were always sure to find random old stuff. Things from your childhood that you'd forgotten about, like board games, your great-grandma's old Tupperware, and even toys you picked up with fast food kids' meals. Lindsey and Derek were having a good time telling each other stories about their lives as they found things to reminisce over.

She'd learned more about Derek in the past three hours than she'd learned during those three months they'd been seeing each other in college. That time around it had been all about the now. The fierce attraction between them during stolen moments between classes, on the weekends, and over Thanksgiving break had left little time for getting-to-know-you conversations. At the time she hadn't minded or even considered it because it was too much fun to kiss and touch. Ironically, it was the things they didn't discuss that had been their undoing.

Today she was beginning to get a sense that Derek's childhood hadn't been the easiest. Not that it had been bad, but a few of his comments about his father had left her wondering if there was much love between them. That made her sad, because although her mother had left her and her father was . . . a handful, she never doubted she was loved. Not for one second.

Lindsey glanced around the large room, trying to decide if she should just give up for today. This floor didn't have much in the way of large furniture. It was mostly kitchenware and textiles.

Ahead of her Derek walked over to a section of vintage clothes. One entire display rack held an assortment of retro ladies' undergarments. He picked up a rather constrictive-looking bra and held it up to show her.

"This is sexy as hell," he said with a smirk. "I really wish cone-shaped boobs would make a comeback."

Lindsey laughed and so did he. "Can you imagine?" Lindsey stepped closer and touched the thick fabric. It was quite a piece of work. "This almost looks like a torture device."

Derek hung the hanger back on the rod. They continued to walk around in silence. Occasionally Lindsey reached out to touch an interesting fabric. Every sensation seemed to go on high alert as she and Derek stole glances at one another over the aisles made up of random items.

They entered an area that reminded them of rummaging through a grandmother's overstuffed attic. Rusted tricycles, a beat-up china cabinet, and stacks of boxes. They continued on, each of them glancing around at the various junk, but somehow Lindsey knew neither of them were really focused on the items being displayed.

Toward the back of the room she watched Derek stop and turn toward a row of wooden crates. She stepped closer and peeked around him. The crates held piles of old comics and instantly she smiled, knowing that he would enjoy this immensely. His long fingers ran across the cover of the one on top, a Green Lantern from the seventies.

After a second he picked it up, gently flipping the pages. The edges were bent and the pages yellowed, but still he handled it as if it were fragile. And she guessed it was, just on the cusp of falling apart.

He carefully laid it to the side and picked up another, looking through it in the same manner, occasionally stopping to read a certain page.

Somewhere in a box nestled safely in the corner of her closet, Lindsey had a stack of comics of her own. But hers had never been published as these were. No, her comics were more special than that. Written and drawn by the man standing next to her.

It had become a fun way for them to communicate during class. He'd leave her part and she'd fill it out. Every time they'd get together he had new pages for her, was always so excited to share. She'd often asked why he wasn't pursuing it as a career, as good as he was. He'd always brushed it off, saying it was nearly impossible to break in. There was no money to be made. But she'd seen in his eyes how happy it had made him. That had to have been worth something.

"Do you still have all the comics you collected?" she asked quietly.

"Some. I'm saving them for Tanner."

"Oh, that's nice. He enjoys them also?"

Derek gave an awkward laugh. "He humors me is probably more accurate. He's a great drawer but he prefers video games."

Lindsey smiled, watching patiently as he continued to thumb through another box. He pulled out various copies of Spider-Man, Wolverine, and the Fantastic Four.

"I used to have quite a collection but my father got rid of a bunch one day."

Lindsey glanced up at him, shocked at this admission. "Why would he do that?" she asked.

"Thought they took up too much space. Wanted me to get over my obsession. Who knows? I quit trying to understand the man a long time ago."

Lindsey bit at her lip. "I'm sure he just didn't realize that they were special."

Derek turned to face her, shoving his hands in his pockets. "He knew *exactly* how special they were."

"That's horrible. I'm sorry." She glanced back down at the box and reached in front of him to pick up one of the comics. "You could buy some of these. They're not in very good condition but it would be . . . something." She wasn't sure what else to say. It was another layer of Derek's past with his father revealed. Each one seemed to be sadder than the last. What kind of man could be that thoughtless and uncaring?

"Some things can't be replaced." His voice was quiet. "I've learned that the hard way because I've had to give up a lot of things I want."

Lindsey put the comic down just as Derek turned and grabbed her hand. She looked up into his eyes. He stared back and slowly lifted her fingers up to his mouth.

She shivered as his lips brushed against one knuckle, than another. He lingered there, his eyes peering over the back of her hand. Lips pursed against her skin. She felt the warmth of his breath all the way down to her toes. And she couldn't move, could barely breathe. With his touch and his lips he'd now made her fingers into an erogenous zone.

His other hand came around her waist, gently pulling her closer. She let him, unable to think clearly as she continued to stare into his heated gaze. She knew what this meant. Things could never be the same if she allowed him to take this any further. She should stop him.

She couldn't.

"Lindsey, I won't break your rules any further," he

said, lowering their joined hands. He twisted his wrist, pulling her hand in to lean against his chest. She swore she could feel the pounding of his heart. "But . . . I'd really love for you to break mine. Please."

He had her. His request was so desperate, his voice so quiet, and his eyes so hopeful. She knew that in this moment she was willing to give this man anything. Damn the past and everything that had happened between them for whatever reasons. This was now. They'd both been hurt in so many ways. Some she was beginning to understand, some she probably never would.

No matter what may result from it, she knew that more than anything she wanted to kiss Derek again. Had known it all along. There had never been anything better than the feel of his lips against hers, and if she got hurt in the end, at least she would enjoy it right now. Refusing to look away, she lifted up on her toes and slowly leaned in, her lips touching his. Tentatively at first, soft. A kiss here, there, here again.

She let her eyes close as she remembered exactly how perfectly they fit together. It was like reliving a dream, the silken texture of his lips, the way he responded slowly, nipping at her bottom lip as he did now. Languidly sucking it into his mouth.

Her body responded instantly, heat pooling in her core. She let out the quietest moan and angled her head to give him all the permission he needed. He took graciously at first, unlocking their hands pressed between them and smashing her chest against his. The now free hand slid to her scalp and shoved into her hair, controlling the angle of her head to just where he wanted it.

And then his kiss turned ravenous, his mouth opening

over hers, his tongue filling her, demanding she reciprocate.

God, it had always been like this, Derek knowing the
exact way to handle her body to leave her desperate and
needy. Making every movement of his mouth feel as intimate as sex itself.

And as willing as she was right now, this was the exact reason she'd tried to keep her distance. This was
what she was afraid of. Losing herself to his charms.
Her body to his intense passion. Her heart to all of him.
She knew she would if given the chance.

Voices behind them had Lindsey suddenly pulling
away, extricating herself from his firm grasp. For a moment she wasn't sure if he'd let her go, but finally he re-
leased his hold.

She took a deep breath, her heart nearly breaking
through her chest as she looked at him. His eyes were
lidded, but his chest was moving just as rapidly as hers.

"I'm sorry. That was probably not a good idea."

"Lindsey—"

"Oh, look at this dress, Tina," a woman said only a
few feet away.

"How about we take a break for some lunch?" Lindsey said, her tone purposely light. She stepped away in
the direction they'd entered.

She turned back to see if Derek was following. He
stood in place for a moment, his eyes giving her a
warning stare. She raised an eyebrow and when the
two women shoppers came closer he followed Lindsey
across the room and down the stairs.

"How do you feel about street tacos?" she asked, her
tone light.

"Whatever you want," he said. They headed down three more flights and then out into the sunshine. Her body was keyed up to the point of humming, but she didn't want him to know that.

Slipping her sunglasses onto her face, Lindsey glanced around for her favorite truck. The streets were now nearly full to bursting, the scent of kettle corn, Indian food, and of course Mexican filled the air. When she spotted what she was looking for she nodded for Derek to follow. If he was as frustratingly unsated as she was at the moment he didn't show it. Cool and calm, that was the only thing she could find in his expression.

"If you trust me I have a favorite. I'm friends with Ruby, the owner."

"Of course I trust you," he said.

She smiled, and led them toward the crowd. Lindsey had gotten to know Ruby a few years ago when she'd just started consigning at the Pink Pearl. They'd hit it off right away and the rest was history. They'd become friends and helped each other when they could. Ruby often hung flyers for Lindsey's booth and Etsy shop, and in return Lindsey had painted some art on the woman's big red taco truck a year or so ago. For small, local entrepreneurs, building these kind of relationships was so important.

They walked side by side, dodging people coming from the opposite direction. Finally they made their way up to the bright red truck with the giant RUBY TACOS across the back. Every time Lindsey spotted the dazzling paint she smiled.

"Wow. That's some paint job," Derek said.

Lindsey smiled to herself but didn't comment. The

truck was a shimmering ruby red and the company logo
was done in a vintage font that also featured a cartoony
light-brown-skinned version of Dorothy from *The Wizard of Oz,* holding a taco. The best part was that Ruby's
tacos were authentic, just like Lindsey's grandmother
from Mexico used to make. Fresh corn tortillas, lots of
lime juice, and the various salsas were nice and hot, just
the way Lindsey liked it.

She pointed the menu out to Derek. All the varieties
were named after characters in the story. There was a
Dorothy, a Tin Man, Toto, and so on. The biggest meal
was, of course, the Wizard. Luckily the line wasn't too
bad, and within ten minutes they were at the window.

"Look who it is, our most beautiful customer and the
highlight of every First Friday," a handsome young man
said from the window.

"Hi, Rico. How are you?" she asked with a grin.

Rico was Ruby's youngest son, and at nineteen way
too young for Lindsey. That never kept him from flirting with her. "I'm a lot better now that you're here." He
leaned his arms on the metal counter, grin wide and
charming.

Lindsey glanced at Derek, who was staring the poor
kid down. She decided to intervene and opened her
mouth to speak when Ben, Ruby's older son, appeared
at the window. He was twenty-two and just as adorable
as Rico. He shoved his little brother out of the way and
gave Lindsey his biggest smile.

"Hey, girl. We were starting to think we wouldn't see
you today."

That was the moment Lindsey felt Derek's hand
snake around her waist, pulling her close to his side. She

hesitated a moment but pulled herself together. After that kiss she wasn't entirely shocked by this, but it still surprised her a little.

"Ugh, hey Ben." Lindsey glanced up at Derek quickly and he raised an eyebrow at her. She turned back to the window. "This is . . . my friend Derek."

"What's up, man?" Ben gave him a chin lift and then his eyes went straight back to her. He obviously didn't notice or didn't care about Derek's possessive display of affection.

"Not much, good to meet you," Derek replied anyway, and Lindsey didn't miss the annoyance in his tone.

"Is your mother not here?"

"Nah, she went to visit her sister in Dallas."

"Oh, that's nice." Lindsey glanced behind them in line. There was a group of women waiting, but they were all too engrossed in their conversation to notice what was going on in front of them. When she turned back to the window, Rico was back. "Well, I want—"

"Please, as if you need to say." Rico grinned, winked at her, and then called over his shoulder to his brother. "One Lindsey Taco, extra juice."

"Really?" Derek said under his breath, his hand clamping down on her waist.

"It's really good. I always order the same thing with extra lime juice, so he just started—"

"Yeah, I get it. You forget I was a young guy once. They think they're being cute. It's not cute." Derek's tone was dry as sand, and Lindsey found herself grinning in spite of herself. Yeah, she'd known when the guys had started describing her special meal the way they did, with a wicked smile, that they thought they were getting away with the innuendo, but she'd been on to them.

Rico put his head back through the window. "What can I get you, man?"

"Well, I guess if it's that good, I'll get a Lindsey Taco, too. In fact, make it two of them."

Rico grinned and raised an eyebrow before saying, "You want the extra juice?"

Derek glanced down at Lindsey before turning to Rico. "Absolutely."

Rico laughed and gave them a wink. "You'll love it."

"I intend to," Derek whispered against her hair. His warm breath tickled behind her ear and she shuddered against him. So much for no flirting and touching. Every rule they'd set had just been blown to pieces.

The Lindsey Taco was amazing, but nowhere near as delicious as the woman herself. And he wanted her again. All of her. But he could tell she was trying desperately to pretend they hadn't just had their tongues down each other's throat.

They were seated at one of many folding tables lining the sidewalk that had been set up for the day. He guessed that while they were in public he could play along with their denial for a little while, but as soon as he got her alone it was back on.

"So what do you think?" she asked.

"It's really good. So you just started ordering this exact thing?"

Lindsey shrugged. "Yeah. I got the Glenda for a while, which is made with chicken also, but this was the way my *abuelita*—my grandmother—used to make it.

She kept it very simple, just cooking the chicken with tomatoes, lots of lime juice, and onions. She also made fresh *guajillo* chile salsa and then topped it with slices of avocado and cilantro."

He loved listening to her say Spanish words, the shape of her lips as she formed the vowels. He'd like to hear her say something dirty. Instead he continued with their conversation. "It tastes really fresh. Nothing like the drive-thru tacos I grew up on."

She laughed. "Most certainly not. Americanized tacos are good, but these, these are the real thing. Completely different."

"So how do you know those yahoos that work the truck?"

She shook her head, hiding a small grin. "Those are Ruby's sons. I'd gotten to know her just from stopping and getting lunch, and one day I just told her about how I remembered my grandmother's tacos and so she made one for me. We kind of became friends after that."

As if his ears had been burning, the youngest of the sons—Rico maybe—walked up to their table and leaned on an empty chair. Derek's body went on alert.

"Everything good?" Rico asked.

"Wonderful," Lindsey said. Derek nodded his agreement, wondering what the guy wanted and wishing he hadn't come by.

"Hey, Linds, I meant to tell you that Pete over there asked me about our truck. But don't worry, I told him we were your one and only. Just wanted to warn you in case he caught you and started putting the pressure on."

Derek glanced across the street to where Rico had nodded. A rather ugly white truck with the words PETE'S

BBQ stenciled onto the side sat parked on the curb. Things started to click into place in Derek's head. He glanced at Lindsey who appeared embarrassed.

"You're right, no more food trucks for me. I just love your mama. Tell her hi for me, will ya?"

"Will do, Linds," Rico said. He turned to Derek. "Later, man."

"Yeah, later."

Derek was in shock and he waited for Lindsey to explain, but when she didn't he put his drink down and stared at her. "Lindsey, were you really not going to tell me you painted that truck?"

She lifted a shoulder. "I don't know."

Derek's shoulders dropped in annoyance. "Don't bullshit me, Linds. I mentioned the paint job, the least you could have done was say it was your work. It's beautiful."

She gave him a smile. "Thank you. But if you must know, part of the reason I didn't say anything was because I didn't want the cartoon genius critiquing my work."

Derek went silent. They stared at each other for a long moment and he was surprised she didn't look away. "Did I ever critique your work?"

She shook her head. "No, I guess not."

"All right, then. So next time you brag when you do something amazing."

Twelve

The following Wednesday evening, Derek stepped out the front door of his office, locked up, and then immediately headed around the side of the building toward his best friend Mike's shop.

Derek had purchased his building about five years ago, mainly because it seemed like a sound investment. Also because he'd thought moving to a smaller town would be nice for Tanner when he visited. Seemed a little silly now because he didn't see Tanner enough.

But he didn't regret the purchase. He did like the small town of Preston. And he'd remodeled the building to house his office and meeting space in the front, leaving a large empty bay and second office in the back.

It just happened to have been ideal, because not long after he'd bought it Mike had needed a space. Since then Derek had leased the rest of the building to his buddy so he could use it to continue his car restoration business. It had worked out well for both of them. Mike was the perfect tenant. On time with his payments, and when he felt like it, Derek could walk around the corner and shoot the shit.

The weather was surprisingly mild so today he found the garage bays open and Mike on his back underneath an orange Camaro.

"You about done for the day?" Derek asked in greeting.

Mike slid out from under the chassis and grinned. He had a dark streak of God knows what greasy substance running the length of his cheek. "I think I am. And you're just in time. Wanna take a test-drive with me?"

Derek shrugged. "If we drive it to a place that serves beer."

Mike chuckled. "How about I'll test-drive it tomorrow and we can walk over to Smokey's."

"Even better," Derek said. "But wash your damn face first."

Fifteen minutes later, Mike had showered, changed, and together they started the five-minute walk down the alley to Smokey's. Wednesday night was wing night, so Derek intended to get a dozen extra hot, the largest beer they served, and try not to think about how he hadn't seen or heard from Lindsey since Friday afternoon.

They'd both been quiet for the rest of their shopping excursion although she had ended up finding a piece for the island. Seeing her happy about that had made things a little better. He'd even loved watching her haggle over the price. That was a side of her he hadn't expected, but it had been sexy as hell.

The thing that was irritating him was that on the drive home she'd been noncommittal about when they could get together to work on the island. And the total radio silence since then. That was really starting to piss him off.

He knew she'd been a little freaked out by the kiss, but he'd never imagined it would affect her this long. He'd texted her Monday but she hadn't responded. Later that night he'd realized he'd made the critical error of sending an open-ended text by saying *Let me know when you want to start on the island* instead of something more definitive. Something that required a response.

And now he was overanalyzing everything. Not cool. This was Lindsey. They'd had rules. They broke them and now she was pulling back. The two steps back had now become five. He was beyond ready to start moving forward again, but that required her cooperation.

Derek followed Mike through the bar, giving the bartender a quick wave as they headed toward a table near the back. Several televisions showed various basketball games, one Dr. Phil. Weird. In no time they'd ordered and were sipping a cold beverage.

"Now that hits the spot," Mike said as he set down his glass.

"Agreed."

"So, how goes it with the house? I've been so busy lately, I haven't had a chance to see it. It sure has been nice having you on the project. It's nice knowing I don't have to worry about a damn thing. Anne tells you and Lindsey what she wants and that's that."

Derek appreciated his friend's trust. "Yeah, it's looking good. You guys need to come out."

"Yeah, Anne wants to this weekend." Mike took another drink of his beer and then hesitated for a moment before speaking. "So she said you and Lindsey have been working together?"

Derek had yet to discuss the developments between him and Lindsey with Mike, but it was no surprise he knew. "We have been. And it's been good."

Mike raised an eyebrow. "Good? How did this transpire exactly? If you recall I was there last fall when she lost it in Anne's kitchen when you showed up."

Derek couldn't help but smile a little at the memory. Lindsey had most certainly lost it. Once he'd realized that his friend's girl knew her, he'd arranged to be there at the right time. It had backfired. Big-time. Looking back, he should have known better. Eight years was a long time, but not long enough for what he'd done, and she hadn't taken well to having him surprise her.

"So when you say good, do you mean *good* good?" Mike asked.

Derek was saved from responding when the bartender delivered their baskets of wings. "Extra hot, extra ranch, extra napkins," Aiden said.

"Thanks, man, you're the best," Derek replied.

Aiden saluted them and headed back to the bar. Derek and Mike came into Smokey's a few times a month, usually on Wing Wednesdays.

Aiden owned the place and served a very small menu of food that he'd created himself. Funny thing was, the guy looked like he belonged in a biker gang with his huge muscles, goatee, and closely cropped hair. Mike and Derek liked to quietly try and guess Aiden's story. They'd had him as an ex-con, a former priest, and even involved with the Witness Protection Program. More than likely it was nothing even half as crazy as any of those, but it was fun to guess.

"Thank God Aiden learned how to make these wings when he was touring with that death metal band," Mike said.

Derek shook his head, reaching for a piece of chicken. "I'm pretty sure he got this recipe from the shaman of an indigenous tribe in the Amazon."

"That does sound right now that you mention it," Mike said, grabbing a napkin off the large stack on their table. He nodded toward the bar. "Check out our man. Whatever his story is, he sure does well with the ladies."

Derek turned in his seat to find three women sitting at the bar laughing at whatever Aiden was saying. He looked back at Mike who was tearing into another hot wing. "Yeah, we've noticed that before. Seems women like that badass-motherfucker look he's got going on."

"No lie. I couldn't grow facial hair like that if I tried," Mike said.

"Nope, you're destined to look like a frat boy without an inheritance."

"Screw you, just because I don't wear a suit to my fancy office every day. I work with my hands, chicks dig that."

"You think I don't work with my hands?" Derek said, wide-eyed. "I'll have you know I spent all last week staining *your* kitchen floor and cabinets. How manly you feel now?"

"Hey, thanks for reminding me. So, is this going to turn into something with you two?" Mike asked, unwilling to let Derek off the hook.

Derek sighed. "Things are complicated."

Mike stared at him. "Tell me you haven't slept with her."

"No." Derek shoved a piece of chicken in his mouth, not liking where the conversation was going. What he wanted to say was *If I did it would be none of your damn business.* He kept that to himself. He knew Mike meant well.

"Have you guys done anything?"

"She kissed me Friday," Derek said. It was the truth. For the most part. No need to clarify that he'd asked for it. Practically begged.

Mike choked. "The hell you say."

They both chuckled. When they were younger that had been Mike's dad's favorite saying. He'd always had the cool father and Derek had enjoyed spending time at their house. Mike's mother had died when he was young so his father had stepped up and been the ultimate parent. Strict but understanding, fun but demanding respect. Derek had always wished his own dad had been more like Chuck Everett. Sadly, his best friend's father died from a sudden heart attack their senior year of high school. Derek remembered how it had destroyed Mike. They'd actually lost touch for a time while Mike dealt with his grief.

"But no, seriously. I can't believe she kissed *you.* We're talking about Lindsey, right?"

"Obviously I played a pivotal role. But the point is I didn't push. We've been getting closer the past couple of weeks."

"Is this gonna turn into something?" Mike asked.

Derek sat up and listened for a moment. "You ever notice that U2 plays like every third song in this joint?"

Mike lifted his chin toward the bar at the front. "Aiden loves this shit. And stop trying to change the subject."

Derek sighed. "I want it to be something. I didn't at first. Or at least I didn't want to admit I did. But I've never gotten over her." Damn. It felt good to say it out loud. Just put it all on the table.

Mike nodded as he loaded up another sauce coated drumstick with ranch. He held it up as he spoke, dressing dripping off the end. "If she kissed you she must want it, too." He stuffed the chicken in his mouth.

Derek shook his head. "I don't know. There's an attraction definitely, but she's fighting it. I can't tell what she really wants, but if the fact that we haven't spoken since the kiss is an indicator, the forecast isn't good."

"You don't know that. Maybe she's just processing it. You know they are all at Pie Mia right now having their blog meeting. After this we can surprise them."

Derek gave Mike a long stare. "How the hell did you manage to get yourself engaged to a woman like Anne? You have no clue about women and you eat like a caveman."

Mike grinned. "You're just jealous."

They laughed together and tucked back into their food and drink. But the truth was, Mike was right. Derek was jealous as hell. He wanted Lindsey and the kiss had only served to solidify his feelings. It looked like he might have to ambush her again.

Lindsey grabbed her third piece of chicken, onion, and goat cheese pizza. Callie had just revealed their bachelorette party idea to Anne.

"You guys, I can't tell you how much I appreciate that idea. Hanging out with the girls and Mike sounds like the best of both worlds. Besides, I'm too old for the typical bachelorette shenanigans."

"Hold up," Callie said. "Just because your man's going to be there doesn't mean you get out of wearing a giant penis pacifier around your neck!"

Anne's eyes went wide in horror.

"I'm kidding, silly." Callie laughed. "Oh, speak of the devil."

Anne and Lindsey both turned to see Mike walking through the small restaurant toward them. And he wasn't alone. Derek trailed behind him, sending Lindsey's heart racing. She'd been avoiding him the past few days since that mind-boggling kiss. But apparently—in typical Derek fashion—he was taking the situation into his own hands. She really couldn't deny that she was happy to see him.

"Hey, babe," Mike said, leaning down to kiss Anne. "How's the meeting going?"

"Good," she replied with a big grin. "I'm so glad you're here. I haven't seen you all day."

Lindsey couldn't watch anymore. She looked at Callie who put her finger in her mouth, faking a gag.

"Oh please," Lindsey said in a whisper. "Like you can talk."

Callie only winked before her eyes traveled over Lindsey's shoulder and up. Lindsey glanced up to see Derek staring down into her eyes, giving her a quick wink. She smiled back, catching the faint masculine scent of him.

"Hey," she said quietly.

"Hi."

"Why don't you guys pull up a chair," Anne said, grabbing an empty chair from the table next to them. Mike immediately took it and sat down. "We've wrapped up all of our official business. Actually, we were just discussing something exciting. Tell them, Callie."

Lindsey didn't look but she sensed that Derek was pulling another chair over right next to her. She wondered what all of their friends were thinking. Had he told Mike that anything had happened between them?

"So basically Lindsey and I just decided we should have a coed bachelor party." Callie grinned at the table. "All of us together at the new casino in Mayville."

"That sounds like a good idea," Mike said, before reaching out and resting his arm along the back of Anne's chair. He glanced across the table at Derek with a grin. "Sorry, Walsh. Your stripper idea is out."

Lindsey's body instantly froze at the comment but before she could react Derek reached out and squeezed her thigh under the table.

"Screw you, man." Derek shook his head, his big hand still resting on Lindsey's leg, his fingers grazing her inner thigh. He glanced over at Anne, whose eyes had gone wide once again. "Anne, he's kidding. I never had that idea."

"He's right, perfect. I was teasing you." Mike leaned to the side and kissed Anne's cheek. Her happy smile as she bunched her shoulders and tried to pull away made Lindsey a little jealous.

She allowed Derek to rest his hand on her thigh. Was tempted to reach below the table and touch him back, but she didn't. She wanted things to be easy. Couples like Anne and Mike had no baggage to overcome. No resentment. Was it possible that this could just be fun? She had a sinking feeling that she was getting in too deep.

"Come outside with me," a low voice said close to Lindsey's ear. She looked over to find Derek leaning in close to her. Lindsey glanced over at Callie, who gave her a raised eyebrow and then a quick nod.

"Okay." Lindsey stood, effectively knocking his hand away. She grabbed her cardigan and followed him through the dining area.

It was now March and as they stepped out the front door they were greeted by a row of vintage-looking street lamps, wooden bench seats, and hanging baskets waiting to be filled with spring blooms.

Pie Mia's was one of the newer tenants in the buildings that lined the adorable Main Street that ran through the center of Preston. It was a fun little boutique town that served as a weekend getaway for people from Kansas City and other local towns. It was home to independently owned restaurants, antiques stores, an old barber shop, a beauty salon, Callie's Confections, and several little one-of-a-kind shops. One of Lindsey's favorites was Sweet Opal, owned by their friend Brooke, who graciously took many of Lindsey's creations in for consignment sale.

It was a lovely town, the kind that made you want to settle down, have a family. Have picnics on the weekend, pick up coffee before work, and go to football games in the fall to cheer on the local team. It elicited feelings of happiness and contentment. Something Lindsey so desperately wanted but wondered if she'd ever have. Not that she was unhappy, but didn't most people dream of having a happily ever after with someone by their side?

"Let's sit," Derek said, motioning to a nearby bench.

She followed him without a word and sat, leaving a few feet between them. She heard Derek's annoyed sigh and then he was scooting closer to her. Before she knew it he was throwing an arm over the back of the bench and staring down at her.

"What are you doing?" she asked quietly.

"I'm getting close to you. What's it look like?"

She looked up at him. His pupils were large and his eyes focused on her. The days were slowly getting a little longer so the streetlights hadn't yet kicked on, the sun hanging low, just out of sight behind the row of old buildings.

It was really ridiculous how handsome he looked all the time. How was a girl supposed to do the right thing? Today he wore dark blue jeans and an ivory sweater, the color perfect against his lightly tanned skin and five o'clock shadow.

"I think we need to discuss something," he said.

"Oh?" She was playing coy but they both knew better.

"Was it really so bad kissing me?" he asked quietly, his voice low and husky.

Lindsey's eyes flew up to his. She hadn't expected him to be so blunt about it. She found him trying to hold back a smile.

"Of course not."

"Okay, then why have I not heard from you?"

"Well, we weren't really in the habit of chatting on the phone."

"No, we weren't. But I know you've been avoiding me."

She shrugged. "I just needed to think."

"Fair enough. But I want you to know that no matter what, you don't have to pull away from me."

"Of course I don't have to, but I needed to."

"So while you were thinking . . . did you come to any grand conclusions?"

She nodded. "A few."

He looked surprised. "Interested in sharing?"

"I think it was probably not a good idea. Something we shouldn't repeat." That wasn't all she'd thought but it felt like the wisest response.

"Eh, I'm not so sure about that. Want to know my theory?" He reached out to touch a lock of hair that rested on her shoulder.

"I guess," she said. The movement of her hair sent tingles through her scalp all the way down to her toes.

"I think that kiss scared you. It was amazing and now you want more. And you hate wanting me as bad as you do."

Lindsey swallowed. His left hand slowly slid into her hair, his fingers caressing the back of her neck. She knew at any moment he was going to pull her toward him. She should stop him. In just a minute.

"And just so we're clear, it scared me too, but for another reason." His eyes went molten with each of his words. "I enjoy wanting you this bad. But I worry that I may never have you again."

She had no words. Would he ever have her again? The right answer was no, no, no. She couldn't handle the pain of losing him all over again, and he said nothing of loving her or wanting something more. A casual fling with Derek would just never work.

"What can I do to make it better?" he asked. His body angled closer to hers, their faces only inches apart.

Lindsey's heart began to hammer in her chest. This was his power, this persistent seduction of her mind and body. She had to be stronger.

A car full of teenagers drove down Main, voices whistling out of the windows as they passed by. "Get a room," one called.

Like a splash of cold water, those words reminded her that they were quickly entering dangerous territory.

"You could give me some space," she said.

He hesitated a moment and then pulled back. His hand dropped from her lap but he continued to stroke the back of her neck. "If that's what you need."

"It is."

He nodded, looking down at the ground. Finally he turned back to her with a sly grin. "I think I liked that punk's idea a little better."

Lindsey groaned in mock annoyance and then they both laughed quietly.

"Things are just—"

"Moving too fast," he finished for her. "I understand." She was grateful that there was no annoyance in his tone. "I want to give you exactly what you need, Linds. What you deserve. What you want. I wish that was me, but if it's not, I'll accept that. Either way I want us to be friends."

Her insides quivered at his statement. The serious look in his eyes. Finally she nodded her head. "Okay."

Behind them the front door of Pie Mia opened, the warm glow from the restaurant casting light onto Derek's face. He was still staring at her but he pulled back.

"Oh boy, what a lovely evening," Callie said, a little too loudly. Lindsey knew she was sending her a warning.

Lindsey stood and faced the building.

"How about we get back to work tomorrow?" Derek asked behind her. "No sense in not finishing what we started."

Lindsey nodded and glanced up at him. "What we started with the island," she clarified.

Derek winked. "Of course."

She gave another nod. "Okay. I guess I'll see you in the morning."

"In the morning, then." Derek pulled his keys out of his pocket. "Good night, Lindsey."

"Good night, Derek."

He walked away toward his Mercedes. She wasn't sure which she liked better, that car or his truck.

"Everything okay?" Callie squeezed Lindsey's hand.

Lindsey let out a cleansing sigh. "I think so."

"You two looked pretty cozy."

"Too cozy."

"For what it's worth, I don't think he's the same guy from eight years ago."

"That's what I'm afraid of."

Thirteen

Lindsey watched as Derek stood up from his sanding and stretched. They'd been out in the barn working on Anne's island for nearly two days. Amazingly, Derek had kept his promise and behaved. He hadn't flirted or touched her once, and she'd enjoyed herself. Even if she occasionally wished he'd might make a tiny move. But she was pleased that he'd respected her wishes for space. They'd talked, laughed, and gotten a lot of work done.

She still couldn't believe they'd found this amazing piece for the island and she was so excited for it to be completed. Lindsey honestly wasn't sure what it had been in its former life—some sort of one-of-a-kind workspace—but it was perfect. It was just a touch higher than counter height, had small cabinets on each end, two sets of drawers in the center and a large stainless steel shelf across the entire bottom. It would hold a ton of kitchen stuff and Anne was going to love it.

"I think I need a break. What about you?" Derek asked.

The weather had warmed considerably over the course of the afternoon, leaving the barn a little stuffy. The minute Derek's fingers went to the button on his plaid flannel shirt Lindsey's eyes went back down to the drawer she was working on.

After a moment she was unable to help herself and she let her eyes peer up through her lashes quickly. He almost had the last button undone. A light gray tee came into view, and when he pulled the shirt off Lindsey noticed how it squeezed against his biceps and shoulders. Derek ran a hand through his hair and turned to look down at the island.

Good Lord, why did the man have to be so beautiful? She remembered his naked body like it was yesterday. A blessing, because it was a wonderful memory, a curse because now she wanted to see it again. And here he was in the flesh, tempting her.

The dark hair on his arms drew her attention as he used a hand to absently scratch his stomach, pulling up his shirt, revealing just a trace of his abs and happy trail.

She picked up her sanding block and refocused on the small trim running around the drawer face. She should probably sand it again just to get her body under control. Yep, good idea.

From the corner of her eye she saw his feet coming toward her. His boot kicked at her tennis shoe and she looked up, faking surprise, as if she hadn't been watching him intently just a moment ago.

She pulled her dust mask off her head and looked up.

"I said break. My back's killing me from sitting on the ground."

She glanced down at the dirt beneath her. Now that

she thought about it, the ground was pretty uncomfortable. Almost as much as her unfulfilled lust. She moved to set her drawer aside but Derek leaned down and grabbed it from her.

"Let's go for a walk," he said.

"Oh, okay."

He held a hand out and she grabbed it so he could haul her up. She made sure not to fall against him, quickly letting his hand go. "You lead."

"Gladly." Derek headed out the back door of the barn. Lindsey instinctively lifted her face up to the sun, loving the feel of it on her skin.

She walked forward, following Derek as he cut across the yard. Taking in the property, she admired the garden as they walked by. It was basically a wildflower garden, untamed and random but so beautiful. It led up to an adorable little courtyard at the back of the house and the plants were just starting to come alive again.

"See that white line of fencing on the back of the garden?" Lindsey pointed to her right and stopped.

"Yeah," Derek replied.

"Those are all lilac bushes running alongside it. Anne and Mike will get married with that as the backdrop. The plan is that they'll be in bloom. Let's hope they are. It would be such a shame if they weren't." She turned to look at Derek, who was now standing close beside her. "Anne loves lilacs. That's where Mike proposed last fall, too."

"Really. Guess he's a romantic. I didn't know. Although it doesn't surprise me too much. I knew the proposal was here but didn't realize that he'd put all that thought into it." Derek started toward the garden taking lazy steps.

Lindsey watched the back of him as he walked in front of her. His jeans were well-worn, with a frayed hole above the back pocket that housed his wallet. She swore she could see navy material peeking through. She knew he used to wear boxers, but that had been a long time ago. He might have changed. Was it briefs? Boxer briefs? She was curious and it suddenly felt like a question that needed an immediate answer.

The muscles in his back flexed as he put out a hand and touched the white fence, giving it a little shake to see how sturdy it was. It struck her that it was an incredibly male thing to do. "I take it this wedding will be on the small side?"

Lindsey thought about that. "I think around fifty people. So fairly small. After the ceremony here in the garden, everyone will head to the barn for the reception. Anne has big plans for it. Lights, tables, chandeliers. It will be beautiful."

"Yeah. It will."

It was a little awkward discussing her friend's wedding with him. What had his wedding been like? Big? Small? Fancy? There was no way she would ask him and it really wasn't any of her business. But it was a reminder that there were still many things about him she didn't know.

"Do you live in Preston?" she asked.

"Just a little ways out of town." They continued their walk as they talked.

"In the country?"

"Not so much the country. We have neighbors. They're just a safe distance away. It's not a big house, but good for Tanner and me. He has lots of space to play outside and his own room. I really don't spend a lot of time at home unless he's there. Usually working late in my office or on a job site. Of course lately I've been with you."

Derek turned and smiled at her as they walked a little farther toward a massive old tree toward the back corner of the property. Stepping up to the giant trunk, which appeared nearly as wide as a whiskey barrel, he reached out with his palm. It almost looked like he was trying to feel its heartbeat. What an odd thing, and yet now she wanted to do it, too. So she did. Placing her hand about a foot away from his.

"What are you feeling for?"

Derek laughed and dropped his hand, like he hadn't even realized he'd done it. "Nothing, I guess it's just something I do. I've always really liked trees. Like to look at them, touch them."

"Really?" That was something she'd never known about him, but she found that she liked it.

"Yeah, is that surprising?"

"No, not at all." She looked at him again, his eyes staring intently at her. He wasn't smiling, but there was amusement in the set of his lips. "I like that you like trees. It's sweet."

He raised an eyebrow, his lips finally turning up in one corner. "In that case, I *love* trees."

Lindsey laughed and shook her head. He grinned wider in response, and he looked so innocent and captivating. She couldn't look away, as if she were young all over again, staring at the most handsome boy in the room. The one that made her feel wanted and precious. In that moment, the only thing she wanted was to feel him. His lips, his body, his arms around her. Lindsey stepped closer.

And closer.

She looked up, watching as his lips came together, his breathing full and heavy from his nose as he realized what she was doing. He smelled wonderful. *Familiar.* Deep inside she'd known it would come to this. Known that she wouldn't escape without once again giving at least part of herself away to this man. It might not be her heart, but a piece of her body. Her soul. Maybe he'd had it all along and she was just searching for it. Wondering if he'd kept it safe all these years.

With the lightest touch, she reached out and settled her hand on his stomach, watching her fingers spread out against the soft cotton. The firmness of his skin felt warm beneath her skin.

His breathing faltered for a second and she looked back into his eyes, speaking softly. "I'm sorry I keep sending mixed signals. I honestly don't know what I'm doing."

"Keep doing it," he whispered. "And don't you dare be sorry."

Her hand began to slide up his torso, chest, and then she felt the weight of his large hand on her hip. He pulled her against him just the slightest bit, and she let him. Wanted it.

Derek stood at the base of the tree, his height accentuated by the incline of the roots. Realizing the predicament, he spun them around and gently shoved her back against the tree. Now their faces were nearly even.

Without hesitating, Derek leaned in and claimed her mouth. It wasn't a tentative kiss like last time. It was the kind of kiss that sent a message. A warning.

If you're going to stop me, better do it now.

She kissed him back and their lips became frantic, catching and pulling at each other. He angled his head and suddenly his hands were on either side of her neck, adjusting her just as he wanted. Just like last time—like every time she could remember—he took over her body and owned it.

With the previous kiss she'd been so focused on what it all meant, comparing it to before. She hadn't fully given herself over to the sensation of it. This time . . . she felt everything.

Wanted to feel everything. Create a new memory with this man. One that she could look back on and smile instead of crying or feeling shame. This was her choice, she was stronger now, and she could take what she needed. He might have meant he'd have her body, and she realized she would have to live with it if that's all he had to give. Right now she wanted him too badly to let that stop her.

His tongue parted her lips and she welcomed it, meeting him, playing with him. Wanting to feel more of his body, she slipped her good hand up his chest and around his neck while her brace rested on his shoulder. The movements had the tree bark abrading her back through her T-shirt, but it didn't matter. He grasped her firmly on the butt and hauled her up his body. The force of his ministrations pulled a moan from her chest and her thighs naturally rested on his forearms as he shoved himself between her legs.

"Oh," she said in a breathy sigh against his lips. He pulled her more firmly against him, his lower body rubbing against her.

"Do you feel me?" His question was nearly a growl against her skin as his lips traveled over her face, chin, and neck, licking and sucking at her. God, how she loved it when he did that and her head dropped back to give him better access. A kiss from Derek Walsh felt like an act of submission and right now that's what she wanted, to give herself to this man. So much for needing space, right now they were as close as they could possibly get.

He angled back, his body holding her against the tree as his hands sought the fullness of her breasts. He watched himself palm each one, squeezing her nipples in the curve of his thumb and first finger. "You're so beautiful."

His breathing came out deep, loud, and labored.

"God, I want you so bad, Lindsey. I've always wanted you."

She sucked in a breath, trying to process his words as his mouth returned to her neck. His tongue lapped at her skin, his teeth nipping. His lips made a trail down her chest, to her T-shirt, and he bent his head while simultaneously gripping her left breast and lifting it to his mouth as he sucked her cloth-covered nipple past his lips.

The pull of his lips made her back arch. "Oh my God," she said with a deep sigh of pleasure. Every nerve ending in her body was on alert, aching, and ready. His right hand slid back to her behind, slipping down and cupping her from the back as his mouth searched out her other nipple. This, she had forgotten. The skillful way he could so easily work her into a frenzy.

Her top and bra were now damp from the wet heat of

his mouth, and her thighs were burning. She wrapped her legs tighter around his waist and locked her ankles together. Derek pulled back and looked at her.

"Is your arm okay?"

She nodded, because she'd honestly forgotten all about her arm. "Yes. It's fine."

He was breathless and she was sure that her weight was probably killing him, although he didn't appear to be straining that much as he adjusted her center to his body, grinding into her. "I know I promised to slow down. Give you space. But damn, Lindsey . . ."

"Forget the space!" she said, her voice breathless.

Derek gave a throaty laugh and leaned his forehead against hers. "You sure, babe?"

"We're outside," she said. Was that her only objection? He pushed his erection against her once more and she gritted her teeth, knowing that she was a complete goner. "Can we go somewhere?"

His eyes jerked up to hers, wide and excited, as if he hadn't really expected her to grant him permission so easily. "Inside."

She nodded and he moved back, allowing her feet to gently fall to the ground. He grabbed her right hand and set off toward the house with such determination, she nearly had to skip to keep up. "You're gonna pull my arm out of the socket."

Derek stopped short and turned to her, dragging her into his arms and kissing her once again. She smiled against his mouth and then kissed him back.

"We're doing this. And you won't regret it . . . I'm going to take good care of you, Lindsey," he whispered against her lips. She wasn't sure what he meant. Good care of her body? She had no doubt. But that was it. She couldn't give him access to anything deeper. Instead of clarifying she let her kiss answer for her. After a moment he let up and resumed walking toward the house. When they rounded the front, he turned to her. "Go wait at the front door, I'll be right back."

Her face fell, and then he spoke again.

"Keys. I'll be back, promise."

Lindsey walked around the porch and up the steps. She stopped outside the door and faced the front yard. She could see the road, where a car drove by. A fly buzzed in her face. Birds were chirping. This was a normal day and normal life was going on.

And now she was officially panicking because she had just agreed to have sex with Derek. The man who had taken her virginity. The man who had broken her heart. The only man to ever have her heart, and here she was subjecting herself to all of that pain again.

She clamped her eyes shut, her hands squeezing into fists. She could do this. Wanted to do this. People had sex all the time and it didn't have to mean something. She could be one of those people and give her body what it wanted. Nothing more.

Derek came around the corner, taking the porch steps two at time. When he saw her face he froze, then slowly stepped toward her and laid a hand on her waist. His head shook just a little. "You changed your mind?"

Lindsey snaked her arms around him and then leaned up to place a kiss on his jaw. "No. I want you."

Derek unlocked the door and held open the screen door for Lindsey. They stepped into the house. It was warm and smelled of construction and age, not really the ideal spot to finally have Lindsey Morales, but right now he couldn't care less about their surroundings. He'd have had her against that tree if she'd let him. He felt her grab onto his hand and he realized he'd just been staring around the entryway.

"Upstairs?" he asked, looking at her.

"At least there's carpet." She smiled and he led them up the staircase, both of them in a hurry.

He stepped around her and headed down the hall, choosing the farthest bedroom. It was also the smallest and had one window that was covered with a sheer pink curtain. The carpet had been vacuumed but it was old and shaggy. He didn't care, right now they were working with what they had, but he decided to leave the light off, the filtered afternoon sun was all he needed. He turned to pull Lindsey into his arms, their loud breathing filling the room, making him think of sex.

Derek ran his hands all over her arms, her neck, and her face. It was like she was a mirage. But the reality was that the woman he'd fantasized about so many times had come to life.

"You have no idea how long I've dreamed of this moment," he said.

"Me, too," she whispered.

He looked into her eyes. "Do you mean that?"

She nodded and Derek covered her mouth with his. He wanted this moment to go on forever, wanted to have her in every way possible. He continued to kiss her as he grabbed the hem of her shirt, gently maneuvered her brace through the armhole, and pulled it over her head.

He looked down between them, drinking in the sight of her. She wore a white bra, nothing fancy, in fact it was very simple, just a lace trim across the top. But damn, it was so Lindsey. Sexy without even trying. Her skin was golden and smooth, unblemished and supple.

"You're even more beautiful than I remembered."

Her eyes fluttered beneath her lashes and finally met his. "Thank you."

He reached around to her back and gently unclasped her bra. Her breasts relaxed as he slid the flimsy garment down her arms, her nipples coming into view one centimeter at a time. He smiled at her. "This is one of my favorite parts."

She smiled, a blush tinting her cheeks. Derek loved that she didn't try to cover herself when he removed her bra completely. He reached up with both hands to cup her soft flesh. Skin on skin was so much better than anything else. Certainly better than his memories.

Lightly he blew on her right nipple, loving her light gasp and the way she arched her back. He watched as her flesh pebbled and puckered in response and then he blew on the other one.

"Oh my . . . that . . ." She couldn't finish and he saw her throat work as she swallowed.

"Feel good?" He ran the tip of his nose along the bridge of hers very slowly.

"It makes . . ." Instead of continuing she smiled and looked away, her hands clamping onto to each side of his waist.

He leaned into her ear and whispered. "Does it make you wet?"

She gave a small nod. "Yes."

"Good. That's what I want, baby. I want you ready for me."

Derek stood straight and pulled his shirt over his head, dropping it on the floor. He loved the way her eyes widened the slightest bit, and he hoped it was because she enjoyed the sight of him. "Lie down. Please."

He quietly thanked the gods of getting lucky when she kicked off her shoes and slid off her jeans before going down on her knees. He held out his hand to her so she could hold on with her good one as she maneuvered herself into a seated position and then rested back on her elbows. She stared up at him, ready, and he'd never seen a more beautiful sight in his entire life.

After slipping off his own shoes, Derek went down on his knees in front of her. He leaned over and placed a hand on each side of her hips, forcing her legs open to make room for him. In this position, with her still leaning back, their faces met perfectly and he kissed her again. He was surprised to find Lindsey's mouth a little more aggressive and he liked it. He kept still for a moment, letting her lips take the lead, her tongue slipping into his mouth. God, she was so good, so hot in the most unassuming way.

He caught her tongue between his lips and sucked it into his mouth, then placed a kiss on her bottom lip. He looked at her. "Lie back."

Derek leaned over and placed a kiss below one breast, loving the way Lindsey's hands went to the back of his head, pulling him down against her. It was so sexy and he felt himself straining against his jeans. He reached down and undid his fly just to be more comfortable and then continued down her torso, flattening his tongue and licking slowly.

Lindsey let out a breathy moan and grasped at his hair. He wasn't deterred by the small pull she gave, continuing down, down, until his teeth caught on the top of her panties.

He bit, holding the elastic between his teeth, and angled his head down, pulling. Using his left hand he worked them over her ass. She reached down to help, pulling them off her right leg. Derek didn't hesitate, immediately lowering his head to her center.

He wanted everything to be about her pleasure. It was the only thing that mattered in this moment. Flattening his tongue he slowly ran it the length of her from bottom to top. Lindsey let out a sharp gasp, her thighs tightening on each side of his head. God, he loved everything about this. Her scent, taste. Even the way she gripped his hair a little too hard until it was almost painful. He continued to lick every inch of her until finally she was trembling against his mouth.

Lindsey's right hand left his hair and dropped onto the carpet as if she didn't have the strength to hold it upright any longer. Derek grinned as he peered up at her. He nuzzled his chin against her clit.

"Oh, oh God, stop. No more," she whimpered.

Lifting up onto his hands, he crawled back up her body, placing random kisses along her torso. Once their faces were aligned he covered her mouth with his, his tongue stroking into her mouth.

Her good hand traveled down his back, his side, and when he registered her intent he lifted off her, making just enough space for her to slide her hand between

them. Her fingers pulled at the band of his boxer briefs
and then he felt her cool skin on the head of his cock.
He held in a groan and looked into her eyes. "Grab it."

She did, wrapping her hand around him, squeezing
lightly, and he blew out a breath before speaking again.
"Harder."

"I don't want to hurt you," she whispered.

Derek chuckled and pressed himself into her grip.
"You won't. Promise."

She squeezed again, her firm grip sending a shiver
down his ass straight to his legs. "I like how you feel in
my hand," Lindsey said. Her voice was breathless and
sexy.

"Mmm, I like it, too," he said against her throat. He
kissed across her neck, up her chin, and then ran his
tongue against her bottom lip. "I like every single thing
about you naked beneath me. You naked on top of me.
You naked anywhere. As long as I'm with you."

"How about you be naked with me?" she asked.

Derek pushed off the floor and stood between her
bent legs. Before going any further he pulled a condom
out of his pocket. Thank God he'd had one in his truck.
He'd retrieved it along with the house key, and he was
grateful she didn't ask if he'd brought it intentionally or,
even worse, kept them on hand.

Lindsey watched as he dropped his pants, his underwear, and then finally as he rolled the condom on. It was
a huge turn-on having her eyes on his movements as he
gripped himself one final time before kneeling back
down between her legs.

As soon as he was in position Derek nestled himself
against her wetness, wanting to feel the heat there, slick

and warm, begging him to enter her. Slowly he grinded against her, running the length of his cock up and down her center. He knew Lindsey enjoyed it when her eyes fluttered closed.

"Derek . . ." she whispered.

"Tell me what you want, Linds."

Her head gave a quick shake, her eyes still pinched shut. He knew somewhere deep inside she was still fighting this need for him.

Derek brought his hand up and gently laid his palm on her neck before applying the slightest amount of pressure. Her eyes instantly flew open but then just as quickly melted with her desire as their gazes met.

"Do you want me?" he asked quietly.

"Yes," she said, her voice breathless. He could feel her neck move under his hand.

"Yes, what?"

"I want you."

His hand slid up the side of her jaw, below her ear, and he cupped the back of her head. Her hair felt like silk between his fingers, and he lifted, angling her mouth up to his as he pivoted his lower body off of hers.

"Put me inside you," he said against her lips.

Her fingers sought his erection once more and she guided him to her entrance. Derek took a deep breath as he pushed inside, his breath catching at the way she instantly pulsed around him.

"Oh God, you feel good." His words were nearly a grunt as he tried to keep himself together. His goal remained the same. No matter how amazing she felt, how tight and hot, he would go slow and please her. All of this was about making Lindsey feel good. If she regretted having sex with him he would never forgive himself.

Her nails now dug into his backside and he went in deeper before pulling out and thrusting back in. As he rested his lips against hers, Lindsey sucked his lower lip into the heat of her mouth and he shuddered against her body.

It had been so long since he'd felt this kind of connection. He'd almost forgotten what real, meaningful pleasure felt like. Lindsey was real. Always had been.

Derek thrust inside her several times, slow and then faster, just reveling in the sensation of her. Her head still lay cradled in his hand and he stared down at her. "I could be inside you for the rest of the afternoon and be a very happy man."

She kissed his neck, squeezing his butt before he heard her say, "I'd forgotten how much you like to talk."

Derek grinned and looked down at her, his strokes steady. "Liar. I don't think you forgot anything about us."

Her smile faltered and he regretted his insinuation. Just because he'd pined for her, missed her, didn't mean she'd done the same. He stilled his movements and continued to stare down into her face. "I'm sorry, I didn't mean—"

"Shhh." She laid a finger over his lips. "Don't apologize. Not for that. You're right. I haven't forgotten anything. Not one second of it, and I missed you so much."

Derek felt his insides lighten at her words, her heart pounding in his chest. This was what he needed. This woman, just like this. His.

Forever.

Fourteen

Lindsey wasn't sure if her heart was going to pound out of her chest or shatter into a million pieces from the look in Derek's eyes as he possessed her body. Was it a mistake revealing that she'd thought of him? Remembered every detail. Missed him. His eyes had gone dark at the words, and now that he knew, where would they go from here? No matter what she'd tried to tell herself up until this moment, the truth was painfully clear. This was more than just sex.

"I missed you too, baby. I thought of you constantly. Needed you," Derek whispered against her lips.

Oh God. What had she done? Her admission—in a moment of pleasure and weakness—had opened up this exchange of emotions that she hadn't prepared herself for. He continued, every word breaking her heart.

"I thought of your face. Your laugh. Your smile." He leaned back, ran his fingertip down her nose, cheek, neck. All the while his pace never faltered, sending her senses reeling.

"I haven't forgotten one thing about you, Lindsey. How it feels to be inside you. How you taste."

Lindsey tried to catch her breath as he sucked her ear-lobe past his lips. Derek had always spoken to her as they had sex and God she'd loved it so much. The deep timbre of his words had been as much her undoing as his body. But these words . . . they were destroying her with their perfection. She'd been so hopeful she could go through with this with her heart remaining intact, but she'd forgotten the way he'd use his voice and his words to seduce her. Did he truly mean the things he was saying right now? Or were beautiful words inti-macy for him?

Reaching down between their bodies, Derek put his fingers to work on her. She let out a moan as he circled her, every stroke bringing her closer.

"That's it, babe. I love the sounds you make."

Between his words and his movements, her body was heading for an explosive release. She used her right hand to pull him harder against her as he thrust, loving the weight of him, the strength in his body.

"How you look when you come with me inside of you. Knowing that I'm the man giving you pleasure. I want to see that again, Lindsey."

Lindsey shut her eyes and tried to focus on her re-lease instead of the memories he was invoking. He al-ways used to say that, how much he loved to watch her finish. Would look deep into her eyes as she came, leav-ing her feeling beautiful and cherished.

But that was then, when things were different, and she couldn't let these words penetrate her heart. This was sex. That was all. Two adults enjoying each other's body. It wasn't about recapturing long-lost feelings. Lindsey began to meet each thrust with enthusiasm, digging her heels into the carpet.

She shouldn't kiss him anymore, it was too wonderful, too real. And she couldn't look at him, so instead she pushed her face into his chest and looped her good hand under his arm and held on to his back for leverage. Within moments she was sucking in deep breaths as her orgasm washed over her.

"Look at me, Linds," he said as he continued to stroke her in time with his words.

She couldn't. In fact she didn't make a noise or move her head so as not to risk meeting his eyes. If she did it would bring her to tears.

"Lindsey." His breathy pleas sounded desperate, only making her come even harder. When the pulsing in her lower body subsided she slowly laid her head back on the floor and glanced up at him.

His expression was pained and confused. And then angry. And she knew what he was thinking. He'd just opened up to her completely. Bared his emotions and then made a simple request. Practically begged her to look at him, and she'd purposely denied him. Didn't he understand that some things were part of nature? A defense mechanism.

Lindsey swallowed hard and turned her head, looking at the wall. The weight of his hurt expression was too much for her to bear. Without saying another word Derek lowered his body and rested his chest against hers, pinning her down onto the floor. He buried his face in her neck and began to rock his pelvis, entering her with quick, frantic thrusts. She felt their disconnection like something beautiful being ripped from her arms. The air around them had changed, and just like that he was simply fucking her.

His body slammed against hers, over and over, forcing her legs wider. His climax was forceful and angry as he pushed into her as hard as he could, his body trembling. She knew he was holding his breath and she gripped his back hard, her nails penetrating his sweaty skin.

Without wasting a second he pushed himself up and rolled off her, lying on his back and looking up at the ceiling. Lindsey glanced at him from the corner of her eyes, noticing his chest hair heaving up and down from the exertion. She couldn't look at the firm set of his lips or the hurt in his eyes any longer. She reached for her shirt, pulled it over her naked body, and turned her head away from him.

"I thought you wanted that," Derek said quietly, his words icy.

She sighed but didn't turn in his direction. "I did. I mean . . . I thought I did."

Lindsey felt him get up off the floor. "You *thought* you did? What the hell does that mean? How did things change that quickly?"

His sudden fury shocked her and the pain in his voice clawed at her conscience. She sat up and looked at him. If they were going to yell she had a few things of her own to say. "You started trying to re-create the past, Derek. You wanted it to be like it used to be between us."

"Of course I did," he said. He'd already put his

underwear on and was now jerking his jeans up. "Things were good then, Lindsey. Apparently you *have* forgotten."

"That's the point, Derek. Things *were* good. Amazing. When we were together I was happy. When we made love I felt it in my soul." Tears began to pool in the corners of her eyes, her nose suddenly stuffy, her voice breaking as she went on. "I don't want to feel that. It will destroy me all over again."

His shoulders dropped, eyes went soft, and he fell to his knees in front of her. "Lindsey, please."

"No, no, don't!" She put her hand out when he reached for her. He jerked back, leaning back on his calves. "Don't feel sorry for me, Derek. I don't need that from you."

"Do you need *anything* from me?"

She shook her head, unsure of how to respond. "I don't know."

"Oh no? How about to haul your shit or stain your floors? You can leave me bitchy Post-it notes when you need me to pay your hospital bills, or maybe I should just tell my best friend I can't be in his wedding so we can never see each other again?"

Lindsey gasped, feeling nauseous as she watched him stand up and pull his T-shirt on. He leaned over and grabbed his shoes off the floor. He was going to leave, not explain himself after that outburst. She finally found her voice and called out before he made it to the door.

"What do you mean, pay my hospital bill?" she yelled. Had he done that for her? Why would he have done that?

"Don't worry about it," he said as he continued into the hall.

"Derek, don't you walk away from me!"

He jerked around and took three long strides back into the bedroom. "Walking away from you is exactly what I didn't want to do. Not then and not now. But this time you're pushing me away so I'm giving you what you want."

"What I want? All I ever wanted was you and you chose someone else."

"I didn't choose her, I chose my son, and you damn well know it," he yelled. She'd never heard or seen him so angry. Ever. As overwhelming as it was to see him enraged, she wasn't afraid of him physically. The only damage Derek Walsh would do was to her heart.

"How many times do I have to tell you I'm sorry? I can't keep trying to prove it to you over and over. Either you believe me, or you don't."

Lindsey pulled herself to her knees, clutching her shirt over her bare breasts. Tears were now falling from her eyes but she wouldn't fully crumble in his presence. "I believe you. That's not the problem. I just can't stop hating the fact that I could have loved your son with you, but you never gave me a chance."

Fury radiated off his body as he filled the doorway. His chest heaved in laborious bursts, his eyes crossing over her entire body, as if committing it to memory before he finally left her for the second time. *Oh God, don't go.*

"Please, just go," she whispered.

Derek turned and stormed down the hallway. She heard him descend the stairs, but before the front door opened she heard a deep, muttered curse followed by the sound of his fist connecting with something.

Lindsey winced at the sound of splintering wood. Or Sheetrock. She didn't know.

The only thing left to do was cry.

Fifteen

Sunday morning Lindsey and Melanie met their dad for brunch. Mel had offered to pay and that was probably why Isaac had agreed to come since he was perpetually broke. Lindsey hated that he couldn't seem to find work. Ever since his heart attack seven years ago he'd been on disability. The problem was that he couldn't afford to not work at all, so he'd taken random minimum-wage jobs here or there, never sticking with one for long. It was irritating, but she felt bad for him. Every year that went by he seemed more and more depressed. She'd been so sure that if he could just get back on his feet, get ahead, he'd feel better.

She should have known better. It was why she'd quit college—thinking that she'd go back after she'd stayed home with him for a while—and also why she'd agreed to help him out last fall. He'd been in a bad place, and without his car he couldn't get to work. She was afraid if he didn't try to keep some sort of normalcy in his life, he would go into a depression he couldn't climb out of.

It was true. She'd given up a lot to help him. She never did make it back to college, the money was just never there. But what else could she do? She and Mel were all he had, but since Lindsey's sister was good at creating boundaries, she never got burdened by his needs. He never even asked Mel for anything, and Lindsey hadn't revealed the depths of his struggles to her sister.

Lindsey smiled as she watched her father make silly faces at Eden, who had recently started giggling at anything and everything. He bounced her on his knee and spoke in a baby voice, kissing her chubby cheeks.

"I'm glad you could meet us, Dad," Melanie said. "You haven't seen Eden in a while."

"I know, I can't let that happen again," he said. "We're best buds, aren't we?" He said in his baby voice again.

Lindsey smiled at Mel and then looked back at her father. "How is the job at the grocery store going?"

"Oh, you know, pretty good. Just keeping busy."

Mel and Lindsey looked at each other, probably both noting how vague his response had been. He looked healthy, seemed happy this morning, and said everything was fine. But something seemed off. And nothing seemed to be improving with his financial situation, which wasn't good news for Lindsey, either.

Melanie usually had a comment where their father was concerned, but Lindsey was grateful she kept her mouth shut today, just sipped her coffee. Lindsey would no doubt hear all of Mel's thoughts later when they were home.

"So, Linds, you're still staying with Mel and Brett?" her father asked.

"Yes. Until I can afford to get a place of my own." It

didn't seem to register with him that she was broke and that loaning him money might have contributed to it.

"It's been such a blessing for us to have Lindsey around to help. It's worked out perfectly," Mel said.

"Of course it has. Lindsey's our girl,"

Lindsey smiled, but his comment struck a nerve. *Lindsey's our girl.* She always had been. Lindsey helps, sacrifices, forgives. It was what she did.

"I think we might have a ripe one," Isaac said, sniffing at Eden with a grimace.

Mel scooted away from the table and laid down her napkin. She reached out for Eden and spoke in her own baby voice. "Be right pack, Abuelo, I need my diaper changed."

He handed the baby right over as Mel picked up the diaper bag and headed to the back of the dining room toward the restroom. Suddenly Lindsey felt nervous sitting alone with her father, especially when he leaned into the table and stared at her.

"You okay, Dad?" she asked.

"I'm trying, mi hija. Always trying," he said.

Lindsey's stomach dropped, her heart began to race. "Did you lie? Are you no longer working at the grocery store?"

He had the decency to look ashamed. "No. They let me go, but I knew it was coming."

Lindsey sucked in a breath. "When did this happen?"

"Last month."

"Last month? Dad!"

"I know, I should have said something sooner. I just

hate having to bother you with my problems." Lindsey glanced around the room. He never did this in front of Mel because he knew she would be pissed.

"Dad, what does this mean? How have you been paying all of your bills?"

"I had to quit paying a few of them."

Lindsey leaned back in her seat, trying not to panic. In some ways her father was like a child, always had been. And she had been his mother. It was infuriating and sad at the same time. Why couldn't she be more like Mel, create healthy boundaries, put herself first? Mel wasn't selfish or ungenerous, she was just . . . strong. Exactly what Lindsey was always trying to be. Often failing.

"I have a job interview Tuesday morning. I think if you could just float me . . . say, three hundred dollars till I can get back on my feet, everything would be fine."

Lindsey felt tears burning her eyelids. She had $300, but she'd spent the past few months saving for when she could afford to move out of Mel's. She had hopes of renting her own place, somewhere with a large space that she could work in. On top of that, business had been slow for her since she didn't have studio space right now. There wasn't really $300 to spare.

And she knew she would never see it again from her father. It was not a loan.

"Dad, I—"

"I promise, mi hija, this will be the last time. The grocery store just wasn't a good fit for me physically, but I feel like this job I got lined up could be the one.

It's just, the city has only given me till the rest of the week before they shut off my water. And the electric—"

"Dad. That's enough." Lindsey couldn't stand to hear it. She saw Mel enter the dining room. "I'm sorry, Dad. I can't bail you out anymore."

Lindsey dug in her purse and slid him a twenty-dollar bill. "Here. It's all I can do. That should cover gas for you to go fill out some applications. Do interviews."

"Lindsey, I need you."

"I'm sorry, Dad. I really am."

She felt like she might cry but managed to put on a smile when Mel came back to the table. Her father also recovered by instantly reaching for Eden once again. But they didn't speak much after that. When it was time to say good-bye he gave Eden and Mel a big hug and a kiss, telling them how much he loved them. Then he turned to Lindsey, gave her a quick sideways hug and told her he'd "see you next time."

The entire exchange had left her feeling cold and guilty. And that wasn't fair. She'd done so much for him. He'd never, ever treated her that way.

Before they walked back to Mel's car, her sister looked at Lindsey. "Everything okay with Dad?"

"Of course, why?" Lindsey said.

"Just felt a little tense between you two. He didn't ask you for money, did he?"

Lindsey reared back, looking shocked. Which wasn't difficult because she definitely had not expected that question from Mel. "No."

And now she was a liar. Which made her feel even shittier.

Mel didn't look entirely convinced. "Okay, well, if he ever does, you don't give it to him. Okay?"

That comment struck Lindsey as odd but she chose not to continue the conversation. She only shrugged. "Okay, whatever."

Sixteen

One week.

That's how long it had been since he'd walked away from Lindsey. Since they'd yelled at one another. And also when they'd had what had started out as totally amazing sex.

Glancing at his watch, Derek stood up from his desk. He had a presentation meeting in twenty minutes that he should be prepping for, but instead he was doing the only thing he seemed to be capable of anymore. Thinking of Lindsey.

He hated himself for how he'd left, but he'd been way too much of a pussy to try and reach out to her since. He'd been pushing her a lot lately and decided that maybe he should try hanging back. Actually give her that space she'd requested. She'd had valid reasons for withdrawing. And maybe he was just straight up stupid for thinking that they could ever get back what they'd had before. He'd gotten wrapped up in her, said things he probably shouldn't have. But damn it, he hadn't been lying. He had missed her. Thought of her. And she'd admitted the same.

His secretary knocked on the door and peeked her head in. "Davis is a little early, shall I send him in?"

"Yeah, that's fine. I'm ready."

Within an hour he was shaking hands with the man and signing contracts to fully design a new building for a new showroom and warehouse for Davis and Jennon Appliances. They wanted something modern and functional and had liked Derek's initial ideas better than anyone else's. Derek was pleased and felt slightly better once he'd walked Neil Davis outside and said good-bye after one more handshake.

Derek inhaled deeply. It was overcast, the sky gray and perfectly matching his mood. He decided to do what he normally did when he felt like crap, so he started to walk around the building. He found Mike leaning on a worktable, phone to his ear, a huge grin on his face. He nodded at Derek when he saw him.

"I love you, too."

Derek angled his body away, annoyed by his friend's conversation with his fiancée. Jealousy wasn't a feeling Derek had often, and really never with Mike. He wanted his best friend to be happy, he deserved it more than anyone, but damn, right now anyone else's relationship bliss pissed him the hell off. He heard Mike say good-bye and turned to face him.

"Hey, man, you're just in time for lunch," Mike said. "How about my treat and then we go get fitted for the tux?"

"Ah, man." Derek sighed. A clothes fitting sounded

like the last thing he wanted to do today. "Do we have to?"

"Anne's been bugging me. It's got to happen this week. Might as well get it out of the way."

Derek almost protested but quickly realized he was being a dick. This was his friend's wedding, he was his best man, and if he needed to go have some old guy push his nuts aside to find his inseam then so be it. "Okay, but you're not treating. If anyone should be doing that it's me."

"You've twisted my arm," Mike said, grabbing a shirt and pulling it over his tee. "I'll drive. Let's do the fitting first."

Twenty minutes later they were crossing the river and heading into Kansas City, and Derek suddenly realized he hadn't spoken one word the entire drive. He forced himself to speak. "So, uh, everything else ready for the wedding?"

Mike gave him a surprised look. "I think so. You looking to help?"

Derek laughed and shook his head. "No. I was just trying not to sit here and be a brooding asshole."

"Yeah, about that. You okay?"

Derek didn't respond right away. Then he decided to just lay it out there. "Linds and I had sex."

Mike's eyes went wide and he glanced quickly at Derek before looking back at the road. "Shit, man. Seriously?"

"Seriously."

"When did this happen?"

"A week ago when we were working at the house."

Mike's brow furrowed. "So, this is bad? Or this is good?"

"Well, it should have been good. But no. It's pretty damn bad."

"Shiiiit." Mike looked out the windshield as he sat at a red light. "What happened?"

"Honestly? I don't even know. I mean, I do, but I don't know when it went wrong or what I can do to fix it. She accused me of trying to get back what we used to have."

"Is that what you want?"

"Well . . . yeah."

Mike seemed to be considering his next comment. "Did she say what she wished you would have done?"

"That's just it, I don't think she even knows. She's hot and cold. I think we both are to a point."

"So she's scared."

"I think so."

"Understandable." Mike took a left turn and headed down 14th Street. "Sounds like you two just need to talk it out."

Derek laughed. "I don't know if she wants to ever see me again."

"Oh please, you know that's not true. It can't be that bad if she hasn't gotten on the horn and bitched about what happened."

"How do you know she hasn't?"

Mike looked confused by the question. "Anne would have told me."

"Why would Anne tell you if Lindsey called and talked about me?"

"Because Anne tells me everything." Mike pulled into a parking garage.

"No way does she tell you everything," Derek argued.

"Wanna bet?" Mike pulled into a spot and killed the engine on his Camaro.

"You seriously think Anne shares everything with you?" Derek turned in his seat, staring him down.

Mike shrugged. "Something like that she would. I know it."

Derek shook his head. "I don't believe that. Girls keep secrets."

Mike opened his car door and looked at Derek. "Yeah, everyone keeps secrets, but now I'm her *person*. You know? The one. And she tells me stuff, especially when it's her friends she's worried about. Believe me, even things I'd rather not know."

"Her *person*, huh?"

"Yeah. And it's good. You need to get yourself a person."

Maybe he did. It sounded good, and he'd never had that with a woman. Had never had that one person to always count on and turn to when you needed to unload. Find support. Just share stupid stuff with. He certainly hadn't had that with Lisa, that was for damn sure. But he wanted it. More than anything.

"Come on." Mike slid out of the car. "Let's get your ass in here and get you all dolled up for my wedding."

They were almost to the tux shop doorway when Mike turned and glared at Derek. "Hold up. Are you telling me you had sex in my new house before I did?"

When Derek didn't respond Mike just shook his head and opened the door. "That's messed up, man."

Lindsey got out of her vehicle and waved at Vanessa who was waiting on the porch of the farmhouse. It was a beautiful mid-March day. The kind that teased at spring just around the corner.

"Thank you so much for coming out on such short notice, and on a Friday evening," Vanessa said, walking down the steps toward Lindsey.

"No problem. Hope I look okay," she said, glancing down at her outfit. She'd chosen a bright red shirtdress that tied around her waist, strappy nude heels, and her hair was long and wavy. The best part was that she'd finally been able to remove her brace. She felt normal again.

Vanessa had called her this morning and asked if she could meet at the renovation site that evening for a quick photo shoot for the following week's house article. Lindsey had been thrilled. She hoped it would give the entire thing a personal touch, boosting interest in her business.

"Please, you look gorgeous. That red is amazing on you." Vanessa smiled before glancing down the road. "Everyone else should be here in just a minute. My photographer was about twenty minutes behind me."

"No problem. Where would you like to do it?"

"Matt's the photographer so he'll know where the best light is, but I was sort of hoping to stand you two out in the yard with the house in the background. Then maybe a few in the garden with the patio behind you. So pretty since the flowers are starting to bud."

Lindsey swallowed before speaking, her stomach turning. "You two?"

Right at that moment a large black pickup pulled into the drive, gravel crunching under its wheels. Lindsey's eyes squeezed shut. *What is he doing here?*

"There he is," Vanessa said in a singsongy voice. Lindsey looked at the ground as she heard the engine turn off and then the door close. "Oh and look at him all dressed up. Girl, you are so lucky."

"Aren't I?" Lindsey faked a smile and turned to see Derek walking up the drive toward them. And of course Vanessa was right. He looked gorgeous in crisp dark jeans and navy suit jacket. The purposely messy hair, hint of facial stubble, and white dress shirt casually unbuttoned at the top made him look like the ultimate playboy. His hands were casually tucked into his pants pockets, but his eyes stared right at Lindsey, anything but relaxed.

"In this next article I'm highlighting the two creative minds behind the project. A little about you and your business and Derek and his. How you're both connected to the couple. I'm assuming you two knew each other before this project?" Vanessa asked as they watched Derek walk toward them.

"Uh, sort of," Lindsey said. She suddenly had a feeling anything she said could be held against her. "We met in college but hadn't seen each other in years."

"Interesting. Okay. Well, I just thought a fun photo of the two of you would look great with the article. Something playful to show off your personalities."

"Sounds good," Lindsey lied.

"Hi, Derek," Vanessa called. If she sensed any tension between her subjects she didn't let on.

"Hello," he said with an easy smile, his gaze turning to the journalist. "Nice to see you again, Vanessa."

Lindsey folded her hands together, suddenly nervous. They hadn't spoken since that day, and she wasn't sure what kind of mood he'd be in.

"Lindsey, you look amazing." Derek's words were quiet and sincere. She wasn't expecting that.

"Thank you."

The crunching of gravel pulled all of their attention to the junky car driving up toward the house.

"Oh good, there's Matt. I'll just go chat with him quickly."

"I'll go with you," Lindsey said, beginning to follow Vanessa.

Her path was suddenly blocked by a massive wall of delicious-smelling man. "No you don't."

Lindsey looked up into Derek's eyes. "Excuse me, please."

"Lindsey. It's been ten days. The only reason I agreed to this photo shoot is because I wanted to see you."

"So, what? So we could be angry at one another again?"

He visibly swallowed, his throat working between the sharply ironed collars of his dress shirt. The skin there looked so warm. So close. Why could he not leave her and her heart be?

"Okay, Matt agrees with me on this spot," Vanessa said over Derek's shoulder.

Lindsey stepped back from him, suddenly feeling the slight chill still lingering in the air.

"Where shall we stand?" Lindsey asked. They needed to get this over with.

Matt and Vanessa took over, moving Derek and Lindsey where they wanted them, moving them. Moving them again. Matt did some test shots, checking the light on his camera, adjusting settings.

"Okay," Matt said. Finally. "Why don't you two stand a little closer?"

Vanessa was standing off to the side holding a massive round reflector. "Looks great, you two. Smile."

Lindsey smiled, feeling way too close to Derek for comfort. Matt took a few shots and then bent over to look at the back of his camera.

"I've missed you," Derek whispered from beside her.

She didn't turn toward him. What she wanted to do was close her eyes and take several deep breaths so she didn't pass out. Had she eaten lunch today? Because she suddenly felt very weak.

Matt stood up. "Looking good, you two," he called from his spot near the road. "Derek, let's try standing a little closer to her."

The photographer took a few more and then stared at them, obviously thinking. "Looks good, there's just . . . I don't know. Something's off. I want you two to look like a team. A little more comradery."

Lindsey turned to face Derek a little more. "This help?" she called out.

"That's a little better." Matt touched his chin. "Derek, how about you put an arm around her?"

"Why would he do that?" Lindsey said. She glanced at Vanessa, desperate for an explanation. "That's not necessary, is it?"

"It'll be cute. We take a lot, see what looks good. Let's just try it."

Derek slid his arm around Lindsey's back and gripped her shoulder. She blew out a hard breath and pasted on a smile.

"Oh, that's cute," Vanessa said. "Lindsey, give it a little more attitude. Put your hand on your hip."

Lindsey sighed but did as Vanessa requested, plastering smile back on as Matt took another round of photos.

"Love it," he yelled across the yard.

"I'm sorry about what happened," Derek said quietly.

"You have no reason to apologize," she said, her smile still tightly in place.

"I disagree. I shouldn't have stormed out like that."

She didn't say anything for a moment, just listened to Matt's directions for another pose.

"I'm sorry, too," Lindsey said quietly. "For freaking out. I might have overreacted."

Lindsey let out a deep breath and then smiled at the camera once again. It felt good to apologize to him. She regretted how she'd acted that day and had played the entire scene over and over again in her mind. Her feelings and reactions had been genuine, but they'd both lost their temper. Having sex with Derek had started out feeling so right and things had just become too intense too fast. She hadn't known how to process it.

"All right, let's get a few in the backyard," Matt called, walking toward them. Lindsey quickly extricated herself from Derek's hold.

"Sounds good," she said, heading for the backyard. Walking through the yard in her heels was far from graceful and she really wished she'd pulled up the rear. As it was she was walking like a moron and having to listen to Vanessa laugh at whatever the hell Derek had just said to her.

Rounding the side of the house, Lindsey forced herself not to glance across the yard at the old tree. She really never wanted to look at it again. Or think about that day. Even though it was pretty much the only thing she'd been thinking about for the past ten days. And now she knew she hadn't been alone in her misery. Or regret. She wasn't quite sure if that made her feel better or worse.

"Dad, my 3DS died. Can I have the car keys?" A small voice came from the opposite side of the house just as they stepped onto the garden patio. Lindsey looked over to see Tanner stepping through one of the overgrown trails in the garden. He had obviously been in the truck.

"Sure, bud." Derek removed the keys from his pocket and tossed them to his son. "But remember, turn it—"

"Just until the radio comes on. I know, Dad."

"Hi, Tanner," Lindsey found herself saying.

"Hey." He smiled in response, almost as if he were surprised she'd said it. He nodded to a row of tulips that had just begun to bloom. "Your dress matches those flowers."

Lindsey smiled. "You're right. It does."

Apparently finished with their conversation, he headed back to the front of the house. Lindsey turned to find Derek watching. She gave him a small smile and he returned it.

"Where should we stand this time?" Lindsey asked, wanting to keep the ball rolling.

"How about sitting on those steps?" Matt motioned to an old stone staircase on one side of the garden. It looked ancient but was surrounded by some beautiful white jonquils. "Derek, you sit first, lean forward resting your arms on your knees."

Derek did as instructed, looking too damn handsome in the process. Matt turned to Lindsey. "Okay, you face this way and lean up against the side of him."

Lindsey nearly rolled her eyes but did walk over to where Derek was seated.

"This is killing you, isn't it?" he teased quietly.

Lindsey didn't respond as she found the least jagged part of the rock to sit on and then carefully leaned back until she rested against Derek's side.

"Let's try one shoe on one step, the other on the lower. Show off those power heels," Vanessa said, peeking over Matt's shoulder. "Lindsey, how about you look over your shoulder at him."

Lindsey glanced over her shoulder at Derek, unsure of what to do with her face.

"Oh no, that won't work," Vanessa yelled. "Derek, make her laugh."

Derek turned to Lindsey, glancing over his own shoulder. "You want me to drop-kick Vanessa?" he whispered so only Lindsey could hear.

At his words she couldn't help herself. She laughed, her shoulder shaking against his. His sexy laugh always lit her body up inside. Just as quickly she got control of herself and smiled at the camera. Damn, maybe that Vanessa knew what she was doing.

They could put on a good show if that was what the job required. But the truth was, being this close to him reminded her of why she'd begun to thaw toward him in the first place. He made it so easy to do.

There had been ten whole days to play it over again and again and Lindsey knew she'd pulled a fast one on Derek. It was something she needed to own up to. It was silly to keep being frustrated with him for everything wrong between them when she was just as responsible for the push and pull between them. She'd initiated things. Touched him. Wanted him.

He hadn't done anything wrong, either. In fact, he was only guilty of making her feel too much. Too good. Too wanted. How could she hold that against him? The question was just . . . what was she going to do now? She'd apologized, but what was next after they'd taken things that far? It wasn't as if they could pretend they hadn't had sex, or certain words hadn't been said.

Ten minutes later they were done and waving good-bye to Vanessa as she backed out of the driveway. Lindsey knew they weren't really alone since she could hear Tanner's video game coming from the window of Derek's truck.

"Can we sit down a minute?" Derek held a hand out toward the front porch steps.

Lindsey nodded and walked over. She sat down and Derek joined her. Not too close, but not too far.

"Before you say anything else there's something you need to explain to me. Why did you pay my hospital bill?" The next day she'd called the hospital, and sure enough, her total had been paid in full. Without insurance it had been nearly a thousand dollars.

He leaned over into the same pose he'd used on the garden stairs, forearms resting on his knees. Turning his head to the side he looked into her eyes. "I wanted to help you."

"Why? What made you think I needed help?"

"Because I overhead you. From the hallway. You said you didn't have any insurance. You sounded worried. I didn't want that stress on your shoulders. Especially when I felt responsible for you getting hurt that day."

Lindsey squeezed her eyes shut. How humiliating. A grown woman, closing in on thirty in a few years, and no insurance. Living with her family. Good Lord. "I plan to pay you back," she said.

"Oh no." He rounded on her, his eyes intense. "I won't take your money so don't ever bring it up again. Got it?"

Lindsey shook her head. "You don't get to decide that. I refuse to be your charity case, Derek. And you can't hide things like that. And as nice as it was, that's part of the problem. You keep being too good to me. I don't know how to handle it or how to interpret it."

"Interpret it?"

"What does it mean? That you feel bad for me?"

Derek laughed. "Good gracious, woman." He squatted down in front of her. "I feel bad for a lot of people in this world. But I'm not paying their hospital bills."

"That still doesn't tell me what it means."

"It means . . . that I care about you. Is that so hard to understand? So maybe I can be a little heavy-handed. I'm a guy and we try to fix things. So tell me to ease up. Hell, pay me back if that will make you feel better. But just don't pull away from me completely."

She didn't know how to respond to that. When Derek realized she wasn't going to speak, he continued. "Lindsey, I don't know if this is a good idea. I don't know what will come of it. And maybe it's a stupid idea. But I want to see if we can try this again."

Her heart began to pound, her fingers fidgeting with the tie on her dress.

"I know you're scared, Linds, but do you really think I'd reinsert myself into your life if I had any intention of hurting you again?"

"I don't think you'd mean to hurt me again. I don't think you *wanted* to hurt me the first time. But you did."

"I know I did. But Linds, there are no guarantees in life. I can only tell you that I want this. Maybe we went about it wrong. Moved too fast. Doesn't mean we can't try again."

"Maybe." Lindsey glanced down at the ground, shocked at the turn in their conversation. When she showed up here an hour ago she would have never dreamed she'd end up having this discussion with Derek. "So you truly want us to try again?"

Lindsey lifted her head to find Derek grinning at her. "Go out with me," he said.

"Like, on a date?"

"Yes. On a date."

Lindsey laughed and glanced over at their cars parked in the driveway. She hoped Tanner wasn't watching and that made her wonder what Derek had said to his son about her. About them. "I don't know . . ."

"Say yes. We'll do this right. Get to know each other again. No sprained wrists, no ambushing, no hiding in the bathroom."

She thought about it for a moment. Or pretended to. There was only one word repeating over and over in her head.

"Yes. I'll go out with you."

Derek grinned. "Yeah?"

"Yeah."

"Good. But just so we're clear, when we go out—on a legit date—I pay."

"I won't argue with you on that one."

Seventeen

After taking Tanner to dinner, Derek pulled onto the road that led to his house with a smug grin on his face. Today could not have gone better considering he'd been nervous as hell when he'd shown up for the photo shoot. He could tell by the look on her face that Lindsey had not been aware that he was coming. But thankfully it had accomplished just what he hoped when Vanessa had called his office. Forced them to speak to one another.

"Do you like that lady, Dad?" Tanner asked quietly from the passenger seat.

Derek smiled over at his son. "I do like her, Tan. What do you think about that?"

Tanner shrugged, looking unconcerned. More just thoughtful. "I think it's okay."

"You sure? I mean . . . I want you to tell me how you feel about things. Always."

"I do," Tanner said, refocusing on his Mario Kart game. After a few moments Tanner spoke again. "Does she like *you*?"

Derek chuckled as he pulled into the driveway of

their house. He put the truck in park and looked over at his son. "I think she does."

"She seems mad a lot."

Okay, he definitely didn't want Tanner thinking that about Lindsey. The circumstances had been unfortunate every time the two were around each other and that wasn't fair to either one of them. "That's not true, Tanner. Lindsey is really nice. Sweet. I think she's just still a little nervous about us liking each other."

"Maybe she likes you but she just doesn't want you to know it. Mom told me sometimes girls do that."

"Your mom told you that? Huh." The idea of Lisa giving their son advice on females made him a little nervous, but she ought to know better than he did what girls were thinking. He had always tried to be honest with his son, but this situation was throwing him a fast one. He'd never dated a woman seriously enough to introduce her to Tanner. In fact, he hadn't really dated much at all. "She's probably right that girls sometimes do that. But I think with Lindsey it's different. When you grow up and like another person it's a little scary. You're afraid that if you start liking them a lot it will be really painful if they stop liking you back. Does that make sense?"

"Like you and Mom stopped liking each other?"

Well, if that didn't gut him, Derek didn't know what would. "Kind of, bud. Sometimes grown-ups just realize that they'd be better people if they weren't married to each other."

Sad but true. And Tanner seemed satisfied with the answer.

"I think Lindsey should like you. You're pretty cool."

Derek ruffled Tanner's hair. "Thanks, bud. You're pretty cool, too. You ready to go in?"

"Yeah." Tanner picked up his backpack off the floor and then paused. "Dad, I hope she stops being nervous about it soon."

"Yeah? How come?"

"Because she seems nice and if you lived with somebody nice you wouldn't be lonely when I'm not here as much."

"What do you mean? You'll always be here as much as you are now." Panic flooded Derek's thoughts.

"I just heard Mom on the phone saying that if she married Lane I wouldn't need to come here so much. But I want to, Dad. I wish I could come here every week."

A hard knot formed in Derek's throat as he took in the fear in his son's eyes. God, he was so damned pissed at Lisa for causing Tanner to worry like this. Derek laid a hand on Tanner's arm.

"Listen, I won't ever let that happen. You understand me?"

Tanner nodded.

"Now let's go inside, it's getting late."

Derek instructed Tanner to brush his teeth, use the restroom, and get a last drink of water. Once that was all finished he tucked him into bed, sitting beside him for a few minutes on the mattress.

"I say we sleep in tomorrow and then go to the bakery downtown for breakfast," Derek said. "Sound like a plan?"

"Can I have two cinnamon rolls?"

Derek pretended to be put out for a moment. "Sure."

Tanner grinned. "Okay. Sounds like a plan." Tanner's brows furrowed once more as they had in the car. "But Dad. I was thinking about something."

Derek angled his body so he could lean one arm on the other side of Tanner, staring down at him. "Okay. What about?"

"Well, just, maybe you should try being *really really* nice to Lindsey so she starts to like you. Mom says you work too much. Maybe she'll let me come here more if Lindsey is here to hang out with me while you're working."

Derek's hands clenched and he pushed one into the bed, furious that Lisa planted these ideas in their son's head. What the hell had she been saying? "Tanner, you know that I own my own business. That does make me busy, but it also means I decide when I work. I can take as much time as I need to be with you. I always will. Maybe your mom doesn't realize that. But I'll make sure she does."

Except she sure as hell did know. It was all Derek could do not to completely trash-talk the woman, but he would never do that to his son. She was his mother and he was already confused as it was.

"Okay. I'll tell her too."

"How about you let me handle that? It's between your mom and me. I don't want you to worry about it. You're the most important thing to me, that's all you need to think about. Okay?" Derek thought for a moment, wondering how to put the next thing into words. "And how about we keep Lindsey between us for now? You know, until she's not nervous anymore. I'll tell your mom when the time is right. Deal?"

"Deal." Tanner nodded, his head slipping against his pillow, and then he rolled onto his side, snuggling into the bed.

"I love you, bud."

"Love you, Dad," Tanner said in a sleepy voice.

Derek leaned over and kissed his son on the forehead before switching off the bedside lamp and going into his own room. Immediately he picked up his phone and opened an e-mail to his attorney. If he'd learned anything about divorce and custody battles, it was that he needed to be proactive not reactive. When she found out about Lindsey, the last thing she'd be feeling was charitable.

So, no, Tanner unfortunately was wrong. Nothing about Lindsey being back in his life would go over well with Lisa. And as bad as Derek felt for asking his son to keep secrets from his mother, he knew it was the only way to handle this right now. He wanted his son in his life more than anything. He also wanted Lindsey.

He was certain that he could have both, but he'd have to move slowly. This time he was going to do things his way, and that meant it was critical that he not hurt Lindsey or his son in the process.

Lindsey turned from side to side in front of the full-length mirror on the back of Anne's bedroom closet, the skirt of her bridesmaid dress draping around her knees. Anne had chosen lovely sage gowns with a delicate eyelet overlay. The dress somehow managed to be classic and modern. It had a fitted waist that led into wide scalloped shoulder straps that showed a generous amount of cleavage. The skirt was full and even had pockets, a fun addition. Lindsey adored it.

"I absolutely love it, Anne," Callie said, squeezing in next to Lindsey to see her reflection in the mirror. "How good do we look?"

Lindsey smiled. "I'm so grateful your mom was able to alter the straps so my boobs don't fall out."

"At least your boobs are capable of falling anywhere. Mine just stick straight out, no hang whatsoever. I *want* hang." Callie cupped her own chest through the material.

"Get pregnant and then give birth," Anne said behind them. "You'll get more hang than you know what to do with."

"I second that. You should see my sister. She's nursing and her boobs are just . . . everywhere. She could carry a wallet underneath there."

"Okay, now that's a visual I didn't need," Callie said with a grimace, while pulling up her hair to imitate her wedding-day style.

"I'm telling you, Cal, you need to have a baby," Anne said. She was sitting cross-legged on her bed watching them try on their dresses. "I give Bennett till the end of the year to propose."

"Good Lord, what if that's not what I want?" Callie asked, sitting down next to Anne on the giant bed.

Anne laughed and then leveled a stare at Callie. "Cal, you've been with me for a lot of my wedding planning, and if I had a dollar for every time you said 'if this was my wedding I would,' I could fly us all to the beach for my nuptials."

"Okay, fine, I do say that. *Sometimes.* But it's fun to

think about. I mean, if you weren't doing this it totally wouldn't have come to mind." Callie's eyes quickly went from uncertain to sparkling. "But if he did, can't you totally see him proposing this fall at halftime during one of his games?"

"So clearly you've given it a lot of thought. Have you and Bennett talked about it?" Lindsey asked.

"Not directly, no. I mean, it's only officially been like five months." Callie pulled her legs around to the side and leaned on her hand. "We talk in dreams. Like, 'someday I want to go to Hawaii,' or 'when I retire I want to travel the country in an RV.' And then the other person agrees, and we discuss what we'll do in detail. Ya know? Like a sort of . . . *implied* forever. Definitive words are scary."

Anne nodded. "That actually makes perfect sense. And you're right, it's not been that long, but it wasn't long for me and Mike, either. But I felt certain and I know he did, too."

"Uh, no kidding, the guy was obsessed with you from day one," Callie said. "Plus Mike is just a really good guy. We all know how much he loves you."

Lindsey smiled at her friends. She would give anything to have what either of them had at this moment. Starting with the confidence of actually being certain of where they'd be sleeping six months from now all the way to knowing who'd be sleeping there next to them.

"Speaking of men," Callie said, turning to Lindsey. "Tell us about your date last night."

"Well, there isn't much to tell." Lindsey couldn't help smiling.

"Uh-uh. I don't believe that, especially with that goofy grin on your face," Callie said.

Lindsey and Derek had now been on two dates. The first had been a Monday-night dinner at a small restaurant on the plaza near her sister's house. Last night—Friday—they'd gone to a little jazz club and had a drink. Just enjoying the music. He'd held her hand. That had been it. On neither date had he kissed her, been inappropriate, or even mentioned the past. It was like they were truly starting over.

"It's been . . . good. He calls me and asks me out. Like official dating style. It's kind of weird, but I like it."

And she did. Derek was sweet and charming. He opened doors, told her she looked pretty, and walked her to the door. If she'd never known him before she'd already be halfway in love with him. He was the perfect gentleman.

But something was missing. That hungry obsession they felt around one another still burned just under the surface. At least for her, and she was pretty sure it did for him, too. Sometimes she would catch him staring at her, his eyes intent.

She knew what he was doing. The right thing. That's what Derek did. And she appreciated it, but as much as she hated to admit it, she missed the way it had been before when they'd been working on the house together. The stolen glances, not-so-accidental touches, and innuendos.

"When are you going out again?" Callie asked.

"Unfortunately not this week. Now that the weather's getting nice again he has a lot of projects starting up in town so he's really busy."

"But the coed party is next weekend, so you'll see him then," Anne said.

"See? I knew what I was doing when I had this idea. Now you guys can get your own room!" The delight in Callie's eyes made them all laugh.

"I don't know about that. Remember, we're trying to do this the right way."

Callie scoffed. "Please. Sometimes the right way is naked."

Eighteen

Thursday morning Derek looked up from his drafting table as his administrative assistant, Molly, walked into his office. Her eyes were wide—panicked—and instantly his stomach knotted.

"What's wrong?" His thoughts immediately went to Tanner.

"Code red just pulled in," she said. "Looks pissed."

Beyond his office they both heard the front door open. Molly scurried back out front.

Derek cursed under his breath and dropped his pencil. Within seconds Lisa was strutting through his office door and stopping him in his tracks. Molly wasn't lying. Lisa was furious.

She walked right up to the table and slammed a folded newspaper on top of the plans he'd been working on. Pencils scattered to the floor.

"Good morning to you, too, Lisa," he said.

"What the hell is this?" She nodded to the photo on the front cover of the Home and Hobby section. Derek hadn't needed to glance down to know what she'd found, but he did. The first thing he noticed was how despite the tension between him and Lindsey that day, the photographer had managed to capture them both looking genuinely happy. They'd chosen a photo from the garden steps. Lindsey leaned against his side, glancing over her shoulder and smiling. Derek smiled back at her. He was pretty sure he remembered what had preceded that moment.

The second thing he noticed was the title of the article: RESTORING THE PAST PT 3: THE COUPLE BEHIND THE RENO. Well, shit.

" 'Restoring the Past'? Are you shitting me, Derek? It says you knew this girl in college. Is she the one? The one you dated?" Lisa screeched. She was nearly shaking. Derek blew out a long breath. The title could not have been more accurate—or awful in this situation— if they'd tried. Lisa had known from mutual friends that he'd been seeing someone before they'd found out she was pregnant. He'd been unwilling to discuss details with her then, not that she hadn't tried to throw it in his face from time to time.

"Lisa, I can explain this."

"Oh, can you? Can you also explain to me why you robbed me of ten years of my life? Because I can't seem to get over that one." That was the understatement of the year.

Derek's fingers clamped down on the bridge of his nose. If she was counting their time together in high school—and obviously she was—ten years was how long they'd been together. God, so damn long. Too long.

"Lisa, what do you want me to say? We've had this conversation so many times. But this"—he pointed to the article—"is misleading. We just happen to be working on the house together. Did you even read the entire article?" And maybe that was a stupid question because he hadn't read it. But what could it possibly say except the truth?

She gave a bitter laugh. "Oh, hooo, oh yes. I read the article. You two are 'just the perfect couple to renovate a house for their good friends,' and 'who knows, Walsh and Morales might be creating more than a beautiful house together.' Do you have any respect for me, Derek?"

"Believe it or not, this has nothing to do with you."

"It has everything to do with me and our son."

Derek felt sick to his stomach. This was exactly what he'd wanted to avoid with his ex-wife. It hadn't even occurred to him that she'd see these photos and realize that Lindsey was a woman from his past. Or even worse, that this Vanessa woman would put her own spin on the story.

But how could he fault the journalist? It wasn't really a spin. Sure she'd taken some liberties, but what she'd picked up on between them was dead-on.

"I just cannot believe you would do this to me. Again."

Blinding fury washed over Derek. To her? If he'd done anything to her it was give her a home, a hefty bank account, and a beautiful son.

"What the hell does that mean, Lisa? The first time I left *her*. Do you get that? I was in love with her and I left her for you!"

Sharp pain filled her eyes and instantly Derek felt like an asshole for the outburst.

"Thank you very much for your sympathy marriage. I'm so sorry I'm not more grateful. I need to remind myself that you did me a favor, because isn't that every girl's dream? To get knocked up and then have her baby daddy marry her out of a sense of obligation?"

"Lisa, damn it. I shouldn't have said that. I'm sorry." He'd never admitted out loud that he'd been in love with Lindsey. He knew Lisa had to have suspected he'd had feelings for someone else, but saying something out loud made it real. And his love for Lindsey had been the most real emotion he'd ever known.

Lisa's lips trembled. "Why did you do that to me?"

Derek knew there was no right answer to this question. He'd tried them all because they'd had this conversation so many times. Every variation of it. "Lisa, please—"

"I hate you for it."

Derek took a step closer. "I know you do, and I sometimes I hate myself for what I did to us. It was wrong. I let my—"

"Stop it." Her face went from heartbreak to rage. "Don't you dare blame your asshole father for your choices. You're a man, Derek. Not a child. Start acting like it."

Lisa stormed toward the door before turning hard. "Speaking of children. If you let that bitch within one inch of my son, your visits are over. Don't think for one minute I won't do everything in my power to make you suffer the way you've made me."

He stood there in complete shock as he listened to the front door and open and close. When Molly peeked her head in he could barely breathe, let alone speak.

"You okay?" she asked quietly.

"No. I'm not okay. But . . . everything's fine, Molly."

"Clearly that's not true, but I won't push. How about I go grab you some lunch? You've been hunched over that table for almost four hours."

He managed a tight smile. Molly was a really good employee. He owed her a lot and hated that she'd had to witness this. She was a single mother herself, since her husband had passed away a few years ago. Derek scrubbed a hand over his face. "I'm not really hungry. But why don't you take off? Use the expense card and get some takeout for you and Katelyn."

Molly gave a sheepish smile. "You don't have to buy our meals, Derek. You pay me, remember?"

"Of course. And I know I don't have to. I want to. I'm sorry you had to be here for that."

Molly stepped into his office. "Don't be too hard on yourself, okay? She'll get over it. There's no way she could have expected you to stay single forever. You're not doing anything wrong."

"Feels like I'm always doing something wrong."

"You're a good guy, Derek. You just need to stop trying to make everyone else happy."

Molly smiled and left the room. After a few minutes he heard her leave and lock up the front door behind her.

All his life Derek had tried to do the right thing. Why did it so often backfire?

Maybe Molly was right, that he just needed to stop trying so damn hard and just live how he wanted. In the meantime he would have to walk on thin ice with Lisa. He didn't want to lose Lindsey again, but if caring for her cost him a relationship with his son he wasn't sure he'd ever forgive himself.

He found himself in the same predicament he'd been the first time he'd loved Lindsey. And it wasn't her fault she was one of the innocent victims of his stupidity. This time had to be different. He just needed to figure out how to do the right thing, not hurt anyone, and get the girl he was in love with.

Friday evening the girls met at Anne's house to have their final meeting before the wedding, which was now only three weeks away. Callie and Lindsey had agreed that for the two weeks prior to the event, and then the week after, they would take over the daily blog business. Anne would post when it worked for her, and luckily they'd prepped all their followers. Everyone knew what was happening and they were all excited.

"I can't believe how many gifts you've gotten from readers," Lindsey said. The entire kitchen table, coffee table, and the corners of the living room floor were covered in packages.

"I know, it makes me feel bad," Anne said. She held up a hand-stitched set of kitchen towels.

"You shouldn't feel bad. You didn't ask them for gifts, in fact you've said 'Please, no need for gifts' if I recall."

Anne sighed. "I did, after receiving the first few. I shouldn't have shared them on social media because now I feel like I need to share everyone's gifts, which only makes people feel the need to send gifts, it's like an ugly cycle I can't break."

"Yeah, an ugly cycle where you get tons of presents," Callie said, confused.

They all laughed at that and then Lindsey spoke again. "Seriously, Anne. People are sending gifts because they want to. Many of them are handmade and when you share online it makes them feel good. Why don't we just save the rest in a pile and then post one big picture of them all with a thank-you after the wedding? We've made it very clear that you're busy."

"That's a good idea," Anne said. "That's what I'll do. I can even include links at the end for the ones that have their own shops online. I'm sure some just really want them featured."

"Are you keeping track?" Lindsey asked. "Or would you like me to come over and make up a list?"

Anne looked relieved. "Oh, would you? That would be wonderful."

Lindsey smiled. "How about I come over tomorrow morning and then we can get ready for that night?"

"Oh well, then I'm coming, too," Callie said. "We can all get ready together and then go check into our room."

Saturday was the day of the coed bachelor party and, after all of her previous worry, Lindsey was now really looking forward to it.

"Okay. Now let's discuss *this*," Callie said. Lindsey looked over to see Callie holding up the newspaper article that featured her and Derek.

Lindsey had definitely seen it. In fact, much to her chagrin the first person to show her had been Mel. Surprisingly she'd been nothing but positive, mainly talking about Lindsey's shoes and hair.

Callie pointed to the photo at the top of the article. "Let's start with these killer heels."

Rolling her eyes, Lindsey laughed. "My sister brought the shoes up also."

"They are really good shoes," Anne said, before taking a bite of her giant salad. She'd committed to a thirty-day no-gluten and no-sugar diet in order to feel good in her wedding dress. They'd tried to convince her it wasn't necessary, but Lindsey could hardly blame her. If she was getting married she'd probably do exactly the same.

They were discussing the article further when Lindsey's phone vibrated on the table. Everyone looked over just as Derek's name popped up on the screen. Callie's eyes flew to Lindsey's, wide and curious.

Lindsey slowly picked up the phone and answered it. "Hello."

"Hey, Linds." Derek's voice rumbled through the line, sending chills through every inch of her body. She looked up to see both of her friends' eyes on her.

"Hey, what's going on?" She figured it was best to make it seem like this didn't happen too often, which was actually the truth.

"I was just thinking about you." Derek laughed, almost as if he were nervous. Was that possible, that Derek felt awkward about calling her?

"Oh well, can you hang on a minute?"

"Sure," he said.

Lindsey put her hand over the phone and stood up before speaking to Anne and Callie who were both smiling. "I'll be right back."

"You better be," Callie teased.

Lindsey stepped into Anne's kitchen and sat down at the table. She brought the phone back up to her ear. "Okay, I'm back."

"Sorry, I should have asked if you were busy."

"It's okay, I'm just with Anne and Callie," Lindsey said.

"Oh good." Was it her imagination or did he sound relieved? "I just wanted to hear your voice."

"Oh . . . okay. Is everything all right?"

Derek chuckled, sounding surprised. "Yeah, of course. Can't I just want to hear your voice for no reason?"

It was Lindsey's turn to laugh quietly. "I guess. Just surprised me, that's all. I'm not used to you calling me."

"We used to talk on the phone for hours," Derek said. Lindsey sucked in a breath, remembering. She'd had the pattern of the cheap ceiling tiles in her dorm room memorized from lying in bed, the phone to her ear. "Do you remember that?"

"Yes."

They were both quiet for a long moment and Lindsey just had a feeling something was off. This kind of behavior wasn't like him. "As much I as like the idea of you just wanting to hear my voice, are you sure everything is okay?"

"Yes. Everything is fine." He sighed into the phone. "I do hate my ex-wife right now but that's not your problem."

Lindsey stayed quiet for a moment, unsure of what to say. Then Derek spoke up again.

"I'm sorry. I didn't mean to say that. I should just let you go."

"Wait. Tell me what happened." She couldn't believe she was inviting this man to tell her his problems about the woman he'd left her for. She closed her eyes for a second. "Please."

"How about you just come over here," he said quietly. There was a hint of seduction in his voice.

Lindsey's eyes flew open. "Now?"

"Yeah, now."

"Derek, have you been drinking?"

"Uh, a little."

"Sounds like a little too much."

"Okay, maybe so, but even if I was stone-cold sober I would still want you here."

"Can you first tell me what happened?"

"Linds," he growled. "I need you."

Lindsey stood up, unable to be still any longer. "Give me your address."

He didn't speak for a second, as if he were surprised she'd agreed. Finally he said, "I'll text it to you. When can you leave?"

"Probably . . . ten minutes or so."

"Then I guess I'll see you soon."

They said their good-byes and Lindsey inhaled a deep breath. Then grinned. Derek had invited her over to his place. And she was going. This was not taking it slow. Or dating. This was simply him needing her and reaching out. It felt a little scary. But it also felt completely right.

Nineteen

As soon as Derek texted Lindsey his address he glanced around his house. It was clean enough, he'd showered after work, and now he needed to brush his damn teeth because drinking three bottles of beer didn't make for ideal breath.

He wasn't drunk, but he was clearly buzzed enough to drunk-dial Lindsey and ask her to come over. Still pretty pathetic.

His intentions had been good when he'd suggested he and Lindsey try dating the right way. He wanted her to feel safe with him. Trust him. They needed to really get to know one another as the people they were now. And they'd started to. But the one thing he knew was that every second he didn't touch her was one he might never get back. He didn't trust himself, he didn't trust fate, and he wanted to have her again the right way. How it should have been a few weeks ago. Not on a whim in an old strange house.

After brushing his teeth, he downed a glass of water and took some pain pills to try and fend off the inevitable headache he'd have in the morning. He didn't drink that often, maybe once a week if that, and really never at home. But ever since Lisa's visit the day before he'd been in a bad mood.

The worst part was the guilt. What he'd done to Lisa was wrong. Just as wrong as what he'd done to Lindsey. But they'd all suffered. He had as much as anyone.

Derek's doorbell rang and he strode over to the front door, pulling it open. There stood the best thing to ever happen to him. Twice now. Lindsey's smile was shy as she stepped inside.

"Hi," she whispered.

"Hi."

And with that out of the way, Derek grabbed the sides of her face and kissed her. Instantly she melted against him, kissing him back. Her lips were warm and wet. Urgent. Or maybe that was him, because if he didn't have this woman soon he was going to explode. He continued to kiss her thoroughly before letting his mouth roam over her chin, down her neck.

"Derek." Her breathy whisper sent a chill through his torso that landed heavy in in his cock.

"What?" Not waiting for her answer, he lifted his head from her neck and sought her mouth again. Her muffled moans got lost in his kiss. Their tongues met in a wet slide against each other and he trailed his fingers down her body.

Lindsey pulled back and looked at him. "Are you sure you don't need to talk? I was worried about you."

And he truly loved that she was concerned for him, but right now only one thing was going to help. "After," he said.

"Can we use a real bed this time?"

Derek huffed out a laugh and grabbed her hand before leading her through the house and up the stairs to his bedroom. Once there he turned on a bedside lamp and then turned to yank her into his arms.

"You feel so good." His palms slipped down her back, over her ass, as he pulled her against him.

Lindsey gave him a gentle nudge and then stepped away. He watched, breath ragged, as she tugged her shirt over her head. He took in her purple bra, nipples straining against the thin material. Her body was enough to make him crazy. But it was her sexy smile that was his undoing.

"Linds . . ." He reached for her. "Come here."

She stepped back into his embrace and lifted her lips to his. Her hands went to his shirt, fingers undoing each button quickly, and before he knew it her palms were sliding over his chest. The fabric fell from his shoulders and he used his hands to pull it off behind him.

Their lips met again and they kissed deeply as she awkwardly fumbled with her jeans. He followed suit, one hand unzipping his pants, the other gripping the back of her head, never letting her lips get away from him.

As soon as both of them were naked and his hands were free, he guided them to the bed and fell back, pulling her on top of him. Her knees naturally fell to each side of his hips, her body straddling his. It was the most natural thing in the world, the way her body fit against his. Derek got a firm grasp of her hips and pulled her down, grinding her against him. She moaned, the sound deep and raw, urging him on. Pressing a kiss to his jaw, neck, chest, Lindsey sat up. He looked up at her, her breasts full and peaked. It was like living a dream.

A dream he had been so certain would never come true. He reached up and palmed her breasts. She lifted her own hands to cover his, her lower body continuing a steady grind against him.

Her head fell back, her mouth dropping open. And God, he wondered if she was going to come from the friction alone. It felt like a forbidden gift, watching her so uninhibited like this. Derek lowered one hand, using his thumb to stroke, helping her along. She bit at her lower lip and dropped her head forward as she continued to ride him.

"Look at me, Lindsey."

He held his breath for a moment, but as soon as she opened her eyes and looked into his he felt his chest expand. Nothing in his life had felt so good. He began to thrust against her. Even like this—rubbing skin to skin—she was so warm and wet, it was almost as good as being inside her. *Almost.* He knew she was close when her chest began to heave, shallow breaths puffing through her lips.

And still she looked right at him. Their gazes never wavered. Her dark hair had fallen over her breasts, one nipple peeking through the soft strands. He wished he could take a photo of her in this moment, her body undulating on top of his, her lips parted, and her lashes fluttering as she pleasured herself.

"This time we're gonna do this right," he whispered. "And I'm going to watch your beautiful face as you come." And in that moment she let out a whimper, then another, her body beginning to tremble. He continued to stroke her as she fell forward, her hands bracing her on his chest.

She never looked away.

Lindsey fell forward trying to catch her breath. Her breasts smashed against Derek's hard chest and she pushed her face into his neck. She was almost embarrassed at the intensity of the moment they'd just shared. She hadn't planned for it to happen that way, but she didn't regret it.

Derek trailed his fingers across her back, one hand resting on her butt. After a moment she sat back up and looked down at him. He grinned.

"What are you smiling about?" She gave his chest a playful slap.

"I'm smiling because that was hot as hell."

Lindsey leaned forward and stroked a lock hair off his forehead. God, this man was too much. Too handsome, too smart, too . . . everything. And she didn't want to let him go. Ever. Something she had to finally admit to herself. She was already in too deep. If things ended right now she'd shatter. It would be worse than the last time. She knew that, but here she was, risking it all.

Reaching down between their bodies, she took hold of his length, positioning him at her entrance before sliding her body down onto him. She stayed spread across his chest, kissing his neck, enjoying the warmth of his breath on her shoulder as he moaned against her.

Derek's hands palmed and grabbed both sides of her ass, using the leverage to lift her body, slamming it back down onto him. She relaxed, allowing him to set the pace, his fingers nearly bruising her skin with their grip.

It was so good. The friction so intense. Within a moment Lindsey was holding her breath and coming a second time. Derek groaned against her neck and she angled her head to kiss him as they found their release at the exact same moment.

He pressed her hard against him and then brought his hands to her head, kissing her deeply. The desperation of the moment subsided, leaving them exhausted, tongues sliding lazily against each other. After a few minutes she pushed herself off his chest and looked down at him.

He grabbed a handful of her hair and brushed it off her face and behind her ear so they could see each other.

"Would you believe I'm already craving you again?" he asked.

Lindsey gave an exaggerated look down between them and then smiled at him before speaking. "I don't know. It kind of feels like you'll need a few moments."

"That's it." He jerked up, rolling them over, and Lindsey squeaked as he pinned her on the bed. In the process he'd left her body, and now he rubbed himself against her inner thigh. "Okay, maybe not quite yet. But it won't be long."

Lindsey giggled and then they became quiet once more as they continued to stare at each other. He stroked her skin, his hands softly pushing at the hair around her face as he leaned over her. It was so peaceful. Gentle.

Perfect.

Finally her curiosity got the better of her. "What happened to upset you tonight?"

His movements faltered for a second but he quickly picked up where he left off, his thumb gently stroking her eyebrows. Temples. Cheeks.

"I got to thinking that . . . I don't want us to try and make this into something it isn't. I just want you. I don't want to overthink it. I already made that mistake once."

"This scares me," she whispered.

"I know. Me, too. But you're here."

"I'm here." She nodded.

"And I'm here. Just me. And there is nothing out there waiting to come between us. I'll make sure of that."

She bit at her lip, trying desperately not to cry.

"Babe," Derek said. He always sensed her emotions before they were obvious. "Don't cry. This is supposed to be good."

Lindsey couldn't open her mouth. If she spoke the sobs would escape. She could only nod once more.

"I'm crazy about you, Lindsey. I always have been. I didn't make it clear then, but I'm telling you now."

He lifted his head and touched her lips with his, light tentative pecks that led into slow, deep, sensual kisses. She felt warm wetness on her cheek. Her tear rolled down her face and pooled where their lips met. Derek turned his head and sucked at the corner of her mouth, making it disappear at the same time his hand came up and touched her face.

Oh God, Lindsey wanted to drown in this man. Everything about this moment unlocked another little piece of her heart and with every touch of his lips he took one of those pieces from her. She was his.

Twenty

Derek carried a mug of coffee up the steps, not surprised when he found the bed empty. He'd heard Lindsey get up and the bathroom door creak shut when he was downstairs. He set her drink on the bedside table and sat down. When she opened the door and stepped out, he smiled.

"Morning, beautiful," he said, nodding to the table. "Your coffee."

"Thank you." She padded over to the bed and slipped under the covers before leaning against the headboard. "I can't believe it's already eight. I haven't slept this late in months."

"Well, after the way you attacked me last night, I can imagine you were exhausted."

Lindsey slid him a look over her mug and he laughed. She took a sip of her coffee and then lowered the mug to her lap. "I do need to get home so I can shower, pack up a bag, and then get back to Anne's."

"For tonight?"

She nodded. "We're all getting ready together. I know guys never do that."

"Hell no. And we don't all go to the restroom at the same time, either."

"That's a shame. Lots of good gossip happens in the bathroom."

They drank in the silence for a moment before he had to ask. "Do they know? About us?"

"Do you mean, as in, *recently*?"

"Yeah."

She shrugged. "They know enough."

" 'Enough' meaning, when you end up in my room tonight they won't be surprised?"

Lindsey smiled and shook her head. "No, they will definitely not be surprised."

Lindsey, Callie, and Anne were all squashed into Anne's hotel room bathroom sharing the mirror. They'd decided to get ready there. If Lindsey did say so herself, they looked fantastic. Digging through her makeup bag, she pulled out a tube of red lipstick and popped off the lid. As soon as she twisted up the base Callie gasped.

"Are you rocking red lips tonight? That will look so good on you."

"Yeah? I was strongly considering it," Lindsey said.

"Definitely," Anne interjected. "With your skin tone and hair color it will be gorgeous."

"It's not fair that you have a tan in March." Callie shook her head and dug into her own makeup bag.

Lindsey looked into the mirror and applied the cherry-red lipstick, popping her lips together a couple times. She applied a light gloss and then took in the full package. She'd curled her hair in wavy spirals, done a smoky eye, and was wearing a short skirt with heels.

"Okay, ladies, I predict free drinks all night." Callie held her cell phone at waist level and arranged her body in an instantly flattering pose. "Get in close. It didn't happen unless we selfie it."

Lindsey and Anne stepped over and leaned in, smiling and giggling until Callie instructed them to smile with their eyes and look sexy. Lindsey tried but was pretty sure she didn't pull it off as Callie snapped the photo and then opened it to look at it.

"Boom. Nailed it on the first try. I'm tweeting this, cool?"

They all agreed and then began to collect their things so they could head downstairs where the guys were waiting for them.

"Is everyone here?" Anne asked, pulling her heels on.

"Yep. Eric just texted me from downstairs and said that he, his date, Mike, and Derek are all drinking at the lobby bar. Bennett should be here anytime."

"Eric's date?" Lindsey asked. "Who is it?"

"Lord knows," Callie said with an eye roll. "For his own sake, hopefully a commitmentphobe."

Eric was Callie's long-time best friend and employee. He'd also become special to Lindsey and Anne as well in the past couple of years. He was attractive, gay, and had a love life that kept them continually entertained and often shocked.

"I still wish he would have stayed with David," Anne said. "He was so sweet. I feel bad for him, too. Eric is so indecisive."

"I know, the guy can't see a good thing even when it's slapping him upside the head," Callie replied. "He's not gonna be hot forever, then what's he going to do?"

Lindsey and Anne laughed, but the comment really stuck with Lindsey. Was this a good thing she had right now? She wanted to think it was. Just because something was scary didn't make it bad. And she certainly didn't want to be like Eric, letting a good thing slip away. She'd done that once before. Hadn't even put up a fight for Derek. Now that she knew the truth she figured it wouldn't have done much good, but she could have let him know how much she'd loved him.

"Well, we look good," Anne said. "Now, everyone, please be safe. Watch your drinks, don't get too far away from the guys, and keep your phones on you at all times."

"Yes, mom," Callie said.

Anne rolled her eyes and then looked around. "Everyone have a room key?"

Callie and Lindsey held theirs up.

"Feel free to come back to this room until . . . say . . . midnight. But after that, if you open that door, I won't be responsible for what you walk in on," Anne said with a wink. "But seriously, this room is open if you girls need it. You hear?"

Anne's gaze lingered on Lindsey and she gave her a small smile. The three of them left, walked down the hall, and then watched the elevator doors close as they headed down to the hotel casino lobby.

Derek turned to glance at the elevator one more time. An old white-haired couple stepped out. He sighed.

Lindsey had left shortly after they'd woken up this morning and he'd been thinking about her all day long. He was pretty sure he'd never felt as close to another person as he had with her last night. Astonishing considering their past. But damn, he was glad. He finally felt like they were on their way to overcoming what they'd been through. What he'd done.

Right now he intended to take things one day at a time. He had said he'd let nothing come between them, and that was his plan. But that didn't mean he didn't have baggage, and his son to think about. He just needed to figure out how to make everything work. He knew it was possible. For the time being he saw no reason to talk to Lindsey about what Lisa had threatened until he was sure what was happening. He'd contacted his lawyer, prepped him for all the potential disasters, and was now going for what he wanted.

"Oh man, take a look at this." Mike leaned over and held his phone in front of Derek on the bar. It was a picture of Anne, Callie, and Lindsey, obviously in the bathroom of their hotel room. They all looked very pretty, but he did a double take on seeing Lindsey. She looked incredible. Her lips looked like ripe-fruit, her hair was sexy and wavy, and she was wearing some sort of tight dress that showed off her amazing cleavage. The day of the photo shoot she'd been wholesome sexy, but tonight . . . goddamn, tonight she looked like a siren.

"Where did you get this?" Derek asked.

"Twitter." Mike pulled his phone back in front of him.

"Since when do you have a Twitter account?" Derek asked in shock.

Mike shrugged. "Since I wanted to start following Anne. They have a blog account all the girls post on."

Derek heard laughter from the lobby and turned. And there she was. The minute their eyes locked she smiled and intense relief and happiness fell over him. This was the feeling he wanted to have forever when he looked at the woman he loved. And damn, he loved her.

Mike got up as soon as Anne stepped near him, and Derek tried not to watch as his friend nuzzled into his fiancée's temple. "Happy Bachelorette Party, Perfect."

At the same moment Derek saw a large guy come up behind Callie and grab her around the waist. She laughed and turned in his arms before plastering a kiss on his lips. Derek hadn't met Bennett yet, Callie's ex-pro-football-playing boyfriend, but clearly this was him. Mike liked him so Derek figured he would also.

Everyone was now coupled up and that left him and Lindsey. She stood next to the bar holding a little black purse in front of her. Her dress was black, tight, and strapless. He lifted a finger and beckoned her over to him.

She took the few steps up to him and he grabbed her hand before leaning into whisper in her ear. "You look so good I want to eat you."

She laughed. "I borrowed this dress from Mel."

He stepped back and looked down her body. "You should keep it. Although I'll bet I like you better without it."

He pulled her against him and laid a quick kiss on the top of her head. He waited, expecting her to get upset. Be embarrassed. She did neither, just smiled up at him.

"David!" Callie yelled, startling them. Derek and Lindsey turned to see Callie rushing over to throw her arms around Eric's date. "We were just talking about you."

Derek looked at Lindsey questioningly. "Eric and David have been off again on again. We would like it to stay on."

"Ah," Derek said.

They waited a few more minutes and then Emma— another employee of Callie's bakery—showed up with a friend of hers and they all headed to the steakhouse at the other end of the building. Derek grabbed Lindsey's hand, threading their fingers. He slowed them down so they could hang in back as they walked the length of the casino.

"Have you been here before?" Lindsey asked

"Once. It was some conference for developers, but it was a year or so ago. It's different now. New owner. And I'm not much for gambling so I haven't been back. You?"

She shook her head. "No, never. It's pretty cool. Is this what the casinos in Vegas look like?"

"You haven't been there, either?" Derek asked.

"Nope. I've lived kind of a sheltered life," Lindsey said.

"This is pretty much what they look like. More flashy though, and probably more crowded. Oh and definitely more half-naked women."

Lindsey laughed. "Sounds really boring."

"Oh yeah, definitely nothing fun to do in Vegas."

Derek liked that they could joke like this. She was

so easy to talk to, that was what he remembered liking about her the first time. She was just . . . sweet. And funny.

They continued to talk about the casino as they walked and by the time they made it to the restaurant he had his arm around her waist. The group congregated at the hostess stand, and Derek caught Mike watching him and Lindsey. His friend gave Derek the classic sly Mike grin. Lindsey must have caught it too because she looked up at him and whispered.

"How long have you and Mike known each other?"

Derek considered this. "Since second grade, I think. Damn, a long time."

"Really?" Lindsey looked shocked. "I had no idea."

"Yeah, we lived down the street from each other. Used to play outside almost every day. We stayed friends all the way through high school. Lost touch a little after that but we caught up again. It's nice having a friend that's known you that long."

"I bet," Lindsey said. Derek put his arm around her shoulder and pulled her in close to him. He placed another kiss on the top of her head and inhaled the sweet fruity scent of her shampoo. It was hard to keep his hands off her. He'd like to kiss her for real but wasn't sure if she was ready for that kind of public display of affection.

Soon they were seated and enjoying an amazing dinner. He was quick to inform their server that he and Lindsey were together, and she smiled, grabbing his leg under the table before leaning closer to him. So maybe she didn't have a problem with them being obvious. He gave her a wink. Once everyone was finished, they decided to head over to the nightclub.

The club required a walk through the main casino floor, and Derek watched Lindsey taking in the lights, sounds, and flash of it all.

"Wanna try some slots?" he asked.

"No way, I can't."

"Blackjack? Poker?" Derek pointed to the rows of tables. "If I was inclined to gamble, poker would be my game. At least then you feel like skill plays a part, although it's still mainly luck."

"The odds are not in your favor no matter what," she said. Derek stopped and pulled her close. He glanced ahead to see that their group had kept moving. The lights of the room flashed in her beautiful eyes and he leaned down to kiss her. She kissed him back, her lips tasting like cherry lip gloss. He lifted his head and rested his nose against hers.

"Everything's a gamble, Linds. You just have to decide if it's worth the risk."

She nodded. Their voices were fairly loud due to the noise, but there was no way anyone would hear their exchange. They could only hear one another. "I think you're worth the risk," she said.

He gave her a slow grin and then squeezed her hand in his.

A siren went off behind them, and everyone in the near vicinity turned to the corner of the room where a giant board of lights began to flash on top of a cluster of quarter slot machines. Several people started clapping and cheering.

Derek leaned down and spoke to Lindsey over the

noise. "Some lucky bastard just won the ten-thousand-dollar jackpot."

When he looked at her face he frowned. She just stared toward the corner where the lights flashed, her eyes narrowing. "That's my dad."

Twenty-One

Lindsey felt like she was going to pass out. At first she thought she'd been seeing things, but no, there he was, grin wide, as a casino employee headed over and shook his hand. The two men laughed and chatted. And still she watched in shock. They appeared to know each other. Lindsey started toward them.

"Linds, wait." Derek tried to grab her arm but she shook him off.

When she was near enough she spoke. "Daddy?"

Her father's head jerked in her direction and instantly he looked ashen. His eyes scanned the crowd but as soon as he made eye contact with her again his expression went from horror to panic. "Lindsey, I just won. Can you believe it?"

"No, Dad. I can't. What are you doing here?"

Just then another older man with a floral Hawaiian-style shirt smacked her father on the back. "Isn't this your second win this month, Isaac?"

Lindsey gasped and her father's eyes darted right to her, full of shame. She was going to be sick. She felt

Derek squeeze her hand again, but she yanked it from his grasp.

"Daddy, please tell me you haven't been gambling every time I give you money. Please." The words didn't even make sense as they came out of her mouth. He'd been broke. Down on his luck. She'd been helping him.

"Answer me, damn it."

Everyone had gone silent. Even the gaming around them had stopped, only the jingle of unused machines could be heard. He didn't say a word. His face was full of shame, his mouth falling open. She knew it had shocked him to hear her speak like that but she couldn't bring herself to care. Finally he stepped forward.

"Mi hija, I can explain. I only come here once in a while."

"Once in a while? Is that why you've already won twice this month? Why this guy knew your name?" She pointed at the idiot in the ridiculous shirt.

"It's not like that, Lindsey." He shook his head. She noticed the crowd had begun to thin and she knew their confrontation was making a lot of them uncomfortable.

"Dad, do you know that I'm broke all the time? Can you explain to me why my dreams have all been put on hold while I continue to loan you money? You told me your water was going to get shut off."

"That was the truth!" He had the audacity to look indignant.

"So you thought the answer was throwing my money into the toilet?"

"I just won, didn't I?" He held his hand up to the flashing $10,000 sign.

"But how much have you lost in order to win? And I

have a hard time believing I would have ever found out about this win. That's my money, Dad." This time she pointed at the sign. "But obviously you would have sunk it all back into these stupid machines."

His eyes darted from side to side. And he looked so lost. And old. She hated that she stood here still feeling sorry for him when all he deserved was her anger.

"I can't believe you would do this to me, Daddy."

Her father reached out an arm. "Lindsey . . ."

She stepped back, out of his reach, as tears began to roll down her face. She had truly thought this man had needed her. Always had, and she'd been there for him time and again. Sacrificed so much to care for him. Not just recently, but her entire life.

The warm wall of Derek's chest closed in around her, his hand going to her waist. She'd almost forgotten he was there, and now her shame deepened.

"Who are you?" her father asked, his eyes on Derek. As if he had a right to question anything about her or her life.

"I'm the man that your daughter's going to be able to count on." His voice rumbled against her back and she didn't miss the anger in his words. "Come on, Lindsey."

He pulled her away from her father, causing her a mix of relief and sadness. They headed back the way they'd come, and before she knew it they were getting on the elevator. "What are we doing? The party . . ."

"I'll deal with that," he said. Derek pulled her into his chest and wrapped his arms around her. Closing her eyes she leaned her forehead into his chest.

"How much have you given him?" Derek asked.

She shook her head against him, not wanting to say it out loud. She was so ashamed for falling for her father's lies.

"Please tell me it's not as much as he just won."

"Half that."

"Goddamn it," Derek said under his breath. "I can't believe how much I wanted to punch your dad."

"Please, can we not talk about it anymore?"

He squeezed her tighter. "I'm sorry. I shouldn't have said that. I would never hurt your father. Probably."

She would laugh but she was too overcome with anger and sadness. Mel would just die when she found out, and that thought only added to Lindsey's humiliation.

In the past year alone she'd given her father nearly $2,000. Since she'd dropped out of college it had been even more. Close to $6,000. And that didn't even take into account that she'd moved in with him and gotten a job after his heart attack so he could take time off and recover. She'd given up so much for her father and here she'd found him gambling it all away.

When they stepped out of the elevator, she registered that Derek was on the phone beside her. It sounded as if he were speaking to Mike, probably telling him what had happened. But she didn't even care, her emotions were all she could focus on.

Her phone vibrated. She looked down. It was her dad. She ignored it. He immediately called again but she ignored that one also. When they got to Derek's room he pulled out a card key, quickly sliding it in and out. As soon as the door opened Lindsey slipped inside. The room was identical to the girls' room and she walked

right into the bathroom and shut the door, locking it
behind her. And then she cried.

"Linds. Let me in, babe." Derek knocked softly on the
bathroom door. She'd been in there for thirty minutes.
At first he'd let her be, realizing that she was in pain.
But now he was starting to worry.

After he'd called Mike, the girls had come up
wanting to see her, but Lindsey hadn't wanted to talk
to anyone so he'd convinced them to go ahead and
have fun. Just as he'd told her father, he planned to be
the one to take care of her. And he meant it. This was
his woman, the only one for him, and he would do
whatever he had to do to keep her happy.

Keep her his.

He leaned his forehead against the cold metal door
just in time to hear some shuffling, the water turn on for
a moment, and then the lock click. Standing straight,
he waited for her to appear in the doorway. As soon as
she did he opened his arms, and sighed in relief when
she walked right into them.

"Talk to me," he said.

"In a minute," she whispered, her arms squeezing his
waist. Derek laid his cheek on the top of her head and
inhaled. God, he loved holding her.

This was what he wanted, to be the person she went
to when she was upset. He wanted to fix whatever was
wrong for her. Take care of her. He wanted a second
chance to be her everything.

After a long moment Lindsey tilted her head up to
him, her eyes red and her cheeks a little splotchy. Still
she was beautiful. Derek pulled some hair out of the

wet tears on her face and motioned for her to lie down on the bed. He lay down beside her and was grateful when she reinserted herself into his arms without any hesitation.

"I guess my dad has a gambling addiction." Her voice was small and resigned.

"That's what it looks like. I'm so sorry."

"I am mad. So *mad*. All this time I truly thought I was helping him. I knew he was bad with money, but I never dreamed he was knowingly taking advantage of me."

Derek continued to stroke her hair as he spoke. "I'm not going to stick up for the guy, but you have to remember that it is an addiction. He didn't want to hurt you."

She shook her head. "I'm sure he didn't want to. Doesn't make me feel any better."

The unspoken truth in the room was that he'd done the same thing. Hurt her even when he didn't want to.

"I still don't know how he could do this to me," she whispered.

Derek pulled her tighter into his arms when her tears started up again. Unsure of how else to comfort her, he kissed her temple, her cheek. When she finally lifted her face to his he kissed her gently. He was afraid she might stop him, and if she did that would be fine. But he was grateful when she kissed him back. At first their lips lazily slipped against one another but it wasn't long before she scooted up on the bed, her kiss becoming feverish and wild.

"Lindsey, we don't have to do this," he whispered. She was licking down the side of his neck, working her fingers under his pants.

"I want you. Please. Make love to me, Derek."

There was no denying that request from this woman's lips. He couldn't have stopped himself if his life depended on it. He unzipped her dress, sliding it down her shoulders as she clawed at his clothing.

"Slow down, babe. I don't want to rip your dress."

"I don't care. Rip it off." Her hands were pulling at his shirt like she couldn't get enough. Derek rolled her onto her back, grabbed her hands and held them over her head.

"What are you doing?" she asked, her voice breathy. He loved how full and swollen her lips were from kissing him. Probably from crying also.

"I'm making you slow down. Now don't move." He leveled her with a stare. "Promise?"

She closed her eyes in annoyance. "Promise," she whispered.

"Not even your hands. Keep them right here."

"Okay."

Derek pushed off the bed, never taking his eyes off hers as he slid her dress down her body. The dress he loved even more when he noticed that it required no bra. Her panties came next, and he kissed the arch of her foot as he pulled them off and dropped them on the floor. And still her eyes stayed on him. He almost couldn't tell if she was focused on him or thinking. He didn't want her thinking or worrying. Only feeling.

"You with me, Lindsey?" he asked, his hands going to his shirt. She nodded. Now he allowed himself to take in the sight of her there, laid out for him on the bed. She shifted her body, obviously a little embarrassed at being on display.

"Good. I know you just want an escape right now. And I'm going to give it to you."

He pulled his shirt off, his pants, and his underwear, all the while watching her breasts rise and fall. When he was completely naked he crawled back up the bed and laid his body down on hers.

"Touch me, Linds," he said quietly. She did, her fingers caressing his back, sliding down to cup his ass.

Derek angled up, holding his weight on his forearms, and nudged her thighs apart with his knees. Instinctively she pulled her legs up, wrapping them around his waist, giving him all the room he needed to slide into her.

"This is what I needed," she whispered.

Derek looked down at her upturned face, her eyes bright and intense. "I'll give you this anytime you want." He pulled back out before pushing in once more.

He began a steady rhythm of slow thrusts and before long she began to arch her body up to meet him. "That's so good, Linds."

She gripped his waist, pulling him down harder against her. "Faster."

He grinned down at her and then nuzzled into her neck. "I like it slow."

"Please, Derek." Her nails pierced his back and her breathy moans finally urged him on. He pushed up and rested on his fists before he began to pound into her.

"Oh God." Lindsey smiled and let her eyes close.

They climaxed together and for a long moment she seemed unable to catch her breath.

Derek rolled over and pulled her against him. Within moments she was fast asleep.

Twenty-Two

The following Tuesday Lindsey pulled into a parking spot on Main Street. Before exiting her car she flipped open her vanity mirror and checked her face. She looked a fright, mascara shadows under her eyes, her hair tangled because after her shower this morning she'd let it air-dry in chunks.

She'd been up late the night before doing very important things. Such as perusing Pinterest, updating her Etsy site with a few new pieces she'd made, and basically trying not to feel sorry for herself.

Trying and failing because today she felt pretty damn sorry for herself. She was angry and still in shock over her father gambling all her money away. He'd continued trying to call her Sunday but had finally given up. Thank goodness, because she just wasn't ready to speak to him and wasn't sure when she would be. She was certain he wouldn't show up at Mel's because he wouldn't want Mel to know if he could help it.

Lindsey hadn't even told her sister. Not to protect her father, but because she was so ashamed. She would tell her . . . eventually. She was just waiting for the right time. Preferably when they didn't live under the same roof. Although now even that felt further and further away.

After putting on a little lip gloss, she got out of the car and headed down the sidewalk toward Callie's Confections. It was nearly two o'clock and she'd spent the day at the farmhouse doing her last project, which was a cute little entryway table for inside the front door. She'd found it on someone's curb last week and knew that it would be perfect with some love and care. After three hours of work this morning she was in need of coffee and cookies.

She pulled open the door, the familiar jingle sounding her arrival, and then stopped dead in her tracks. Derek and his son were standing at the counter chatting with Eric. Just as she was contemplating how she would handle the situation, Tanner turned and saw her.

He smiled wide. "Hey, look, Dad. It's Lindsey."

Stunned, Lindsey glanced from face to face. Derek looked as surprised as she did. Catching Eric's eye she saw him put a finger up to his mouth, drawing a smile. *Oh, right.*

She obeyed, forcing out a smile, and after a second, Derek reciprocated. They'd only spoken once on the phone since the morning she'd left the casino, but it was fine. He had informed her that Tanner was on spring break this week and he'd be a little occupied.

"Hi, guys." Lindsey stepped farther into the bakery. "What a surprise." It was, and in that moment she remembered how awful she looked. She lifted a hand to her ratty hair, wishing she'd never walked out the front door in such a state.

"It is a surprise." Derek grinned.

Although they were supposed to be dating, they had yet to discuss how to handle being around his son. She decided to just pretend they were friends.

Behind the counter Eric cleared his throat. Lindsey looked up to find him holding out a to-go coffee cup. "Have you come for this?"

She stepped up to the counter and took the cup. "I did. Thank you." She looked down at Tanner and then up at his very handsome father. She still couldn't get over how similar they looked. "What are you guys up to today?"

"We're going to a movie," Tanner said. "But we came here to get cookies. That's why I have this hoodie on, so I can stuff them in my pockets."

"Smart. I'd take Callie's cookies over Milk Duds any day. But I'd still need movie popcorn, that's my favorite."

Tanner looked up at his father—who'd been staring at her the whole time—and then back to Lindsey. "Dad, she should come with us."

"Oh, that's so nice, but . . ." She smiled down at him and he looked so hopeful. She quickly raised her eyes up to Derek, hoping he'd be ready with an easy out for her.

"You *should* come. It's a good idea," he said. Lindsey's mouth dropped open in shock.

Her reaction must have been humorous because Derek gave a silent chuckle and then looked down at his son. "It's okay, bud, I'm sure Lindsey is just really busy."

"No! I mean, okay. I'll come with you." If he was willing to include her with his son, she was going to accept.

Derek's eyes darted back to hers. "Really?"

"Sure. What are you seeing?"

"Horned Troopers."

Lindsey blew out a breath, her first bit of doubt creeping in. But she laughed it off. "Okaaay. But first, I'll have to get some cookies for me."

Eric stepped over to the counter, ready with a bag. "What kind?"

"Peanut butter," she said.

When Eric walked down to the register Derek was already standing there with a five-dollar bill. Eric took it without question.

Derek didn't even bother looking at her as he took the change and shoved it in his pocket. "When Tan and I take a woman on a movie date, we pay. Right, bud?"

"But this is the first time we've been on a date, Dad."

At that, Derek did turn and wink at Lindsey. "Hear that? First movie date. You must be real special."

"I feel special," she said, smiling at Tanner. "Before we go can you guys give me a minute? I'm gonna use the restroom and I'll be right back."

Lindsey headed back through the kitchen door, tossing her empty coffee cup in the trash can. Callie always let them use the employee restroom in the back and that was right where she went. Lindsey flipped on the light and began digging through the basket on the small shelf near the door.

"Thank God," she whispered to herself when she found a bag of beauty products. She couldn't imagine

Callie not having something back here. She unzipped it and found some random makeup, a brush, and thankfully some toothpaste.

Within four minutes Lindsey looked much better. It was a fine line between freshening up and not looking like she'd gone into the kitchen as one person and come out as another. She didn't want it to be that obvious. She washed her hands, checked herself one more time, and made her way back out front to find Eric alone behind the counter.

"They're waiting in the car. They've got your cookies," he said.

Lindsey walked over to Eric. Thankfully the store was empty at the moment. She spoke quickly. "Tell me it's okay, Eric."

"To go out with a hottie? Obviously it's okay."

"A hottie and his *son*," she clarified. "That's different. It means something."

"It means this man is into you. Let him be."

"Thank you." She reached up and kissed Eric on the cheek before heading toward the front door. She stepped outside and suddenly the weather appeared to be a whole lot nicer, the sun brighter, and her body felt light.

"Over here," a deep voice called from her right.

Derek stood beside his Mercedes waiting for her, Tanner was already inside. She walked over, nerves tingling. She was going to go somewhere with Derek and his son. She was either crazy or insanely crazy. He was blocking the passenger side door and remained there when she walked off the curb and up to him.

He'd put sunglasses on but she could still feel his eyes on her. "I'm glad you said yes."

"Me, too. But are you sure this is a good idea?"

"No idea. I've never had another woman around my son, ever. But sure as hell feels right. What do you think?"

She nodded.

"Okay then."

"I want him to like me."

Derek reached out and gave her hand a quick squeeze. "Pretty sure he already does."

She hoped that was true. Derek opened her door and Lindsey sat down. She immediately turned and looked into the backseat. Tanner was focused on a small game device in his lap.

"Hey, thanks for letting me tag along."

He looked up at her. "You're welcome."

She straightened and put her seat belt on just as Derek opened the driver side door and got in. "We ready?" he said to no one and started the engine.

They were all awkwardly silent on the drive into the city, save for the sounds coming from Tanner's game and the low hum of the radio. After a while Derek glanced in her direction. "You should really learn not to talk so much."

Lindsey glanced at him and then over her shoulder before whispering, "Sorry. I'm just a little . . . nervous."

"Don't be nervous," Tanner said. "Right, Dad?"

Lindsey's eyes went wide and she knew she was blushing. She gave a quiet laugh and looked down at her lap. She'd been so sure Tanner was too engrossed in his game to hear, but apparently not. Derek reached over and grabbed her thigh. She caught his hand with hers and squeezed.

Ten minutes later Derek pulled into the parking lot. Once out he opened Tanner's door and they all walked toward the giant theater building, Tanner skipping ahead.

"You think you can handle *Horned Warriors*?" Derek said with a grin.

"Well, considering I've never even heard of them, it should be interesting."

"You're in for a treat, Ms. Morales."

Their hands brushed as they walked and Lindsey felt the contact zing through her entire body. Derek was in full dad mode today, wearing jeans, T-shirt, and tennis shoes. She liked him like that. She was starting to see that he could pull off any look he tried, although naked was probably her favorite.

They stepped up to the ticket counter and she hung back and let him get the tickets. Tanner stood beside her so she glanced down at him. She wasn't sure what to say, but she wanted him to be comfortable. "Is this the first *Horned Warriors* movie?"

"Second," he said.

She waited to see if he added anything else but he didn't. Okay. So he wasn't much of a talker. She was so used to Claire, who said whatever popped into her head. But she liked that about him, he was a cool little guy. Both of these guys were cool and even more so as a pair.

Once they were inside, loaded with drinks and popcorn, they found the correct theater. Lindsey started to feel nervous about the seating arrangement. Derek went in first, walking up the steps and then taking a center row. Tanner had run ahead and sat down right next to his father. If Lindsey took the next available seat that would leave Tanner between them. She didn't want to assume so she began to sit down in the first empty seat.

"Don't you wanna sit by my dad?" Tanner asked, looking up at her.

"Oh, okay." She scooted in front of his legs, then Derek's—which of course she brushed against—and then sat down next to him. He turned his head to look at her.

"Relax," he whispered.

"What do you mean? I'm totally relaxed." Lindsey set her drink in the cup holder and then got situated in her seat. She felt Derek's eyes on her the entire time so she finally looked over at him.

"I know I already said it. But I'm really glad you're here," he whispered.

"Me, too."

"You been okay?"

"Yes."

"Have you talked to your dad?"

She shook her head. "Not yet. I will eventually. Just not ready."

Before he could respond Tanner pulled Derek's attention away. Just as well, since she didn't really want to discuss anything depressing. She just wanted to enjoy her first date with Derek and his son.

Twenty-Three

Nearly two hours later they walked out into the bright sun, squinting as they found their way through the parking lot toward Derek's car. He glanced over at his son and Lindsey who were discussing the movie.

Lindsey hadn't been the only nervous one today, although he'd tried really hard not to show it. Derek knew it was risky, taking her out with Tanner. He wasn't sure what he'd tell his son later. But no matter what, he was happy as hell she was there. It felt like this was how things were supposed to be. As if she were meant to walk into that bakery and plug herself into his and Tanner's world.

The adorable look on Lindsey's face when she'd seen them there was just an added bonus. And he'd known full well she'd been embarrassed about how she looked, but damn, she looked good no matter what. It was cute but unnecessary that she'd obviously gone into the restroom and tried to fix herself up.

"So, was it as good as you expected?" Lindsey asked as she opened the car door for Tanner.

His son's face scrunched up in contemplation. "It was okay. The plot was a little weak, but the CGI was amazing. I give it a C plus."

Derek laughed at the shock on Lindsey's face. "We're kind of movie buffs around here. Right, Tan?"

"Yeah, we see one almost every Dad weekend. My mom is glad because she never wants to see boy movies."

He was happy that Lindsey didn't react to the comment about Lisa. Once they were all in and buckled up he headed back to Preston, Tanner absorbed in his 3DS. Derek reached out and grabbed her hand, pulling it over to rest on his thigh. She glanced up at him quickly but he caught a hint of a smile on her face.

"Dad, do you think it was realistic that Keletron was able to kill him with that saber? I thought he went down way too easy."

Derek grinned and looked over at Lindsey. "He usually has to let things marinate a while before he wants to hash it out."

For the next twenty minutes the three of them discussed the probability of three mutated frogs managing to save the world from aliens. These were the conversations he loved having with his kid and he was surprised at how quickly Lindsey jumped in and joined them.

Tanner laughed at Lindsey's comments and the two of them even shared some opinions. It was nice. Way too damn nice. Derek was so used to feeling like it was he and Tanner against the world, or even just him trying to figure out parenting as a single dad while simultaneously dealing with his ex. Lindsey was just so sweet, and easy to be around. He could tell his son liked her. In fact, he was pretty certain he owed Tanner something awesome for inviting her along. Derek wasn't sure what he'd have said if his son hadn't spoken up. Now he didn't want their date to end.

"How about we get some dinner and take it home?" Derek asked. He turned to Lindsey. "You have plans for tonight?"

"Uhhh, no. I guess not."

Derek glanced in the rearview mirror. Tanner was looking down at his game. "What about you, Tan? Cool if Lindsey has dinner with us?"

"Yep." He didn't even look up from his 3DS.

"Sounds unanimous. We can swing by and get your car and pick something up in Preston," Derek said. "How about Chinese? Tanner and I can take down chicken fried rice like it's our last meal."

"And egg rolls," Tanner called out. Obviously he was catching everything even though he looked completely absorbed in his device. He'd have to remember that.

"And egg rolls." Derek nodded. "How about you, Lindsey?"

"Well, I like chicken fried rice. But I also like vegetables."

"Vegetables, gross!" Tanner made a gagging sound from the backseat. Lindsey laughed along with Derek.

"Don't worry, I'll buy you all the vegetables you want." Derek gave Lindsey a wink.

Full of fried rice, egg rolls, and a mountain of moo goo gai pan, Lindsey began to gather up all of the empty cartons on Derek's kitchen table.

"You don't need to do all that." Strong arms wrapped

around her from behind and Lindsey leaned back into Derek's chest.

"I don't mind picking up," she said. She laughed as he kissed the side of her neck, nipping playfully with his teeth. She lowered her voice and glanced around. "What if someone comes in here?"

Derek removed the trash from her hands and then turned her in his arms so they were facing one another. "Someone is taking a shower."

"Oh, well. In that case." Lindsey angled her head and kissed Derek. His mouth was warm and inviting. His tongue teased her lips until she opened up to him. She was pretty sure she would never get tired of kissing this man.

"I wish you could stay the night," he whispered against her lips.

Lindsey pulled back, looking into his eyes. "Me too, but I can soon enough."

"True, but I really want you now."

She slapped at his chest and then shoved him out of the way so she could throw all of the cartons she'd stacked in the trash can.

"A little over a week until Anne and Mike's wedding," Derek said. He leaned against the counter. "Hard to believe."

"I know. Seems like we just started on that house."

He smiled. "Turned out good, though. What did Anne think of the island?"

Lindsey gave him a long look. "What do you think? She loved it. As I knew she would."

"I'm glad. You did great on that house, Lindsey."

"We both did." Lindsey picked up one of the fortune cookies on the table for herself and handed one to Derek.

He shook his head. "I don't do fortune cookies."

"How come? They're just for fun. There's no truth to them."

He shrugged. "Just don't. Never have."

"What a party pooper." And how odd of him. Lindsey cracked open her cookie and pulled the paper out. She read it quietly to herself.

"Well?" Derek urged.

"Why should I read it? You don't do fortune cookies."

Derek snatched the paper from her fingers and read it aloud. " 'You are about to embark on a delightful journey.' "

He looked her in the eye, dropped the paper, and then snatched his own cookie off the table. After ripping the cellophane open, he pulled out the cookie, cracked it, and extracted the paper. " 'If a turtle doesn't have a shell, is it naked or homeless?' What the—"

Lindsey giggled and picked up another cookie. "Try again."

She opened the wrapper and handed it to him. He stared at it a minute and then read. " 'If you want the rainbow, you must put up with the rain.' "

"See, that's a good one." She stepped closer to him.

Derek grabbed her hand and pulled her to him. "I hope I'm your delightful journey."

"I hope I'm your rainbow."

He looked into her eyes. "Always. Or you can be my naked turtle. Take your pick."

Footsteps pounding down the steps quickly separated

them. Derek gave Lindsey a quick wink and then lifted the full trash bag from the can. "I'm going to run this outside."

"Okay, Dad," Tanner said.

Derek went out through the garage door and Lindsey glanced at the boy sitting down at the kitchen table. She had no idea what to say to him. With his hair wet from his shower he looked so young. She handed him a fortune cookie and he began to open it.

"My dad likes you." Tanner looked at Lindsey, his words shocking her. She sat down so she didn't hover over him.

"Oh. Well, I like him, too." She watched as he turned the folded cookie over in his small fingers. She could tell that this conversation was important to him.

"Good. I'm glad. Don't worry, I promised Dad I won't tell Mom about you. It'd just make her madder, and she'd call her lawyer again."

Lindsey's mouth dropped open and she shifted in her seat, suddenly dizzy. *Call her lawyer.* The words buzzed in her head. *Again.*

Lindsey knew that things weren't great between Derek and his ex, but could she be part of the problem?

The garage door creaked and footsteps announced Derek was back in the kitchen. She couldn't turn around. Couldn't look at him. Things were just starting to seem so good, so strong, but could she make things even worse for him and Tanner? She blinked a few times.

"What's up?" Derek said. He must have sensed something was off. She decided right then she'd save the conversation for later. Having it in front of Tanner wouldn't be good.

"Nothing," she said. She glanced at Tanner who had taken a bite out of his cookie.

Derek frowned. "Hey, Tan, why don't you go brush your teeth."

"I already brushed."

"And you just took a bite of that cookie. Go brush again." Derek's words were strained and a little harsh.

Lindsey watched as Tanner's worried eyes darted from her to his father. Here Lisa was already causing stress between them. After a moment's hesitation Tanner got up and she heard him run up the stairs.

Derek instantly squatted down in front of her chair. "What happened?"

"Tanner told me . . . It's not his fault. But he said . . ." She wasn't even sure how to explain the conversation they'd just had. "Is seeing me going to upset your ex-wife?"

Derek sighed, his shoulders dropping. "Lindsey."

"What? If my being here is going to affect your relationship with your son you need to tell me."

"What did Tanner say to you?" he asked.

"He told me that he wouldn't tell his mom I'm here. That she'd be mad and then call her lawyer again."

"Damn." Derek stood up and ran his hands through his hair. "I don't want you to worry about this, Linds."

"How can I not? A child—*your* child—just told me that he planned to keep me a secret so his mother wouldn't get mad." Her words came out a clipped whisper. "And I'm not blaming him. Just so we're clear. I feel horrible that he even had to think those things about me. It's humiliating if you want me to be honest."

"Don't say that. This is not about you, this is about

me and her. She's angry at me. Only me. Has been for a long time."

"Does it really matter who she's angry at? If I make it worse . . . I can't live with that, Derek."

All these years she'd convinced herself that the only person who was hurt when she and Derek had broken up was her. She was wrong. Derek had cared for her, but he'd loved his son more. How could he not? This little human that looked like him, laughed like him, and smiled like him. It was apparent to her now that he might have to make that choice again.

And he shouldn't.

"What will she do if she finds out?" Lindsey asked. Derek had pulled a kitchen chair around and sat down across from her, their knees touching.

"She's already found out. She saw the newspaper article, which made it seem like we were already a couple. And damn it, it wasn't wrong. You are mine."

"What did she do, Derek?"

"She threatened to keep Tanner away from me." His words were quiet. Low. Lindsey couldn't believe what she'd heard. With that admission he now looked so anguished. Exhausted. Still, he reached out and touched her, wrapped one of her hands in his.

"Is she capable of that?" Lindsey asked.

"I'd like to say no." Derek began to play with her fingers as he spoke. Outlining them with his own, down the side of one, into the crevice between them, and over the next. "I pay child support and alimony. Never miss. If she asks for extra I give it. But I've learned not to underestimate her. She blames me for ruining her life by marrying her. She's never forgiven me for it. And now, the fact that you and I are seeing each other again . . . it makes her angry because she knows we dated after I broke up with her in college. Knows I always cared for you even though I married her."

Lindsey almost couldn't blame Lisa for some of her anger. She would be devastated to find herself caught in a loveless marriage with a small child. But they'd both made the decision. It wasn't only Derek's fault.

Lindsey let her head fall forward. This relationship was a roller coaster. They were like two ships that continued to collide in the night, throwing passengers overboard right and left. It was madness, and while every part of her screamed at her to fight for this man, could she do that knowing it might mean he'd potentially lose more time with his son?

"I don't know what to think right now," she said.

"You don't need to think about this at all, Lindsey. I'll handle this. I promise."

She couldn't believe what he was saying. "I'm not interested in being in a relationship where you deal with all the problems, Derek. This affects me. It affects your son. That's the most important thing in your life. Maybe the universe is trying to tell us something."

"Ughrrrr." A painful growl came from deep in his throat. "Fuck the universe. I love you, Lindsey. I loved you then. I love you now. It just needs to be that simple. It *is* that simple."

"Except it's not. We keep trying to make this happen and everything keeps reminding us that this isn't working. It didn't work the first time. Why did we think it would work now?"

Derek looked into her eyes. "Because you're the

woman that makes me happy. Because I want to make you happy. Because when I see you teasing and joking with my son I feel a peace inside that I didn't know I could ever have."

Oh God, his words were going to rip her in two. But she needed to be strong. For him. For Tanner. Most importantly, for herself.

"I think you need to get this figured out with Lisa before anything else. I can't be the person that takes your son from you. Then you'll end up resenting me the way Lisa did you. That won't work."

"Do you love me, Lindsey?" His eyes never left hers, waiting intently for her answer.

She considered lying. Or not answering. She'd never told him she'd loved him and wasn't sure this was the time. But she couldn't keep secrets from him. The things they didn't share were destroying them from the inside out. "Yes. I love you very much. Which is exactly why we have to give this time."

Derek scooted forward onto the edge of his chair and grasped her face, one hand cupping each side. "If you love me then don't pull away from me."

"I'm not pulling away. I'm giving us room to figure things out."

"That sounds a lot like pulling away."

Lindsey rested her forehead on his. "Derek. Right now the only thing that matters is doing what's right for Tanner. And he needs you."

He shook his head against hers. "The last time I did that I lost you. I can't lose you again."

"Then don't," she whispered. "I'm trusting you, Derek. Start trusting yourself."

With those words lingering between them Lindsey placed a kiss on Derek's forehead, stood, and left.

Derek grabbed Tanner's bag from the back of his truck and followed his son up the sidewalk to the front door of his mother's house. Tanner walked right in but Derek stood on the step, waiting for Lisa to appear.

Derek was apprehensive about the task before him, but there was no going back. After Lindsey had left Tuesday, he'd agonized over the best way to handle the situation with Lisa. He'd quickly come to the conclusion that the only option was to deal with it head-on. Lying and omission had only hurt the people he cared about in the past, and he wouldn't make that mistake again. There was too much at stake. Even more importantly, Derek had completely sent the wrong message to Tanner and now he needed to make things right. You didn't hide the truth or deny the one you loved for any reason. You fought for it, and he intended to make Lisa understand that he was willing to deal with whatever came his way, with Lindsey beside him.

"Mom," Tanner yelled from the entryway. "I'm home."

Lisa came down the stairs and smiled at their son, genuine love and happiness on her face. "Hey, baby. I missed you so much."

"I missed you, too." Tanner immediately wrapped his arms around his mother's waist. Lisa's eyes met Derek's over Tanner's head.

"Hi," Derek said. "Can we talk a minute?"

"I guess," she said, her tone neutral. Probably for Tanner's benefit.

"Hey, bud, can you give me and your mom a minute?" Derek asked.

Tanner grabbed his bag off the floor and eyed them both for a second. "Sure." He headed up the stairs.

"Join me?" Derek nodded toward the steps out front.

Lisa didn't respond but came outside. Today she sported gray yoga pants and an oversized T-shirt. She looked younger, but then again, he supposed she *was* young, barely thirty. She'd become a mother way too soon and been thrust into a life neither of them had been prepared for.

Derek sat down on the top step and motioned for her to do the same.

"What's going on, Derek?" she asked.

"I just felt like we should talk." He was grateful that she seemed calm. Willing.

"You do realize we're not very good at that," she said, her tone dry.

"Yeah, I do, but that doesn't mean it's impossible."

When they were both comfortable, both facing the yard, not looking at one another, Derek spoke. "Lisa, I want to apologize to you."

The air changed as her body tightened next to him. She lifted her hands in front of her and became a little too interested in her cuticles. But he knew she was listening.

"To be clear, I don't regret the past. We have Tanner and that makes everything we went through worth it. But I wish . . . I wish I had handled things differently back then. I thought we were doing the right thing by getting married. I know we were both scared . . ."

"And pressured," she said quietly.

"Yeah, there was definitely pressure. But I should have been looking out for both of us. And our son. And I failed. Failed me, failed you, and failed another person that was important to me."

When Lisa didn't reply, Derek turned to face her, forearms resting on his knees. "You were right. I knew Lindsey back then. We dated right after you and I broke up and I was completely in love with her. Still am. It wasn't fair to you that we married under the conditions we did. But I tried, Lisa. I did."

She swiped a tear from her eyes and turned away so he couldn't see her face. "I know you did. But so did I."

"You did. I know that. But we didn't love each other and we have to forgive one another or we're never going to be able to move on."

They were both silent for a moment, the only sounds the trees rustling in the breeze and the occasional sniff from the woman sitting next to him. He wasn't going to comfort her physically, but her tears did make him sad. The whole thing was sad, but they could get past it. If they tried.

"I want us both to be happy, Lisa. Did you mean it about this Lane guy? Does he make you happy?"

Finally she sat up straight and sucked in a breath. "Yes. I think so. Sometimes I'm not even sure what a healthy relationship is supposed to feel like."

"Does he make you happy, Lisa? Is he there for you? Support you, care about your feelings?" Derek paused before he went on. "Does he love Tanner?"

Lisa nodded and finally met Derek's eyes. "He does. They get along really well. Even when Tanner talks about you, which is often." She let out an awkward laugh.

Derek grinned. "I will always be the coolest guy in his life. You know that."

She rolled her eyes. "Whatever."

He'd never considered how difficult it would be to be the other person trying to fit into an already made family. It had to be hard, scary. He didn't want Lindsey to feel that way, only wanted her to know she was needed. Wanted. Derek lowered his voice before he spoke again. "Lisa, I want you to be happy. If it's with Lane, great. If not, I want you to find the person that will give you that. But I need you to respect the fact that I still love Lindsey and want her in my life. In Tanner's life."

When she didn't respond he continued. "I can't constantly fear that you're going to take time with Tanner away from me. I'll fight you, you know that."

Finally she nodded. "I know. And I won't, okay? Is that what you need to hear? Tanner loves you. Needs you."

Derek nodded. Relief settled heavily throughout his body. "Yeah. It is what I need to hear."

Lisa sighed and then slapped her hands on her thighs. "Are we done, then?"

Derek glanced at her. They would probably never be friends. But he hoped they could be allies instead of enemies. Their son deserved that. They deserved it, too. "I mean it, Lisa. I am sorry. I never wanted you to be unhappy."

Lisa looked at him, her lips quirked. "I know you didn't."

With that she went inside.

Twenty-Four

Thursday morning Lindsey carried Eden down to the mailbox. It was a beautiful day, spring was in full swing, the sun bright and the flowers blooming. She kneeled down by a patch of bright pink tulips and let Eden touch the soft petals.

"Aren't they pretty, Ediepoo?" Lindsey asked.

Before she knew it Eden's fat little hand wrapped around the tulip, crushing it. "Uh-oh," Lindsey said, glancing around to make sure no one had seen. She knew Mel and Brett's complex took their landscaping seriously. She quickly pried open Eden's fingers and frowned at the sad state of the poor tulip. She pecked a kiss on Eden's cheek before speaking in her baby voice. "Sorry, tulip."

They continued down the sidewalk and Lindsey pulled the mailbox key out of her pocket. She grabbed the stack of mail, noticing the letter on top was addressed to her. Instantly she recognized Derek's boxy architect handwriting. Her heart fluttered and she couldn't hold back her smile.

Hitching Eden up on her hip, Lindsey ripped the envelope open. She pulled out the carefully folded paper and gasped. It was a two-paneled comic strip. The first panel showed a guy standing in front of an old house leaning against the porch. A girl sat on the steps looking up at him. She had long brown hair, red lips, and big eyes. The male's dialogue bubble read "Have we met before? My name's Derek."

Lindsey smiled instantly. He'd put so much detail into the scene and it was clearly the farmhouse. The second panel showed the female alone with an empty dialogue bubble. Below it was a note.

Your trust means everything to me. I finally trusted myself.

I love you. Always have, always will.

Tears began to pool in her eyes as she turned the envelope back over to make sure it had his complete address. It appeared to be his office.

When she'd left his place the other night she'd actually felt at peace. Sad, yes, but in her heart she'd known that things weren't over. Just on pause. She wanted to be a priority for Derek, but she could wait for him to do what he needed to do. She hoped this note meant that he'd done it. She said she'd trusted him, and despite everything they'd been through, she did.

Before she could lock the mailbox back up, a car pulled up to the curb. Her father. Lindsey took a deep breath and walked over to him. He got out, looking tired and thin. She hadn't noticed it before. Maybe she should have.

"Hi, Linds,"

"Dad," she said. Even though she'd had some time to think on it, she was still angry with him.

He walked up onto the sidewalk and grinned at Eden before looking at Lindsey.

"I came to apologize to you, Lindsey. You have no idea how ashamed I am."

She really wasn't sure how to respond. She couldn't say "it's okay" because it wasn't. She couldn't say she'd forgiven him, because she hadn't yet. But she was tired of being angry.

"Thank you for apologizing, Dad."

He nodded, lifting his hands to his hips. She knew this was difficult for him, but he would never understand how devastated she'd been by his betrayal. Funny that she found herself in this position with all the men in her life.

"Hey, Dad." Mel walked up behind Lindsey. "What are you doing here?"

Hearing Mel's voice, Eden rooted around searching for her mother, so Lindsey handed her over while she waited to see if her father was planning to own up to the reason for his visit. She figured there probably was no time like the present to get it all out there. Despite the fact that she knew Mel would let her have it when they were alone.

"Uh, I actually just came by to apologize to your sister."

Lindsey's stomach flopped. She really couldn't believe he was going to say it, but she had to admit, she admired him for it. She knew her father tended to live in denial so this was pretty huge for him.

Mel turned to Lindsey, pushing Eden's fist out of her face. "What for?"

"Melanie, I'm not proud of it. But your sister's been

helping me out the past six months. Well, she's always helping me out, but it's been . . . more, lately."

"Helping you out?" Mel asked, confused. She turned to Lindsey. An awkward silence hung in the air between them and finally their father continued.

"I also need to admit to you girls that I have . . . a gambling problem."

Mel's eyes closed slowly as she whispered, "Dad."

"I know, Mel. I know you're ashamed of me."

"Dad, stop," Lindsey said, hating the pitiful tone of his voice and the sadness in his face. No matter what, he was their father. "We're not ashamed. Just—"

"No, Lindsey," Mel interjected. "Don't cover for him. Dad, this is a load of crap. Did you know Lindsey is broke? How could you stomach taking money from your daughter when she doesn't even have a home to live in anymore?"

Lindsey fell silent. It was hard to argue her sister's logic. But at the same time, she needed to stop letting Mel stand up for her. She could handle this herself.

"Dad, Mel's right. I am broke and I was accepting that for now because I thought you truly needed my help. And you do need help, Dad. But I can't be the one to help you. You need to get some counseling."

"You're right, Linds." He looked off to the side, not wanting to meet their eyes. "Guy at the casino overheard our conversation. Said he's had a problem for years. Gave me a flyer with a number on it."

"So he was still at the casino, but giving out advice?" Mel asked dryly.

"Hey, didn't say he'd cured himself. Just said he understood," Isaac Morales bit back. "I'm not expecting you girls to understand. I'm not asking for your sympathy. I just don't want this to come between us for good."

"It's a good place to start, Daddy. Call the number. It can't hurt. But you can't ask me for money ever again."

"Or me," Mel said. "We love you, Dad, but you can't do this to your kids again."

Lindsey looked at Mel in shock. Had their father been swindling them both?

"You're right, girls. I'm gonna knock this. I'm gonna try. And I am sorry, Linds. I mean it when I say I never meant to hurt you."

Those words sounded familiar "I know, Daddy."

He reached into his pocket and pulled out a check. He handed it to Lindsey and she read the amount. Four thousand dollars. Instantly she was flooded with relief for her own situation, but then concern for her father's. "Dad, did you use the rest of the money—"

"The rest of the money caught all my bills up and then went into the bank. I need to find a new job. I left the casino immediately after I cashed out. Haven't been back yet."

"Yet," Mel said. She glanced over Lindsey's shoulder at the check. "So you won this money?"

Isaac nodded. "It's a little hard to go out on a win like that. Makes me want to go again, but I realize that's the problem. I'm trying, girls."

Lindsey sighed. "You can do this, Dad. I know you can. And thank you."

She gave her dad a quick hug and after a few moments he got in his car and left. Mel, Eden, and Lindsey headed back up to the condo.

"Why didn't you tell me, Linds?" Mel asked.

"Well, clearly you've given him money, too. I didn't know that."

"It was a few years ago and I told him it was not going to become a habit."

It made Lindsey feel marginally better that she hadn't been the only sucker in the family. Just the most consistent.

"You know you can stay here as long as you need," Mel said as they went up the steps.

"I know, but you guys are a family. I need more space and I need to figure something out soon."

"I want you to tell me if you're struggling. Okay?"

Lindsey nodded, grateful to her sister.

"One more word of advice?" Mel said before they went up the stairs. "Get that check cashed ASAP."

Lindsey laughed. "Already planned on it."

Once she was back in her room she pulled out Derek's comic and placed it on her bed. Her life had been in such limbo lately. So many things had come to a head and she wasn't sure what was right or wrong any longer. Thankfully, her resentment toward her father had now ebbed a little. It would take time, but she wanted to forgive him. Everyone messed up and everyone deserved forgiveness. She'd recently learned that forgiving someone relieves a real physical burden. It takes a lot of strength to carry anger on your shoulders and she didn't want that any longer.

She owed that insight to Derek as strange it seemed. It made her smile to think how far they'd come together. His comic was a true starting over. And she missed him, thought of him. And she knew for certain that she was deeply in love with him.

She recalled the last thing she'd said to Derek. *Trust yourself.* Right now she planned to take her own advice.

For the fourth time Friday afternoon Derek walked to his office doorway and looked at Molly. She obviously didn't even have to lift her head to know he was standing there because her gaze stayed on her computer as she spoke.

"You've asked me four times. Don't you think if it had come I would have brought it to you? Good grief."

"Sorry. Of course you would." Derek sighed.

Molly finally glanced over, her face full of concern. "What are you hoping will come today?"

"Just . . . something. Nothing to be worried about."

"*Right,* you pacing the floor is very convincing." She laughed and then shook her head. "Go focus on something else. I can see the mailbox from my window so as soon as he pulls up I'll know."

Derek nodded. "Okay. Thank you, Molly." He stepped over behind her desk and looked out the window.

"Scram. I can't work very hard at perusing Pinterest while you're standing here. I feel guilty."

"Sure you do," Derek said.

He walked back into his office and plopped down in his desk chair. It was ridiculous to be so anxious. He wasn't even certain Lindsey would reply. Then again he hadn't been certain she'd reply eight years ago. But she had.

The problem might be the timing. She'd have gotten his mailing yesterday. For him to get something back today she'd have had to put it right back in the mail. Why had he put his office address? It was Friday. If she happened to put it in the mail today he wouldn't get it until Monday. No, he'd just have to swing by tomorrow and check the box. He made a mental note to get the key from Molly before she left.

Good Lord, he was going insane.

He heard Molly's chair creak from the front room, followed by her footsteps. He shot out of his chair and into the front office.

"You gonna race me?" she asked with a grin. Derek could see the mail truck out the window.

"Give me the key. Hurry." He held out his hand.

"If you go now you won't need it. He'll just hand it to you."

Derek picked up his pace and headed out the front door. Their mail guy was chatting with Mike as he dug through the piles in his truck.

"Hey, man," Mike said with an odd grin. "What are you doing out here?"

"Just getting the mail. Obviously," Derek said. He'd never met the mailman, but apparently Mike spent a lot of his workday shootin' the breeze.

"Well, like I was sayin', Jack." Mike gave Derek a sidelong glance as he continued to speak. "Have your son just bring it over. I can look at the brakes."

"Thanks, Mike. I appreciate it. Never can be too safe."

Derek wanted to yell for them to hurry it up but waited patiently. Finally Jack the mailman reached out and handed Mike the mail.

"Later," Mike said to Jack as he pulled away. Derek waited anxiously as his friend took his sweet-ass time sifting through the envelopes.

"Man, I was really hoping for some catalogs today. Or a magazine. I haven't gotten a magazine in a while."

Derek sucked in a breath. "Can you hurry?"

They shared a mailbox. Or rather, Mike used Derek's office mailing address since technically the back of the building didn't have its own. Finally handing over the stack, Mike gave him an odd look.

"Fine. Here. What's gotten your ass in a twist?"

"Nothing. Just need to get back to work."

Mike gave him a smirk and turned around. He spoke over his shoulder as he walked back toward his shop. "Quit freaking out, man. It's in there."

Derek froze and turned to Mike. His best friend turned and began to walk backward. He held up his hand and pointed at Derek. "I told you Anne tells me everything."

Shaking his head, Derek walked back into his office as he sorted through the mail. Mike had said it was in there.

"Find what you're looking for?" Molly asked from her desk.

Finally his hand closed around a small blue envelope and his entire body exhaled when he saw Lindsey's name in the upper right corner. "Yes, I did."

Derek tossed the unimportant mail on Molly's desk and instantly retreated to his office. He thought he heard her mutter something about him being no fun but he didn't have time to care. Shutting the door, he rounded his desk and sat down while carefully opening the envelope.

Inside was the same paper he'd sent her. Same two-paneled comic, his side filled out and hers . . .

His tense expression slid into a grin as he read her response.

"We have met. One of the best days of my life, actually. I'm Lindsey."

Derek felt as if he could nearly cry with relief, but it was her note at the bottom that did him in.

I love you, too. Always have, always will.

Without hesitation Derek picked up his pencil and began a new drawing. The first time they'd played this game it had lasted a while. And they'd both enjoyed it, passing the comics back and forth, flirting through their words. There was no hurry this time. They'd botched this second chance enough already and he wasn't going to do it again.

Mike and Anne's wedding was the following weekend. They would see each other at the rehearsal and of course at the wedding. She would be dressed up, beautiful, as she always was. It was meant to be a happy occasion, but he wouldn't survive it if he wasn't able to touch her. Kiss her.

That meant he had exactly one week to woo the woman of his dreams. The woman he loved. He had to convince her that this time it would be worth it. This time they would come out on the other side together.

Twenty-Five

Lindsey pulled into the driveway of Anne and Mike's completed farmhouse. She'd seen it so many times, in so many stages, but today it finally looked like a home. Twin black rockers sat to the left of the front door, lilac pennant banners ran the length of the porch railing, and two giant urns flanking the steps were filled with ferns.

Mike had moved in a few days ago—along with almost all of their possessions—but Anne and Claire wouldn't officially move in until after the wedding.

Callie burst through the front door and ran down the steps toward Lindsey's vehicle, blond curls flying around her head. Lindsey opened her driver side door and waved.

"Need help?" Callie asked, a little breathless.

"Sure. There's a box in the back you can grab."

The past few days all of the girls had been busy tackling odds and ends for the wedding. Callie had obviously baked the cake, as well as various cupcakes and cookies for the dessert table, and also helped Anne with whatever came up. Lindsey had been in charge of various decorations and place cards. For that she'd found the most perfect giant vintage frame with ornate fili- gree. She'd painted it, run burlap twine strings across the width, and hung each hand-printed kraft paper card on the strings with a mini clothespin. Another of her projects had been preparing all the various signs for the ceremony and reception, and the past few days had been a flurry of spray and chalkboard paint, glue guns, and ribbon. She and Mel had done a lot of the work to- gether on the deck at home—it had been fun. And she loved how everything had come out.

Anne, Lindsey, and Callie had agreed to meet today to do some staging so they could get a few teaser pho- tos for the blog. The official wedding post would come when the professional photographer had their photos ready from the actual day. But the readers were clam- oring for a peek. They'd shared the process with them, asked for their input, and now everyone was anxious.

Lindsey grabbed a handful of handmade signs from her backseat and followed Callie up to the house. Once inside she couldn't believe the transformation. The ambiance of the space had changed dramatically. It felt . . . happy. Complete. Anne had clearly been there decorating, since many of the pieces from her current home hung on the walls. The entryway table Lindsey had made held a selfie of Mike, Anne, and Claire from the day of the proposal. Next to it sat a painted Mason jar full of fresh flowers.

In complete awe, Lindsey walked down the hallway to the living room. She sucked in a breath as she took it all in. Together Anne and Mike had purchased some new furniture. It was gray linen, a bit modern but warm and inviting lined with pillows of various coordinating fabrics. The mantel Lindsey had stained was also covered with silver picture frames. Of course against the wall sat a massive flat-screen TV. Totally Mike's touch.

"What do you think?" Anne said beside Lindsey.

She turned and grinned at her friend. "I think I want to move in."

Anne laughed and threw her hands around Lindsey's shoulders. "Thank you so much for helping me create my dream house."

At the sound of tears in Anne's voice Lindsey turned and hugged her back. "Oh Anne, don't cry. It was my pleasure."

They held each other for a long moment until Anne pulled back and swiped at her eyes. For the first time Lindsey took in Anne's outfit. Sweats and a dirty T-shirt. She didn't think she'd ever seen Anne in such disarray and she couldn't help laughing.

"I know!" Anne protested, her tears melting into a laugh. "I'm a mess. I've been a mess for months and that's why I'm so thankful for you. And Callie."

Lindsey looked over to where Callie leaned against the door frame of the living room. "We'd do it all again for you, Anne," she said.

"I know you would. And I can't wait to return the favor for both of you. I've just been so overwhelmed with the blog, my daughter, Mike, planning a wedding, renovating a new house. I really don't know what I'd have done without both of you."

Anne turned to Lindsey. "I knew you would take my wishes for this renovation and just . . . take care of everything. And even though you had to work with Derek. Oh Linds, you don't know how much it means to me. And Mike, too. We are both so happy with how the house looks."

Lindsey smiled, wiping a tear from her eye. "I'm so glad. And it wasn't so bad. You know . . . working with Derek."

All three of them laughed through their tears.

"No kidding," Callie said. "You should be thanking Anne!"

Anne smiled. "Did you get another comic today?"

"I did. And I've already replied." Every other day she received mail from him and had continued to reply the same day. It was so much like the first time, and she knew he was trying to make up for all the ways things had gone wrong for them. Start fresh.

"So what now?" Anne asked. "Mike said Derek hasn't said much, but he does know that he had a talk with Lisa."

Lindsey nodded. She'd been pretty certain he did but it was nice to have confirmation.

"I know it's not my place to tell you any of it, but I wanted you to know. He's trying to make everything right."

Lindsey smiled. "I know. We'll get there. I know it."

Derek leaned back on Mike's new couch, beer in hand, and took a deep breath. He'd taken Friday off to be there for his best friend on the day before his wedding. Rehearsal day. They'd planned to spend the afternoon at the house hanging out while various vendors came by to drop things off for the wedding on Saturday.

Today there would be no reply in the mail. She would have received the last envelope herself this afternoon. And while he was pretty damn certain she would give him the response he wanted, he was still nervous as hell. And anxious. In fact, waiting was making him crazy. He glanced at his watch.

Four more hours.

"You want another sandwich?" Mike called from the doorway.

"Nah. I'm good. Thanks." Derek blew out a breath.

"Dude. You need to chill out. It's gonna be fine. You know this girl's crazy about you."

"Is that something else Anne has told you? Did she say if Lindsey will show?"

Mike pulled a hesitant face. "That she did not, but dude, calm down. I have a good feeling about this. She's been replying so you know she'll play along with this."

A few hours ago Derek had thought he'd had a good feeling about it also. Mike was right. She had replied to every letter. Filled in dialogue and even added her own drawings. Had even said she loved him. But every second that ticked by he got a little more nervous. He'd put it all on the line for this woman. Something he should have done long ago.

After an hour of lounging around, then setting up tables and chairs, and then finally getting ready, Derek walked out of the upstairs bathroom to find Mike walking out of the master bedroom.

Instantly Derek's face broke out in a wide grin.

"Do I look pretty?" Mike asked, hands out to the sides to showcase his outfit. He was wearing pressed flat-front khaki pants, a light blue button-up shirt, and a tie with a muscle car on it.

"Beautiful. You can take the grease monkey out of the garage but you can't take the garage out of the grease monkey. Isn't that how that saying goes?" Derek teased him.

"You shut your mouth," Mike said. "My . . . *stepdaughter* gave me this tie for Christmas. I'm just now getting the chance to wear it."

"Stepdaughter? Are you just now trying that word on for size?" Derek grinned. It made him realize how much he wanted Lindsey to say something similar about Tanner.

"It feels weird, saying it," Mike said as they walked down the stairs. "But good. I mean, she can't call me uncle forever. That would be fucked up."

"No kidding," Derek said, as they made it to the first floor. "So uh . . . I'm just gonna . . . go do this thing. *Hopefully.*"

Mike turned in the entryway and stuck out his hand. "She'll be here. I mean, obviously she'll be here. It's the wedding rehearsal. But I have no doubt she'll be out there for you."

Derek took his friend's hand and Mike pulled him into a guy hug, slapping him on the back. They pulled apart and Derek took a deep breath.

"Now don't go crying on me," Mike said.

Derek glared at him. "I'm not gonna cry."

Mike grinned. "I don't know, dude. Need I remind you about—"

"Good God, yes, I cried at *Forrest Gump.* Can we never discuss that again?"

Mike chuckled as he headed down the stairs, speaking over his shoulder. "You're a sap, Walsh. But I love you."

Derek shook his head and followed Mike down the stairs before walking down the hall, through the kitchen, and out the sliding doors. He passed through the garden, which was loaded with fully blooming bulbs and the white fence was bursting with lilacs. Their sweet scent filled the air. It really was a beautiful place to get married.

Hitting the grass, Derek crossed the yard and headed right for the giant tree. This was where the comic version of him asked Lindsey to meet him. He took a deep breath and let it out slowly. He was in knots over this woman. Had been for years, and he was resigned to the fact that he didn't ever want to live without her. And now all he could do was hope she felt the same way and was ready to finally be his for good.

Twenty-Six

Lindsey was late. Fifteen minutes late due to a rush-hour accident on the highway out to Preston. On top of that she'd left her phone at home. Of all the damn days. This was not fate trying to tell her something. Definitely not. Heart pounding and palms sweating, she pulled into the driveway, threw open her car door, and began to run up the gravel driveway.

In a dress. And heels.

This could end badly.

"Girl, slow down, you're gonna fall," Callie called from the porch steps.

"Can't . . . have to go," Lindsey yelled as she rounded the side of the house. Before she turned the corner she stopped short and took a breath. And another. And then pushed her hair out of her face.

"Okay," she whispered to herself, her voice breathless.

She turned the corner, rounded the garden, and stopped. From this spot in the yard she could see the tree. It was by itself. He wasn't there. Her shoulders dropped.

"Lindsey."

Jerking her head to the side, she saw him. He was walking from the opposite side of the house. He looked so gorgeous in dress pants and a white button-up shirt. It was unbuttoned at the top, just the way she liked it, the smooth tan skin of his collarbone exposed.

"Derek." She ran straight to him. Right before she collided with him, he held out his arms, pulling her into his embrace. "I was afraid you'd left."

"No, babe." He squeezed her hard, crushing their chests together so tightly she had to turn her head to the side. "I'd gone out front looking for you. Waiting."

"I'm sorry I was late. Eden had spit up on my dress . . . and then there was a highway accident, I forgot my—"

She was shushed by Derek's arms firmly grabbing her shoulders as he pushed her away far enough to look down into her eyes. "It doesn't matter. You're here. Had you not come out back, I'd have gone inside and hunted you down, Lindsey Morales."

She grinned before wrapping her arms around his neck. Their lips met softly and his hands went into her hair. They kissed long and slow, taking turns nipping at one another.

"I missed you," she whispered, nuzzling into his neck. She would never get enough of the scent of his cologne, the strength of his arms around her. The feel of his lips on hers. Finally Derek leaned his forehead on hers, touching her lips with his thumb.

"I missed you more," he said.

"I loved the comic strips," she said.

He grinned. "I'm glad. I loved getting yours back. I was so afraid you wouldn't respond."

"How could I not? It's how we started. And you already knew I loved you."

"I hoped it was enough," he said.

He kissed her once more. When they finally pulled apart she looked up at him. "I heard you talked to Lisa."

"I did. And it went surprisingly well. For now at least. I'll tell you all about it, but right now, I want this moment to be about us. Nothing else."

She nodded. "Okay. I think I like that."

"Good. I want you to understand, Lindsey, this is it. We've been apart way too long and eventually I want us to be a family. Me, you, Tanner . . . and all the other babies we manage to create."

Her mouth dropped open and then she choked out a laugh. "I think we could probably manage that. Or at least give it a try."

He grinned. "Lots of tries sounds good," Derek said, kissing her lips, nose, cheek. She loved how he never neglected any part of her body.

"Are you sure, Derek?" Lindsey asked, her eyes closed as his lips touched her eyelids.

He angled her face up and she opened her eyes to find him staring at her. "I think that's what I've always wanted."

Lindsey smiled. "Good. I want it, too."

"It won't be easy."

She laughed. "None of it has been."

"True. But I know it's worth it." He stroked a finger down the side of her face. "You're worth it."

"So are you. And so is Tanner. And all those babies we're gonna make."

"*All* of those babies." He agreed with a nod. "Let's start now."

"Derek." Lindsey slapped at his chest and he drew her back into his arms, resting his chin on her head. The scent of him mixed with the flowers left her with a feeling of tranquility and happiness.

"I love you so much, Lindsey. I'm not letting you go ever again."

She squeezed him back. "Don't worry. I won't let you."

Epilogue

Anne and Mike's wedding couldn't have been more perfect if they'd tried. From the lace on Anne's dress down to the black Camaro groom's cake, it was lovely in every way. They'd written their own vows and Mike's were delivered to both Anne and Claire, promising to love and care for the two of them. There hadn't been a single dry eye in the entire place.

During the reception the drinks flowed, the food was delicious, and the decorations made the space feel like a chic, woodland fairy tale. Anne and Mike had just shared their first dance under the twinkling lights that filled the rafters of the barn. With a smile on her face Lindsey took the opportunity to step out back to get some fresh air.

The sun hung just beyond the field that backed up to their property, leaving streaks of pink and blue across the sky. It was the most beautiful evening and Lindsey wasn't sure she'd ever felt lighter or happier.

She stood, drink in hand, staring at the horizon until

she heard footsteps behind her. Turning, she smiled as she took in Derek and his minime, Tanner.

"I still can't get over how handsome you two look tonight," she said.

"I'm kinda tired of this vest. Can I take it off?" Tanner asked, tugging at the tie at his neck.

Derek patted his son's head. "Sure, bud. Why don't we get out of here, go for a drive? The three of us."

Lindsey shrugged. "Okay. But just for a little bit. I still want to spend some time with the girls and I have to help clean up."

Derek held his hand out to her. "We'll get you back here. I have something to show you."

"Something to show me?" Now she was intrigued. "Well, in that case, let's go."

Ten minutes later they pulled in front of Derek's office. She slid him a confused look.

"Trust me," he said with a wink.

All three of them got out of the car, but instead of walking to his door, he began to walk around back toward Mike's shop.

"Where are you going?" she said.

Derek stopped, held out his hand, and waited for her to take hold before they proceeded. "Sorry, I'm just anxious. Come on."

They came to the big black door in back and Derek pulled out a key. Lindsey had been to Mike's shop before a few times. It was not exciting. Actually, it was always a mess, as car garages tended to be. But as they stepped inside she found that it was empty.

"Mike moved all his stuff out, huh?"

"He did," Derek said, flipping on all the lights. The

space that Mike had used as his office had been freshly painted a dark cream color and rustic wood flooring had been laid over the concrete. It reminded her of all the old flooring in the buildings at the West Bottoms.

"I chose the flooring because . . . I thought you'd like it. But the rest is a completely blank space. For you."

"For me?" She was in shock. Complete and utter shock. Sucking in a quick breath, Lindsey turned in a circle, taking in the room. It wasn't huge, but it was big enough to display many things. Instantly she could picture it full of her creations. He must have been working like crazy to get it all done so quickly.

"Follow me, we aren't done." Derek was grinning, holding his hand out to her. "Come on, Tan. Let's show her the rest."

The boys led Lindsey into a smaller room. "Mike's former bedroom is now . . . your office." He flipped the light on to reveal more wood flooring and more ivory paint. Lindsey couldn't help laughing. In shock, excitement. She wasn't sure.

"Keep moving." Derek pulled on her hand, leading her back through the bigger room, down a small hallway, and out to what used to be Mike's garage. "Here's the best part. Your workshop."

"Derek," Lindsey whispered. The space had been mostly cleared, but it was still basically a garage. Concrete floors, giant bay doors, lots of shelving, a utility sink.

It was perfect.

"Where is Mike going to work?" she asked.

"Well, he took two weeks off to spend with Anne and

Claire and during that time he's having a Morton building put up on their property. He's going to work at home, move the business there. And now you're going to work here. With me."

He pulled her against his chest and looked into her eyes. "At least . . . I hope you will."

She smiled. "Are you kidding me? This is the most beautiful space I've ever seen. There are drains in the floor for easy cleanup!"

Derek laughed and kissed her on the nose. "If I'd known drains made you happy I'd have given them to you earlier."

Lindsey smiled. "How much is the rent here?"

Derek made a face. "I don't know, I hadn't thought about it."

"Well, you must think about it. I'm paying rent," she said. And she meant it. She had also set aside a chunk of the money her dad had paid her back to pay Derek for her hospital bills. She wouldn't let him argue about it, either.

"I'm sure we can come to an agreement." He grabbed her hand and gave it a squeeze.

"Dad, can we stay the night in here? This is awesome."

"No way, bud. We have to get back to the wedding." Derek looked back down at Lindsey. "But maybe Lindsey will let you hang out in here with her sometime."

"Absolutely," she said. "I might have to take Tanner Dumpster diving. Then we can create something awesome together."

"Dumpster diving?" Tanner asked, completely confused.

"Yeah, it's fun. Maybe we'll make something cool for your dad's office," Lindsey said with a wicked grin.

Derek gave her a sidelong glance. "That sounds like a great idea."

They stood there a long moment, holding on to one another as they watched Tanner explore the space. She looked up to Derek once more. "Final request. Next Valentine's Day I will need chocolate, a card, and flowers."

He chuckled. "You're not high maintenance at all."

She feigned offense. "I'm not! I've just never gotten any of those things before on Valentine's Day."

"Never? You're kidding?" he asked. Obviously surprised.

"Not kidding at all."

"I'm kind of glad. You were waiting for me."

Lindsey rolled her eyes and laid her head back on his chest. "Don't disappoint."

Derek groaned and then whispered against Lindsey's temple. "Never again. You're mine now."